Good Cheer Stories Every Child Should Know

Various

Editor: Asa Don Dickinson

Contents

GOOD CHEER STORIES EVERY CHILD SHOULD KNOW

BY

Various

Editor: Asa Don Dickinson

THE CHILDREN'S BOOK OF
THANKSGIVING STORIES
THE KINGDOM OF THE GREEDY

BY P. J. STAHL.

TRANSLATED BY LAURA W. JOHNSON.

This fairy tale of a gormandizing people contains no mention
of Thanksgiving Day. Yet its connection with our American
festival is obvious. Every one who likes fairy tales will
enjoy reading it.

The country of the Greedy, well known in history, was ruled by a king who had much trouble. His subjects were well behaved, but they had one sad fault: they were too fond of pies and tarts. It was as disagreeable to them to swallow a spoonful of soup as if it were so much sea water, and it would take a policeman to make them open their mouths for a bit of meat, either boiled or roasted. This deplorable taste made the fortunes of the pastry cooks, but also of the apothecaries. Families ruined themselves in pills and powders; camomile, rhubarb, and peppermint trebled in price, as well as other disagreeable remedies, such as castor ---- which I will not name.

The King of the Greedy sought long for the means of correcting this fatal passion for sweets, but even the faculty were puzzled.

"Your Majesty," said the great court doctor, Olibriers, at his last audience, "your people look like putty! They are incurable; their senseless love for good eating will bring them all to the grave."

This view of things did not suit the King. He was wise, and saw very plainly that a monarch without subjects would be but a sorry king.

Happily, after this utter failure of the doctors, there came into the mind of His Majesty a first-class idea: he telegraphed for Mother Mitchel, the most celebrated of all pastry cooks. Mother Mitchel soon arrived, with her black cat, Fanfreluche, who accompanied her everywhere. He was an incomparable cat. He had not his equal as an adviser and a taster of tarts.

Mother Mitchel having respectfully inquired what she and her cat could do for His Majesty, the King demanded of the astonished pastry cook a tart as big as the capitol--bigger even, if possible, but no smaller! When the King uttered this astounding order, deep emotion was shown by the chamberlains, the pages, and lackeys. Nothing but the respect due to his presence prevented them from crying "Long live Your Majesty!" in his very ears. But the King had seen enough of the enthusiasm of the populace, and did not allow such sounds in the recesses of his palace.

The King gave Mother Mitchel one month to carry out his gigantic project. "It is enough," she proudly replied, brandishing her crutch. Then, taking leave of the King, she and her cat set out for their home.

On the way Mother Mitchel arranged in her head the plan of the monument which was to immortalize her, and considered the means of executing it. As to its form and size, it was to be as exact a copy of the capitol as possible, since the King had willed it; but its outside crust should have a beauty all its own. The dome must be adorned with sugarplums of all colours, and surmounted by a splendid crown of macaroons, spun sugar, chocolate, and candied fruits. It was no small affair.

Mother Mitchel did not like to lose her time. Her plan of battle once formed, she recruited on her way all the little pastry cooks of the country, as well as all the tiny six-year-olds who had a sincere love for the noble callings of scullion and apprentice. There were plenty of these, as you may suppose, in the country of the Greedy; Mother Mitchel had her pick of them.

Mother Mitchel, with the help of her crutch and of Fanfreluche, who miaowed loud enough to be heard twenty miles off, called upon all the millers of the land, and commanded them to bring together at a certain time as many sacks of fine flour as they could grind in a week. There were only windmills in that country; you may easily believe how they all began to go. B-r-r-r-r! What a noise they made! The clatter was so great that all the birds flew away to other climes, and even the clouds fled from the sky.

At the call of Mother Mitchel all the farmers' wives were set to work; they rushed to the hencoops to collect the seven thousand fresh eggs that Mother Mitchel wanted for her great edifice. Deep was the emotion of the fowls. The hens were inconsolable, and the unhappy creatures mourned upon the palings for the loss of all their hopes.

The milkmaids were busy from morning till night in milking the cows. Mother Mitchel must have twenty thousand pails of milk. All the little calves were put on half rations. This great work was nothing to them, and they complained pitifully to their mothers. Many of the cows protested with energy against this unreasonable tax, which made their young families so uncomfortable. There were pails upset, and even some milkmaids went head over heels. But these little accidents did not chill the enthusiasm of the labourers.

And now Mother Mitchel called for a thousand pounds of the best butter. All the churns for twenty miles around began to work in the most lively manner. Their dashers dashed without ceasing, keeping perfect time. The butter was tasted, rolled into pats, wrapped up, and put into baskets. Such energy had never been known before.

Mother Mitchel passed for a sorceress. It was all because of her cat, Fanfreluche, with whom she had mysterious doings and pantomimes, and with whom she talked in her inspired moments, as if he were a real person. Certainly, since the famous "Puss in Boots," there had never been an animal so extraordinary; and credulous folks suspected him of being a magician. Some curious people had the courage to ask Fanfreluche if this were true; but he had replied by bristling, and showing his teeth and claws so fiercely, that the conversation had ended there. Sorceress or not, Mother Mitchel was always obeyed. No one else was ever served so punctually.

On the appointed day all the millers arrived with their asses trotting in single file, each laden with a great sack of flour. Mother Mitchel, after having examined the quality of the flour, had every sack accurately weighed. This was head work and hard work, and took time; but Mother Mitchel was untiring, and her cat, also, for while the operation lasted he sat on the roof watching. It is only just to say that the millers of the Greedy Kingdom brought flour not only faultless but of full weight. They knew that Mother Mitchel was not joking when she said that others must be as exact with her as she was with them. Perhaps also they were a little afraid of the cat, whose great green eyes were always shining upon them like two round lamps, and never lost sight of them for one moment.

All the farmers' wives arrived in turn, with baskets of eggs upon their heads. They did not load their donkeys with them, for fear that in jogging along they would become omelettes on the way. Mother Mitchel received them with her usual gravity. She had the patience to look through every egg to see if it were fresh.

She did not wish to run the risk of having young chickens in a tart that was destined for those who could not bear the taste of any meat however tender and delicate. The number of eggs was complete, and again Mother Mitchel and her cat had nothing to complain of. This Greedy nation, though carried away by love of good eating, was strictly honest. It must be said that where nations are patriotic, desire for the common good makes them unselfish. Mother Mitchel's tart was to be the glory of the country, and each one was proud to contribute to such a great work.

And now the milkmaids with their pots and pails of milk, and the buttermakers with their baskets filled with the rich yellow pats of butter, filed in long procession to the right and left of the cabin of Mother Mitchel. There was no need for her to examine so carefully the butter and the milk. She had such a delicate nose that if there had been a single pat of ancient butter or a pail of sour milk she would have pounced upon it instantly. But all was perfectly fresh. In that golden age they did not understand the art, now so well known, of making milk out of flour and water. Real milk was necessary to make cheesecakes and ice cream and other delicious confections much adored in the Greedy Kingdom. If any one had made such a despicable discovery, he would have been chased from the country as a public nuisance.

Then came the grocers, with their aprons of coffee bags, and with the jolly, mischievous faces the rogues always have. Each one clasped to his heart a sugar loaf nearly as large as himself, whose summit, without its paper cap, looked like new-fallen snow upon a pyramid. Mother Mitchel, with her crutch for a baton, saw them all placed in her storerooms upon shelves put up for the purpose. She had to be very strict, for some of the little fellows could hardly part from their merchandise, and many were indiscreet, with their tongues behind their great mountains of sugar. If they had been let alone, they would never have stopped till the sugar was all gone. But they had not thought of the implacable eye of old Fanfreluche, who, posted upon a water spout, took note of all their misdeeds. From another quarter came a whole army of country people, rolling wheelbarrows and carrying huge baskets, all filled with cherries, plums, peaches, apples, and pears. All these fruits were so fresh, in such perfect condition, with their fair shining skins, that they looked like wax or painted marble, but their delicious perfume proved that they were real. Some little people, hidden in the corners, took pains to find this out. Between ourselves, Mother Mitchel made believe not to see them, and took the precaution of holding Fanfreluche in her arms so that he could not spring upon them. The fruits were all put into bins, each kind by itself. And now the preparations were finished. There was no time to lose before setting to work.

The spot which Mother Mitchel had chosen for her great edifice was a pretty hill on which a plateau formed a splendid site. This hill commanded the capital city, built upon the slope of another hill close by. After having beaten down the earth till it was as smooth as a floor, they spread over it loads of bread crumbs, brought from the baker's, and levelled it with rake and spade, as we do gravel in our garden walks. Little birds, as greedy as themselves, came in flocks to the feast, but they might eat as they liked, it would never be missed, so thick was the carpet. It was a great chance for the bold little things.

All the ingredients for the tart were now ready. Upon order of Mother Mitchel they began to peel the apples and pears and to take out the pips. The weather was so pleasant that the girls sat out of doors, upon the ground, in long rows. The sun looked down upon them with a merry face. Each of the little workers had a big earthen pan, and peeled incessantly the apples which the boys brought them. When the pans were full, they were carried away and others were brought. They had also to carry away the peels, or the girls would have been buried in them. Never was there such a peeling before.

Not far away, the children were stoning the plums, cherries, and peaches. This work, being the easiest, was given to the youngest and most inexperienced hands, which were all first carefully washed, for Mother Mitchel, though not very particular about her own toilet, was very neat in her cooking. The schoolhouse, long unused (for in the country of the Greedy they had forgotten everything), was arranged for this second class of workers, and the cat was their inspector. He walked round and round, growling if he saw the fruit popping into any of the little mouths. If they had dared, how they would have pelted him with plum stones! But no one risked it. Fanfreluche was not to be trifled with.

In those days powdered sugar had not been invented, and to grate it all was no small affair. It was the work that the grocers used to dislike the most; both lungs and arms were soon tired. But Mother Mitchel was there to sustain them with her unequalled energy. She chose the labourers from the most robust of the boys. With mallet and knife she broke the cones into round pieces, and they grated them till they were too small to hold. The bits were put into baskets to be pounded. One would never have expected to find all the thousand pounds of sugar again. But a new miracle was wrought by Mother Mitchel. It was all there!

It was then the turn of the ambitious scullions to enter the lists and break the seven thousand eggs for Mother Mitchel. It was not hard to break them--any fool could do that; but to separate adroitly the yolks and the whites demands some talent, and, above all, great care. We dare not say that there were no accidents here, no eggs too well scrambled, no baskets upset. But the experience of Mother Mitchel had counted upon such things, and it may truly be said that there were never so many eggs broken at once, or ever could be again. To make an omelette of them would have taken a saucepan as large as a skating pond, and the fattest cook that ever lived could not hold the handle of such a saucepan.

But this was not all. Now that the yolks and whites were once divided, they must each be beaten separately in wooden bowls, to give them the necessary lightness. The egg beaters were marshalled into two brigades, the yellow and the white. Every one preferred the white, for it was much more amusing to make those snowy masses that rose up so high than to beat the yolks, which knew no better than to mix together like so much sauce. Mother Mitchel, with her usual wisdom, had avoided this difficulty by casting lots. Thus, those who were not on the white side had no reason to complain of oppression. And truly, when all was done, the whites and the yellows were equally tired. All had cramps in their hands.

Now began the real labour of Mother Mitchel. Till now she had been the commander-in-chief--the head only; now she put her own finger in the pie. First, she had to make sweetmeats and jam out of all the immense quantity of fruit she had stored. For this, as she could only do one kind at a time, she had ten kettles, each as big as a dinner table. During forty-eight hours the cooking went on; a dozen scullions blew the fire and put on the fuel. Mother Mitchel, with a spoon that four modern cooks could hardly lift, never ceased stirring and trying the boiling fruit. Three expert tasters, chosen from the most dainty, had orders to report progress every half hour.

It is unnecessary to state that all the sweetmeats were perfectly successful, or that they were of exquisite consistency, colour, and perfume. With Mother Mitchel there was no such word as *fail*. When each kind of sweetmeat was finished, she skimmed it, and put it away to cool in enormous bowls before potting. She did not use for this the usual little glass or earthen jars, but great stone ones, like those in the "Forty Thieves." Not only did these take less time to fill, but they were safe from the children. The scum and the scrapings were something, to be sure. But there was little Toto, who thought this was not enough. He would have jumped into one of the bowls if they had not held him.

Mother Mitchel, who thought of everything, had ordered two hundred great kneading troughs, wishing that all the utensils of this great work should be perfectly new. These two hundred troughs, like her other materials, were all delivered punctually and in good order. The pastry cooks rolled up their sleeves and began to knead the dough with cries of "Hi! Hi!" that could be heard for miles. It was odd to see this army of bakers in serried ranks, all making the same gestures at once, like well-disciplined soldiers, stooping and rising together in time, so that a foreign ambassador wrote to his court that he wished his people could load and fire as well as these could knead. Such praise a people never forgets.

When each troughful of paste was approved it was moulded with care into the form of bricks, and with the aid of the engineer-in-chief, a young genius who had gained the first prize in the school of architecture, the majestic edifice was begun. Mother Mitchel herself drew the plan; in following her directions, the young engineer showed himself modest beyond all praise. He had the good sense to understand that the architecture of tarts and pies had rules of its own, and that therefore the experience of Mother Mitchel was worth all the scientific theories in the world.

The inside of the monument was divided into as many compartments as there were kinds of fruits. The walls were no less than four feet thick. When they were finished, twenty-four ladders were set up, and twenty-four experienced cooks ascended them. These first-class artists were each of them armed with an enormous cooking spoon. Behind them, on the lower rounds of the ladders, followed the kitchen boys, carrying on their heads pots and pans filled to the brim with jam and sweetmeats, each sort ready to be poured into its destined compartment. This colossal labour was accomplished in one day, and with wonderful exactness.

When the sweetmeats were used to the last drop, when the great spoons had done all their work, the twenty-four cooks descended to earth again. The intrepid Mother Mitchel, who had never quitted the spot, now ascended, followed by the noble Fanfreluche, and dipped her finger into each of the compartments, to assure herself that everything was right. This part of her duty was not disagreeable, and many of the scullions would have liked to perform it. But they might have lingered too long over the enchanting task. As for Mother Mitchel, she had been too well used to sweets to be excited now. She only wished to do her duty and to insure success.

All went on well. Mother Mitchel had given her approbation. Nothing was needed now but to crown the sublime and delicious edifice by placing upon it the crust--that is, the roof, or dome. This delicate operation was confided to the engineer-in-chief who now showed his superior genius. The dome, made beforehand of a single piece, was raised in the air by means of twelve balloons, whose force of ascension had been carefully calculated. First it was directed, by ropes, exactly over the top of the tart; then at the word of command it gently descended upon the right spot. It was not a quarter of an inch out of place. This was a great triumph for Mother Mitchel and her able assistant.

But all was not over. How should this colossal tart be cooked? That was the question that agitated all the people of the Greedy country, who came in crowds--lords and commons--to gaze at the wonderful spectacle.

Some of the envious or ill-tempered declared it would be impossible to cook the edifice which Mother Mitchel had built; and the doctors were, no one knows why, the saddest of all. Mother Mitchel, smiling at the general bewilderment, mounted the summit of the tart; she waved her crutch in the air, and while her cat miaowed in his sweetest voice, suddenly there issued from the woods a vast number of masons, drawing wagons of well-baked bricks, which they had prepared in secret. This sight silenced the ill-wishers and filled the hearts of the Greedy with hope.

In two days an enormous furnace was built around and above the colossal tart, which found itself shut up in an immense earthen pot. Thirty huge mouths, which were connected with thousands of winding pipes for conducting heat all over the building, were soon choked with fuel, by the help of two hundred charcoal burners, who, obeying a private signal, came forth in long array from the forest, each carrying his sack of coal. Behind them stood Mother Mitchel with a box of matches, ready to fire each oven as it was filled. Of course the kindlings had not been forgotten, and was all soon in a blaze.

When the fire was lighted in the thirty ovens, when they saw the clouds of smoke rolling above the dome, that announced that the cooking had begun, the joy of the people was boundless. Poets improvised odes, and musicians sung verses without end, in honour of the superb prince who had been inspired to feed his people in so dainty a manner, when other rulers could not give them enough even of dry bread. The names of Mother Mitchel and of the illustrious engineer were not forgotten in this great glorification. Next to His Majesty, they were certainly the first of mankind, and their names were worthy of going down with his to the remotest posterity.

All the envious ones were thunderstruck. They tried to console themselves by saying that the work was not yet finished, and that an accident might happen at the last moment. But they did not really believe a word of this. Notwithstanding all their efforts to look cheerful, it had to be acknowledged that the cooking was possible. Their last resource was to declare the tart a bad one, but that would be biting off their own noses. As for declining to eat it, envy could never go so far as that in the country of the Greedy.

After two days, the unerring nose of Mother Mitchel discovered that the tart was cooked to perfection. The whole country was perfumed with its delicious aroma. Nothing more remained but to take down the furnaces. Mother Mitchel made her official announcement to His Majesty, who was delighted, and complimented her upon her punctuality. One day was still wanting to complete the month. During this time the people gave their eager help to the engineer in the demolition, wishing to have a hand in the great national work and to hasten the blessed moment. In the twinkling of an eye the thing was done. The bricks were taken down one by one, counted carefully, and carried into the forest again, to serve for another occasion.

The TART, unveiled, appeared at last in all its majesty and splendour. The dome was gilded, and reflected the rays of the sun in the most dazzling manner. The wildest excitement and rapture ran through the land of the Greedy. Each one sniffed with open nostrils the appetizing perfume. Their mouths watered, their eyes filled with tears, they embraced, pressed each other's hands, and indulged in touching pantomimes. Then the people of town and country, united by one rapturous feeling, joined hands, and danced in a ring around the grand confection.

No one dared to touch the tart before the arrival of His Majesty. Meanwhile, something must be done to allay the universal impatience, and they resolved to show Mother Mitchel the gratitude with which all hearts were filled. She was crowned with the laurel of *conquerors*, which is also the laurel of *sauce*, thus serving a double purpose. Then they placed her, with her crutch and her cat, upon a sort of throne, and carried her all round her vast work. Before her marched all the musicians of the town, dancing, drumming, fifing, and tooting upon all instruments, while behind her pressed an enthusiastic crowd, who rent the air with their plaudits and filled it with a shower of caps. Her fame was complete, and a noble pride shone on her countenance.

The royal procession arrived. A grand stairway had been built, so that the King and his ministers could mount to the summit of this monumental tart. Thence the King, amid a deep silence, thus addressed his people:

"My children," said he, "you adore tarts. You despise all other food. If you could, you would even eat tarts in your sleep. Very well. Eat as much as you like. Here is one big enough to satisfy you. But know this, that while there remains a single crumb of this august tart, from the height of which I am proud to look down on you, all other food is forbidden you on pain of death. While you are here, I have ordered all the pantries to be emptied, and all the butchers, bakers, pork and milk dealers, and fishmongers to shut up their shops. Why leave them open? Why indeed? Have you not here at discretion what you love best, and enough to last you ever, *ever* so long? Devote yourselves to it with all your hearts. I do not wish you to be bored with the sight of any other food.

"Greedy ones! behold your TART!"

What enthusiastic applause, what frantic hurrahs rent the air, in answer to this eloquent speech from the throne!

"Long live the King, Mother Mitchel, and her cat! Long live the tart! Down with soup! Down with bread! To the bottom of the sea with all beefsteaks, mutton chops, and roasts!"

Such cries came from every lip. Old men gently stroked their chops, children patted their little stomachs, the crowd licked its thousand lips with eager joy. Even the babies danced in their nurses' arms, so precocious was the passion for tarts in this singular country. Grave professors, skipping like kids, declaimed Latin verses in honour of His Majesty and Mother Mitchel, and the shyest young girls opened their mouths like the beaks of little birds. As for the doctors, they felt a joy beyond expression. They had reflected. They understood. But--my friends!--

At last the signal was given. A detachment of the engineer corps arrived, armed with pick and cutlass, and marched in good order to the assault. A breach was soon opened, and the distribution began. The King smiled at the opening in the tart; though vast, it hardly showed more than a mouse hole in the monstrous wall.

The King stroked his beard grandly. "All goes well," said he, "for him who knows how to wait."

Who can tell how long the feast would have lasted if the King had not given his command that it should cease? Once more they expressed their gratitude with cries so stifled that they resembled grunts, and then rushed to the river. Never had a nation been so besmeared. Some were daubed to the eyes, others had their ears and hair all sticky. As for the little ones, they were marmalade from head to foot. When they had finished their toilets, the river ran all red and yellow and was sweetened for several hours, to the great surprise of all the fishes.

Before returning home, the people presented themselves before the King to receive his commands.

"Children!" said he, "the feast will begin again exactly at six o'clock. Give time to wash the dishes and change the tablecloths, and you may once more give yourselves over to pleasure. You shall feast twice a day as long as the tart lasts. Do not forget. Yes! if there is not enough in this one, I will even order ANOTHER from Mother Mitchel; for you know that great woman is indefatigable. Your happiness is my only aim." (Marks of universal joy and emotion.) "You understand? Noon, and six o'clock! There is no need for me to say be punctual! Go, then, my children--be happy!"

The second feast was as gay as the first, and as long. A pleasant walk in the suburbs--first exercise--then a nap, had refreshed their appetites and unlimbered their jaws. But the King fancied that the breach made in the tart was a little smaller than that of the morning.

"'Tis well!" said he, "'tis well! Wait till to-morrow, my friends; yes, till day after to-morrow, and *next week*!"

The next day the feast still went on gayly; yet at the evening meal the King noticed some empty seats.

"Why is this?" said he, with pretended indifference, to the court physician.

"Your Majesty," said the great Olibriers, "a few weak stomachs; that is all."

On the next day there were larger empty spaces. The enthusiasm visibly abated. The eighth day the crowd had diminished one half; the ninth, three quarters; the tenth day, of the thousand who came at first, only two hundred remained; on the eleventh day only one hundred; and on the twelfth--alas! who would have thought it?--a single one answered to the call. Truly he was big enough. His body resembled a hogshead, his mouth an oven, and his lips--we dare not say what. He was known in the town by the name of Patapouf. They dug out a fresh lump for him from the middle of the tart. It quickly vanished in his vast interior, and he retired with great dignity, proud to maintain the honour of his name and the glory of the Greedy Kingdom.

But the next day, even he, the very last, appeared no more. The unfortunate Patapouf had succumbed, and, like all the other inhabitants of the country, was in a very bad way. In short, it was soon known that the whole town had suffered agonies that night from too much tart. Let us draw a veil over those hours of torture. Mother Mitchel was in despair. Those ministers who had not guessed the secret dared not open their lips. All the city was one vast hospital. No one was seen in the streets but doctors and apothecaries' boys, running from house to house in frantic haste. It was dreadful! Doctor Olibriers was nearly knocked out. As for the King, he held his tongue and shut himself up in his palace, but a secret joy shone in his eyes, to the wonder of every one. He waited three days without a word.

The third day, the King said to his ministers:

"Let us go now and see how my poor people are doing, and feel their pulse a little."

The good King went to every house, without forgetting a single one. He visited small and great, rich and poor.

"Oh, oh! Your Majesty," said all, "the tart was good, but may we never see it again! Plague on that tart! Better were dry bread. Your Majesty, for mercy's sake, a little dry bread! Oh, a morsel of dry bread, how good it would be!"

"No, indeed," replied the King. "*There is more of that tart!*"

"What! Your Majesty, *must* we eat it all?"

"You *must*!" sternly replied the King; "you **MUST**! By the immortal beef-steaks! not one of you shall have a slice of bread, and not a loaf shall be baked in the kingdom while there remains a crumb of that excellent tart!"

"What misery!" thought these poor people. "That tart forever!"

The sufferers were in despair. There was only one cry through all the town: "Ow! ow! ow!" For even the strongest and most courageous were in horrible agonies. They twisted, they writhed, they lay down, they got up. Always the inexorable colic. The dogs were not happier than their masters; even they had too much tart.

The spiteful tart looked in at all the windows. Built upon a height, it commanded the town. The mere sight of it made everybody ill, and its former admirers had nothing but curses for it now. Unhappily, nothing they could say or do made it any smaller; still formidable, it was a frightful joke for those miserable mortals. Most of them buried their heads in their pillows, drew their nightcaps over their eyes, and lay in bed all day to shut out the sight of it. But this would not do; they knew, they felt it was there. It was a nightmare, a horrible burden, a torturing anxiety.

In the midst of this terrible consternation the King remained inexorable during eight days. His heart bled for his people, but the lesson must sink deep if it were to bear fruit in future. When their pains were cured, little by little, through fasting alone, and his subjects pronounced these trembling words, "We are hungry!" the King sent them trays laden with--the inevitable tart.

"Ah!" cried they, with anguish, "the tart again! Always the tart, and nothing but the tart! Better were death!"

A few, who were almost famished, shut their eyes, and tried to eat a bit of the detested food; but it was all in vain--they could not swallow a mouthful.

At length came the happy day when the King, thinking their punishment had been severe enough and could never be forgotten, believed them at length cured of their greediness. That day he ordered Mother Mitchel to make in one of her co-lossal pots a super-excellent soup of which a bowl was sent to every family. They received it with as much rapture as the Hebrews did the manna in the desert. They would gladly have had twice as much, but after their long fast it would not have been prudent. It was a proof that they had learned something already, that they understood this.

The next day, more soup. This time the King allowed slices of bread in it. How this good soup comforted all the town! The next day there was a little more bread in it and a little soup meat. Then for a few days the kind Prince gave them roast beef and vegetables. The cure was complete.

The joy over this new diet was as great as ever had been felt for the tart. It promised to last longer. They were sure to sleep soundly, and to wake refreshed. It was pleasant to see in every house tables surrounded with happy, rosy faces, and laden with good nourishing food.

The Greedy people never fell back into their old ways. Their once puffed-out, sallow faces shone with health; they became, not fat, but muscular, ruddy, and solid. The butchers and bakers reopened their shops; the pastry cooks and confec-tioners shut theirs. The country of the Greedy was turned upside down, and if it kept its name, it was only from habit. As for the tart, it was forgotten. To-day, in that marvellous country, there cannot be found a paper of sugarplums or a basket of cakes. It is charming to see the red lips and the beautiful teeth of the people. If they have still a king, he may well be proud to be their ruler.

Does this story teach that tarts and pies should never be eaten? No; but there is reason in all things.

The doctors alone did not profit by this great revolution. They could not af-ford to drink wine any longer in a land where indigestion had become unknown. The apothecaries were no less unhappy, spiders spun webs over their windows, and their horrible remedies were no longer of use.

Ask no more about Mother Mitchel. She was ridiculed without measure by those who had adored her. To complete her misfortune, she lost her cat. Alas for

Mother Mitchel!

The King received the reward of his wisdom. His grateful people called him neither Charles the Bold, nor Peter the Terrible, nor Louis the Great, but always by the noble name of Prosper I, the Reasonable.

THANKFUL[1]
BY MARY E. WILKINS FREEMAN.

This tale is evidence that Mrs. Freeman understands the children of New England as well as she knows their parents. There is a doll in the story, but boys will not mind this as there are also two turkey-gobblers and a pewter dish full of Revolutionary bullets.

Submit Thompson sat on the stone wall; Sarah Adams, an erect, prim little figure, ankle-deep in dry grass, stood beside it, holding Thankful. Thankful was about ten inches long, made of the finest linen, with little rosy cheeks, and a fine little wig of flax. She wore a blue wool frock and a red cloak. Sarah held her close. She even drew a fold of her own blue homespun blanket around her to shield her from the November wind. The sky was low and gray; the wind blew from the northeast, and had the breath of snow in it. Submit on the wall drew her quilted petticoats close down over her feet, and huddled herself into a small space, but her face gleamed keen and resolute out of the depths of a great red hood that belonged to her mother. Her eyes were fixed upon a turkey-gobbler ruffling and bobbing around the back door of the Adams house. The two gambrel-roofed Thompson and Adams houses were built as close together as if the little village of Bridgewater were a city. Acres of land stretched behind them and at the other sides, but they stood close to the road, and close to each other. The narrow space between them was divided by a stone wall which was Submit's and Sarah's trysting-place. They met there every day and exchanged confidences. They loved each other like sisters--neither of them had an own sister--but to-day a spirit of rivalry had arisen.

[Note 1: From *Harper's Young People*, November 25, 1890.]

The tough dry blackberry vines on the wall twisted around Submit; she looked, with her circle of red petticoat, like some strange late flower blooming out on the wall. "I know he don't, Sarah Adams," said she.

"Father said he'd weigh twenty pounds," returned Sarah, in a small, weak voice, which still had persistency in it.

"I don't believe he will. Our Thanksgiving turkey is twice as big. You know he is, Sarah Adams."

"No, I don't, Submit Thompson."

"Yes, you do."

Sarah lowered her chin, and shook her head with a decision that was beyond words. She was a thin, delicate-looking little girl, her small blue-clad figure bent before the wind, but there was resolution in her high forehead and her sharp chin.

Submit nodded violently.

Sarah shook her head again. She hugged Thankful, and shook her head, with her eyes still staring defiantly into Submit's hood.

Submit's black eyes in the depths of it were like two sparks. She nodded vehemently; the gesture was not enough for her; she nodded and spoke together. "Sarah Adams," said she, "what will you give me if our turkey is bigger than your turkey?"

"It ain't."

"What will you give me if it is?"

Sarah stared at Submit. "I don't know what you mean, Submit Thompson," said she, with a stately and puzzled air.

"Well, I'll tell you. If your turkey weighs more than ours I'll give you--I'll give you my little work-box with the picture on the top, and if our turkey weighs more than yours you give me--What will you give me, Sarah Adams?"

Sarah hung her flaxen head with a troubled air. "I don't know," said she. "I don't believe I've got anything mother would be willing to have me give away."

"There's Thankful. Your mother wouldn't care if you gave her away."

Sarah started, and hugged Thankful closer. "Yes, my mother would care, too," said she. "Don't you know my Aunt Rose from Boston made her and gave her to me?"

Sarah's beautiful young Aunt Rose from Boston was the special admiration of both the little girls. Submit was ordinarily impressed by her name, but now she took it coolly.

"What if she did?" she returned. "She can make another. It's just made out of a piece of old linen, anyhow. My work-box is real handsome; but you can do just as you are a mind to."

"Do you mean I can have the work-box to keep?" inquired Sarah.

"Course I do, if your turkey's bigger."

Sarah hesitated. "Our turkey is bigger anyhow," she murmured. "Don't you think I ought to ask mother, Submit?" she inquired suddenly.

"No! What for? I don't see anything to ask your mother for. She won't care anything about that rag doll."

"Ain't you going to ask your mother about the work-box?"

"No," replied Submit stoutly. "It's mine; my grandmother gave it to me."

Sarah reflected. "I *know* our turkey is the biggest," she said, looking lovingly at Thankful, as if to justify herself to her. "Well, I don't care," she added, finally.

"Will you?"

"Yes."

"When's yours going to be killed?"

"This afternoon."

"So's ours. Then we'll find out."

Sarah tucked Thankful closer under her shawl. "I know our turkey is biggest," said she. She looked very sober, although her voice was defiant. Just then the great turkey came swinging through the yard. He held up his head proudly and gobbled. His every feather stood out in the wind. He seemed enormous--a perfect giant among turkeys. "*Look* at him!" said Sarah, edging a little closer to the wall; she was rather afraid of him.

"He ain't half so big as ours," returned Submit, stoutly; but her heart sank. The Thompson turkey did look very large.

"Submit! Submit!" called a voice from the Thompson house.

Submit slowly got down from the wall. "His feathers are a good deal thicker than ours," she said, defiantly, to Sarah.

"Submit," called the voice, "come right home! I want you to pare apples for the pies. Be quick!"

"Yes, marm," Submit answered back, in a shrill voice; "I'm coming!" Then she went across the yard and into the kitchen door of the Thompson house, like a red robin into a nest. Submit had been taught to obey her mother promptly. Mrs. Thompson was a decided woman.

Sarah looked after Submit, then she gathered Thankful closer, and also went into the house. Her mother, as well as Mrs. Thompson, was preparing for Thanksgiving. The great kitchen was all of a pleasant litter with pie plates and cake pans and mixing bowls, and full of warm, spicy odours. The oven in the chimney was all heated and ready for a batch of apple and pumpkin pies. Mrs. Adams was busy sliding them in, but she stopped to look at Sarah and Thankful. Sarah was her only child.

"Why, what makes you look so sober?" said she.

"Nothing," replied Sarah. She had taken off her blanket, and sat in one of the straight-backed kitchen chairs, holding Thankful.

"You look dreadful sober," said her mother. "Are you tired?"

"No, marm."

"I'm afraid you've got cold standing out there in the wind. Do you feel chilly?"

"No, marm. Mother, how much do you suppose our turkey weighs?"

"I believe father said he'd weigh about twenty pounds. You are sure you don't feel chilly?"

"No, marm. Mother, do you suppose our turkey weighs more than Submit's?"

"How do you suppose I can tell? I ain't set eyes on their turkey lately. If you feel well, you'd better sit up to the table and stone that bowl of raisins. Put your dolly away, and get your apron."

But Sarah stoned raisins with Thankful in her lap, hidden under her apron. She was so full of anxiety that she could not bear to put her away. Suppose the Thompson turkey should be larger, and she should lose Thankful--Thankful that her beautiful Aunt Rose had made for her?

Submit, over in the Thompson house, had sat down at once to her apple paring. She had not gone into the best room to look at the work-box whose possession she had hazarded. It stood in there on the table, made of yellow satiny wood, with a sliding lid ornamented with a beautiful little picture. Submit had a certain pride in it, but her fear of losing it was not equal to her hope of possessing Thankful. Submit had never had a doll, except a few plebeian ones, manufactured secretly out of corn-cobs, whom it took more imagination than she possessed to admire.

Gradually all emulation over the turkeys was lost in the naughty covetousness of her little friend and neighbour's doll. Submit felt shocked and guilty, but she sat there paring the Baldwin apples, and thinking to herself: "If our turkey is only bigger, if it only is, then--I shall have Thankful." Her mouth was pursed up and her eyes snapped. She did not talk at all, but pared very fast.

Her mother looked at her. "If you don't take care, you'll cut your fingers," said she. "You are in too much of a hurry. I suppose you want to get out and gossip with Sarah again at the wall, but I can't let you waste any more time to-day. There, I told you you would!"

Submit had cut her thumb quite severely. She choked a little when her mother tied it up, and put on some balm of Gilead, which made it smart worse.

"Don't cry!" said her mother. "You'll have to bear more than a cut thumb if you live."

And Submit did not let the tears fall. She came from a brave race. Her great-grandfather had fought in the Revolution; his sword and regimentals were packed in the fine carved chest in the best room. Over the kitchen shelf hung an old musket with which her great-grandmother, guarding her home and children, had shot an Indian. In a little closet beside the chimney was an old pewter dish full of homemade Revolutionary bullets, which Submit and her brothers had for playthings. A little girl who played with Revolutionary bullets ought not to cry over a cut thumb.

Submit finished paring the apples after her thumb was tied up, although she was rather awkward about it. Then she pounded spices in the mortar, and picked over cranberries. Her mother kept her busy every minute until dinnertime. When Submit's father and her two brothers, Thomas and Jonas, had come in, she began on the subject nearest her heart.

"Father," said she, "how much do you think our Thanksgiving turkey will weigh?"

Mr. Thompson was a deliberate man. He looked at her a minute before replying. "Seventeen or eighteen pounds," replied he.

"Oh, Father! don't you think he will weigh twenty?" Mr. Thompson shook his head.

"He don't begin to weigh so much as the Adams' turkey," said Jonas. "Their turkey weighs twenty pounds."

"Oh, Thomas! do you think their turkey weighs more than ours?" cried Submit.

Thomas was her elder brother; he had a sober, judicial air like his father. "Their turkey weighs considerable more than ours," said he.

Submit's face fell.

"You are not showing a right spirit," said her mother, severely. "Why should you care if the Adams' turkey does weigh more? I am ashamed of you!"

Submit said no more. She ate her dinner soberly. Afterward she wiped dishes while her mother washed. All the time she was listening. Her father and brothers had gone out; presently she started. "Oh, Mother, they're killing the turkey!" said she.

"Well, don't stop while the dishes are hot, if they are," returned her mother.

Submit wiped obediently, but as soon as the dishes were set away, she stole out in the barn where her father and brothers were picking the turkey.

"Father, when are you going to weigh him?" she asked timidly.

"Not till to-night," said her father.

"Submit!" called her mother.

Submit went in and swept the kitchen floor. It was an hour after that, when her mother was in the south room, getting it ready for her grandparents, who were coming home to Thanksgiving--they had been on a visit to their youngest son--that Submit crept slyly into the pantry. The turkey lay there on the broad shelf before the window. Submit looked at him. She thought he was small. "He was 'most all feathers," she whispered, ruefully. She stood looking disconsolately at the turkey. Suddenly her eyes flashed and a red flush came over her face. It was as if Satan, coming into that godly new England home three days before Thanksgiving, had whispered in her ear.

Presently Submit stole softly back into the kitchen, set a chair before the chimney cupboard, climbed up, and got the pewter dish full of Revolutionary bullets. Then she stole back to the pantry and emptied the bullets into the turkey's crop.

Then she got a needle and thread from her mother's basket, sewed up the crop carefully, and set the empty dish back in the cupboard. She had just stepped down out of the chair when her brother Jonas came in.

"Submit," said he, "let's have one game of odd or even with the bullets."

"I am too busy," said Submit. "I've got to spin my stint."

"Just one game. Mother won't care."

"No; I can't."

Submit flew to her spinning wheel in the corner. Jonas, still remonstrating, strolled into the pantry.

"I don't believe mother wants you in there," Submit said anxiously.

"See here, Submit," Jonas called out in an eager voice, "I'll get the steelyards, and we'll weigh the turkey. We can do it as well as anybody."

Submit left her spinning wheel. She was quite pale with trepidation when Jonas and she adjusted the turkey in the steelyards. What if those bullets should rattle out? But they did not.

"He weighs twenty pounds and a quarter," announced Jonas, with a gasp, after peering anxiously at the figures. "He's the biggest turkey that was ever raised in these parts."

Jonas exulted a great deal, but Submit did not say much. As soon as Jonas had laid the turkey back on the shelf and gone out, she watched her chance and removed the bullets, replacing them in the pewter dish.

When Mr. Thompson and Thomas came home at twilight there was a deal of talk over the turkey.

"The Adams' turkey doesn't weigh but nineteen pounds," Jonas announced. "Sarah was out there when they weighed him, and she 'most cried."

"I think Sarah and Submit and all of you are very foolish about it," said Mrs. Thompson severely. "What difference does it make if one weighs a pound or two more than the other, if there is enough to go round?"

"Submit looks as if she was sorry ours weighed the most now," said Jonas.

"My thumb aches," said Submit.

"Go and get the balm of Gilead bottle, and put some more on," ordered her mother.

That night when she went to bed she could not say her prayers. When she woke in the morning it was with a strange, terrified feeling, as if she had climbed a wall into some unknown dreadful land. She wondered if Sarah would bring Thankful over; she dreaded to see her coming, but she did not come. Submit herself did not stir out of the house all that day or the next, and Sarah did not bring Thankful until next morning.

They were all out in the kitchen about an hour before dinner. Grandfather Thompson sat in his old armchair at one corner of the fireplace, Grandmother Thompson was knitting, and Jonas and Submit were cracking butternuts. Submit was a little happier this morning. She thought Sarah would never bring Thankful, and so she had not done so much harm by cheating in the weight of the turkey.

There was a tug at the latch of the kitchen door; it was pushed open slowly and painfully, and Sarah entered with Thankful in her arms. She said not a word to anybody, but her little face was full of woe. She went straight to Submit, and laid Thankful in her lap; then she turned and fled with a great sob. The door slammed after her. All the Thompsons stopped and looked at Submit.

"Submit, what does this mean?" her father asked.

Submit looked at him, trembling.

"Speak," said he.

"Submit, mind your father," said Mrs. Thompson.

"What did she bring you the doll baby for?" asked Grandmother Thompson.

"Sarah--was going to give me Thankful if--our turkey weighed most, and I was going to--give her my work-box if hers weighed most," said Submit jerkily. Her lips felt stiff.

Her father looked very sober and stern. He turned to his father. When Grandfather Thompson was at home, every one deferred to him. Even at eighty he was the recognized head of the house. He was a wonderful old man, tall and soldierly, and full of a grave dignity. He looked at Submit, and she shrank.

"Do you know," said he, "that you have been conducting yourself like unto the brawlers in the taverns and ale-houses?"

"Yes, sir," murmured Submit, although she did not know what he meant.

"No godly maid who heeds her elders will take part in any such foolish and sinful wager," her grandfather continued.

Submit arose, hugging Thankful convulsively. She glanced wildly at her great-grandmother's musket over the shelf. The same spirit that had aimed it at the Indian possessed her, and she spoke out quite clearly: "Our turkey didn't weigh the most," said she. "I put the Revolutionary bullets in his crop."

There was silence. Submit's heart beat so hard that Thankful quivered.

"Go upstairs to your chamber, Submit," said her mother, "and you need not come down to dinner. Jonas, take that doll and carry it over to the Adams' house."

Submit crept miserably out of the room, and Jonas carried Thankful across the yard to Sarah.

Submit crouched beside her little square window set with tiny panes of glass, and watched him. She did not cry. She was very miserable, but confession had awakened a salutary smart in her soul, like the balm of Gilead on her cut thumb. She was not so unhappy as she had been. She wondered if her father would whip her, and she made up her mind not to cry if he did.

After Jonas came back she still crouched at the window. Exactly opposite in the Adams' house was another little square window, and that lighted Sarah's chamber. All of a sudden Sarah's face appeared there. The two little girls stared pitifully at each other. Presently Sarah raised her window, and put a stick under it; then Submit did the same. They put their faces out, and looked at each other a minute before speaking. Sarah's face was streaming with tears.

"What you crying for?" called Submit softly.

"Father sent me up here 'cause it is sinful to--make bets, and Aunt Rose has come, and I can't have any--Thanksgiving dinner," wailed Sarah.

"I'm wickeder than you," said Submit. "I put the Revolutionary bullets in the turkey to make it weigh more than yours. Yours weighed the most. If mother thinks it's right, I'll give you the work-box."

"I don't--want it," sobbed Sarah. "I'm dreadful sorry you've got to stay up there, and can't have any dinner, Submit."

Answering tears sprang to Submit's eyes. "I'm dreadful sorry you've got to stay up there, and can't have any dinner," she sobbed back.

There was a touch on her shoulder. She looked around and there stood the grandmother. She was trying to look severe, but she was beaming kindly on her. Her fat, fair old face was as gentle as the mercy that tempers justice; her horn spectacles and her knitting needles and the gold beads on her neck all shone in the sunlight.

"You had better come downstairs, child," said she. "Dinner's 'most ready, and mebbe you can help your mother. Your father isn't going to whip you this time, because you told the truth about it, but you mustn't ever do such a dreadful wicked thing again."

"No, I won't," sobbed Submit. She looked across, and there beside Sarah's face in the window was another beautiful smiling one. It had pink cheeks and sweet black eyes and black curls, among which stood a high tortoise-shell comb.

"Oh, Submit!" Sarah called out, joyfully, "Aunt Rose says I can go down to dinner!"

"Grandmother says I can!" called back Submit.

The beautiful smiling face opposite leaned close to Sarah's for a minute.

"Oh, Submit!" cried Sarah, "Aunt Rose says she will make you a doll baby like Thankful, if your mother's willing!"

"I guess she'll be willing if she's a good girl," called Grandmother Thompson.

Submit looked across a second in speechless radiance. Then the faces vanished from the two little windows, and Submit and Sarah went down to their Thanksgiving dinners.

BEETLE RING'S THANKSGIVING MASCOT[2]
BY SHELDON C. STODDARD.

Beetle Ring had the reputation of being the toughest lumber
camp on the river. The boys were certainly rough, and rather hard drink-
ers, but their hearts were in the right place, after all.

Six months of idleness following a long run of fever, a lost position, and consequent discouragement had brought poverty and wretchedness to Joe Bennett.

The lumber camp on the Featherstone, where he had been at work, had broken
up and gone, and an old shack, deserted by some hunter, and now standing alone in
the great woods, was the only home he could provide for his little family. It had answered its purpose as a makeshift in the warm weather, but now, in late November,
and with the terrible northern winter coming swiftly on, it was small wonder the
young lumberman had been discouraged as he tried to forecast the future.

His strength had returned, however, and lately something of his old courage,
for he had found work. It was fifteen miles away, to be sure, and in "Beetle Ring"
lumber camp, the camp that bore the reputation of being the roughest on the Featherstone, but it was work.

[Note 2: From the *Youth's Companion*, November 30, 1905.]

He was earning something, and might hope soon to move his family into a
habitable house and civilization.

But his position at Beetle Ring was not an enviable one. The men took scant
pains to conceal their dislike for the young fellow who steadfastly refused to "chip
in" when the camp jug was sent to the Skylark, the nearest saloon, some miles down
the river, and who invariably declined to join in the camp's numerous sprees. But

Bennett worked on quietly.

And in the meantime to the old shack in the woods the baby had come--in the bleak November weather.

Night was settling down over the woods. An old half-breed woman was tending the fire in the one room of the shack, and on the wretched bed lay a fair-faced woman, the young wife and mother, who looked wistfully out at the bleak woods, white with the first snow, then turned her wan, pale face toward the tiny bundle at her side.

"Your pappy will come to-night, baby," she said, softly. "It's Saturday, and your pappy will come to-night, sure." She drew the covers more closely, and tucked them carefully about the small figure.

"Mend the fire, Lisette, please. It's cold. And, Lisette, please watch out down the road. Sometimes Joe comes early Saturdays."

The old woman shook her head and muttered over the little pile of wood, but she fed the fire, and then turned and looked down the long white trail.

"No Joe yet," she said, with a sympathetic glance toward the bed. She looked at the thick gray clouds, and added, "Heap snow soon."

But the night came down and the evening passed, while the women waited anxiously. It was near midnight when the wife's face lighted up suddenly at a sound outside, and directly there was a pounding, uncertain step on the threshold. The door opened and Bennett came in clumsily.

The woman's little glad cry of welcome was changed to one of apprehension at her husband's appearance. The resolute swing and bearing of the lumberman-- that had returned as he regained his strength--were gone. He clumped across the room unsteadily on a pair of rude crutches, his left foot swathed in bandages--a big, ungainly bundle.

"What is it, Joe?" the wife asked anxiously.

"Just more of my precious luck, that's all, Nannie." He threw off the old box coat and heavy cap, brushed the melting snow from his hair and beard, and without waiting to warm his chilled hands at the fire, hobbled to the bed and bent over the woman and the tiny bundle.

"Are you all right, Nan?" he asked anxiously.

"All right, Joe; but I've been so worried!"

"And the baby, Nan?"

The wife gently pushed back the covers and proudly brought to view a tiny pink and puckered face. "Fine, Joe. She's just as fine, isn't she?"

A proud, happy light flickered for a moment in the man's eyes as he stooped to kiss the tiny face; then he shut his teeth hard and swallowed suddenly.

"What is it, Joe?" his wife asked, looking at the rudely bandaged foot.

"Cut it--nigh half off, and hurt the bone. It'll be weeks before I can do a stroke of work again. It means--I don't know what, and I daren't think what, Nannie. The cook sewed it up." He glowered at the injured member savagely.

His wife's face grew paler still, but she only asked tenderly, "How did you ever get here, Joe?"

"Rode one of Pose Breem's hosses--his red roan."

"Fifteen miles on horseback with that foot? I should have thought it would have killed you, Joe."

"I had to come, Nan," said the lumberman. "I didn't know how you were getting on, and I had to come."

"I didn't suppose they'd let you have a horse, any of 'em, now sleighing's come."

"They wouldn't--if I'd asked 'em. They don't seem to like me very well, and I didn't ask."

His wife's big, wistful eyes were turned upon him in quick alarm. "I'm scared, Joe, if you took a horse without asking. What'll they think? Where is it, Joe?"

"Don't ye worry, Nan. I've sent the horse back by Pikepole Pete. He'll have him back before morning--Pose won't miss him till then--and I wrote a note explaining. Pose will be mad some, but he'll get over it."

The young lumberman listened uneasily to the storm, which was increasing, looked at his wife's pale face a moment, and added:

"I had to come, Nan. I just had to."

But the woman was only half reassured. "If anything should happen," she said, "if he shouldn't get it back, they'd think you--you stole it, and--"

"There, there, Nan!" broke in her husband, "don't be crossing bridges. Pete'll take the horse back. I've done the fellow lots of favours, and he won't go back on me. Don't worry, girl!"

He moved the bandaged foot and winced, but not from the pain of the wound. The hard look grew deeper on his face. "I'm down on my luck, Nan," he said, hopelessly. "There's no use trying. Everything's against me, everything--following me like grim death. And grim death," he jerked the words out harshly, "is like to be the end of it, here in this old shack that's not fit to winter hogs in, let alone humans. There's not wood enough cut to last a week. You'll freeze, Nan, you and the baby, and I'm--just nothing."

He took two silver dollars from his pocket, and said, almost savagely, "There's what we've got to winter on, and me crippled."

But his wife put her hand on his softly. "Don't you give up so, Joe," she said. And presently she added: "Next Thursday's Thanksgiving. We've seen hard times, and we may see harder, but I never knew Thanksgiving to come yet without something to be thankful for--never."

Outside the storm continued, fine snow sifting down rapidly. "Pikepole Pete" found stiff work facing it, and bent low over the red roan's neck.

"Blue blazes!" he muttered. "Bennett's a good fellow all right, and he's hurt; but if he hadn't nigh saved my life twice he could get this critter back himself fer all of me!" He glanced at the dark woods and drew up suddenly. "The road forks here, and Turner's is yonder--less than a mile. I'll hitch in his barn a spell and go on later," and he took the Turner fork.

But at Turner's Pete found two or three congenial spirits--and a jug; and a few hours later the easy-going fellow was deep in a tipsy sleep that would last for hours.

The following Sunday morning came bright and clear upon freshly fallen snow that softened all the ruder outlines of town and field and woods. Beetle Ring camp lay wrapped in fleecy whiteness.

The camp was late astir, for Sunday was Beetle Ring's day--not of rest, but of carousal. Two men had started out rather early--the camp's jug delegation to the Skylark. Presently the men began to straggle out to the snug row of sheds where the horses were kept. Posey Breem yawned lazily as he threw open the door of his particular stall, then suddenly brought himself together with a jerk and stared fixedly.

"What ails you now, Pose? Seen a ghost?"

"Skid" Thomson stopped with the big measure of feed which he was carrying.

"No, I've seen no ghost," said Breem slowly, still staring. "Look here, Skid!" Thomson looked into the stall, and nearly dropped the measure.

"By George, Pose!" he said. "By--George!"

The news flew over the camp like wildfire. Posey Breem's red roan, the best horse in the camp, had been stolen! The burly lumbermen came hurrying from all directions. There was no doubt about it--the horse was gone, and the snow had covered every trace. There was absolutely no clue to follow. Silently and sullenly the men filed in to breakfast. In a lumberman's eyes hardly a crime could exceed that of horse stealing.

"What I want to know is," said Breem, as he glanced sharply round the long room of the camp, "what's become of that yellow-haired jay--Bennett?"

"By George!" said Skid Thomson, "that's right! Where is the critter?"

"Skipped!" said Bill Bates, sententiously, after a quick search had been made. "It's all plain enough now. I never liked the close-fisted critter."

"Nor I, either!" growled Skid. "Never chipped in with the boys, but was laying low just the same."

"You won't catch him, either," said Bates. "They're sharp--that kind. The critter knew 'twould snow and hide his tracks."

"And I'd just sewed up his blamed foot!" muttered the cook in disgust.

"Maybe we'll catch him. Up to Fat Pine two years ago," began Breem, reminiscently, "Big Donovan had a horse stole. They caught the fellow."

"Yes, I remember," said Skid Thomson. "I was there. We caught him up north." The men nodded understandingly and approvingly.

"Wuth a hundred and fifty dollars, the roan was," said Breem.

Beetle Ring camp passed an uneasy day, the "jug" for once receiving scant attention. Late in the afternoon "Trapper John," an old half-breed who hunted and trapped about the woods, stopped at the camp to get warm.

"Didn't see anybody with a horse last night or this morning, eh, John?" asked Posey Breem.

"Um, yes," responded the old trapper, quickly. "Saw um horse las' night--man ride--big foot--so." Old John held out his arms in exaggerated illustration.

Beetle Ring rose to its feet as one man. "What colour was the horse, John?" asked Breem softly.

"Huh! Can't see good after dark, but think um roan." Breem looked slowly round the silent camp, and Beetle Ring grimly made ready for business.

It was evening when the men stopped a few rods below the shack. A light shone out from a window, lighting up a little space in the sombre woods.

"The fellow's got pals prob'bly," said Posey Breem. "You wait here while I do a little scouting."

Breem crept cautiously into the circle of light, and glancing through the un-curtained window, saw his man--with his "pals." He saw upon the miserable bed a woman with a thin, pale face and sad, wistful eyes, eyes that yet lighted up with a beautiful pride as they rested upon the man, who sat close by, holding a tiny bundle in his arms.

The man shifted his position a little, so that the light fell upon the bundle, and then the watcher outside saw the sleeping face of a baby.

There was a rumour in the camp that Posey Breem had not always been the man that he was--that a woman had once blessed his life. But since they had carried the young mother away, with her dead baby on her breast, to place the two in one deep grave together, he had gone steadily downward.

With hungry eyes Breem gazed at the scene in the poor little house, his thoughts flying backward over the years. A sudden sharp, impatient whistle roused him, and he strode hastily back to the waiting men.

"Well, Pose?" interrogated Skid impatiently.

"He's there, all right," said Breem, in a peculiar tone. "I ain't overmuch given to advising prowling round folks' houses, but you fellows just look in yonder." He jerked his head toward the shack. And a line of big, rough-looking men filed into the little illumined space, to come back presently silent and subdued.

"Now let's go home," said Breem, turning his horse toward camp.

"And your horse, Pose?" questioned Bates.

"Burn the horse!" said Breem quickly. "D'ye think the like of yonder's a horse thief? I ain't worrying 'bout the horse." And the men rode back to camp silently.

The next morning, when Breem swung open the door of the stall, he was not surprised to find the red roan standing quietly by the side of his mate. A bit of crumpled paper was pinned to the blanket. Breem read:

I rode your horse. I had to. I'll surely make it right.

BENNETT.

"Course he had to!" growled the lumberman, and he passed the paper round.

"Oncommon peart baby," said Skid, at last.

"Dreadful cold shack, though!" muttered Bates, conveying a quarter of a griddlecake to his mouth.

"That's just it," said Pose, scowling. "Just let a stiff nip of winter come, and the woman yonder and the little critter, they'd freeze, that's what they'd do, in that old rattletrap."

The men looked at one another in solemn assent. "And I've been thinking," continued Breem, "since Bennett there belonged to the camp, and since we kind of misused the fellow for being stingy--for which we ought to have been smashed with logs--that we have a kind of a claim on 'em, as 'twere, and they on us. And we must get 'em out of that yonder before they freeze plumb solid." He stopped inquiringly.

"Right as right," assented several.

"And I've been thinking," said Bates suddenly, "about that storeroom of ours. It's snug and warm, and there's a lot of room in it, and we can put a stove into it and--" But the rest of Bates's suggestion was drowned in a round of applause.

"And *I've* been thinking, just a little," put in Skid Thomson, "and if I've figured correct, next Thursday's Thanksgiving--don't know as I've thought of it in ten years--and if we stir round sharp we can get things ready by then, and--well, 'twouldn't hurt Beetle Ring to celebrate for once--" But Skid was also interrupted by a cheer.

"And it's my firm belief," reflected Bates with an air of profound conviction, "that that baby of Bennett's was designed special and, as you might say, providential, for to be Beetle Ring's mascot. Fat Pine and Horseshoe have 'em--mascots--to bring luck, and I've noticed Beetle Ring ain't had the luck lately it should have."

Bates paused, and the camp meditated in silent delight.

Thanksgiving morning was a cold one, but clear. More snow had fallen, and the deep, feathery whiteness stretched away until lost in the dark background of the pines and spruces. A wavering line of smoke rose over the roof of the little old shack in the woods.

Bennett was winding rags round the armpieces of the rough crutches. He had dragged in some short limbs the day before for fuel, but in so doing had broken open the wound, which gave him excruciating pain.

"Joe," said his wife, suddenly, "where are you going?"

"I'm going to try for help, Nan. We're out of nigh everything, and my foot no better."

"You can't do it, Joe. You--you'll die, if you try, Joe, alone in the woods. Oh, Joe!"

The look of hope that had never wholly left the woman's eyes was slowly fading out.

"We'll all die if I don't try, Nannie. I'm--"

"Huh!" suddenly exclaimed the old woman, peering out of the little window. "Heap men, heap horses! Look, see 'em come!"

Bennett turned hastily, and saw a long line of stalwart men and sturdy horses threshing resolutely through the deep snow and heading directly for the shack. He looked keenly at the men, and his face paled a little, but he said steadily, "It's the Beetle Ring men, Nan."

His wife gave a sharp cry. "It's the horse, Joe! It's the horse! They're after you, Joe, sure!" She caught her husband's arm.

The men were now filling up the little space before the shack. Directly there came a sounding knock. Bennett opened the door to admit the burly frame of Posey Breem. He said quietly:

"I'm here all right, Pose, and I took your horse, but--"

"Burn the hoss!" said Breem explosively. "That's all right. Shake, pard!" He held out a brawny hand. Bennett "shook" wonderingly.

"Wife, pard?" asked Breem, gently, nodding toward the bed. Bennett hastily introduced him.

"Kid, pard?" Breem pointed a stubby finger at the little bundle.

Bennett nodded.

The lumberman grinned delightedly, then coughed a little, and began awkwardly:

"Pard, th' boys over at Beetle Ring heard--as you might say, accidental"--Breem coughed into his big hand--"about your folks over here, your wife *and*--the baby. They were powerful interested, specially about the baby. Why, pard, some of the boys hain't seen a baby in ten years, and we thought as you belonged to the camp, maybe you and your wife would allow that the camp had a sort of claim on the little critter yonder." He eyed the tiny bundle wistfully.

"And another thing that hit the boys, pard," he went on. "Up at Fat Pine they got what they call a mascot, bein' a tame b'ar; an' up at Horseshoe they got a mascot, bein' a goat. Lots of camps have 'em--fetches luck. And the boys are sure that this baby of yours was designed special to be Beetle Ring's mascot. Now, pard, Beetle Ring, as you know, ain't what you'd call a Sunday-school, but the boys they'll behave. They fixed up that storeroom to beat all, nice bed, big stove, and lots of wood, and so on, and we've got a cow for the woman and baby. Say, we want you powerful. Got a sleigh fixed, hemlock boughs and a cover of robes and blankets, and Skid'll drive careful. He's a master at drivin', Skid is. You'll come, won't you? The boys are waitin'."

Big tears were in the woman's eyes as she turned toward her husband. "Oh, Joe," she said, and choked suddenly; but she pressed the baby tightly to her breast. "I knew 'twould come Thanksgiving."

"There, pard," said Breem, after blowing his nose explosively, "you just see to wrappin' up the woman and the kid, and me and Skid, being as you're hurt, you know, 'll tote 'em out to the sleigh."

The young mother was soon placed carefully in the sleigh, the old woman following. But when Skid Thomson appeared in the door of the old shack, bearing a tiny form muffled up with wondrous care, the whole of Beetle Ring shouted.

Breem led up a spare horse for Bennett's use. The latter stopped short, with a curious expression on his face. The horse was the red roan.

But Breem only said, his keen eyes twinkling:

"Under such circumstances as these, pard, you're welcome to all the hosses in Beetle Ring."

With steady, practiced hand Skid Thomson guided his powerful team through the deep snow, over the rough forest road; and sometimes brawny arms carried the sleigh bodily over the roughest places.

    *   *   *   *   *

At the close of the day an anxious consultation took place in the big main room of Beetle Ring, and presently two men appeared outside.

They walked slowly toward what had been the camp's storeroom, but halted before the door hesitatingly.

"You go in ahead, Skid, and ask 'em," said Breem, earnestly, to his companion.

"No, go ahead yourself, Pose. I'd be sure to calk a hoss or split a runner, or somethin'. Go on!"

Breem knocked, and both went in.

"All right, pard?"

"Right as right, Pose," said Joe Bennett.

"Wife all right?" Breem turned toward the bed, and Mrs. Bennett smiled up at him with happy eyes, and with a bit of colour already showing in her pale face. Breem smiled back broadly. Then he asked, "***And***, pard, the baby?"

"Peart as peart, Pose."

Breem waited a little, twirling his cap, but receiving a sharp thump from Thomson, went on:

"The boys, pard, are anxious about the little critter. They're kind of hankering, pard, and, mum, if you are willin', and ain't 'fraid to trust her with us, why, we'd be mighty glad to tote her--just for a few minutes--over to camp. The boys are stiddy, all of 'em, stiddy as churches. They hain't soaked a mite to-day, mum, and they ain't goin' to; they've hove the jug into a snowdrift, and they'd take it kind, mum--if you are willin'."

The woman, still smiling happily, was already wrapping up the baby.

Breem held up a warning finger when he returned a little later, and again smiled delightedly.

"Went to sleep a-totin'--if you'll believe it, the burned little critter!" he said, softly. "And," he added, "the boys, pard, are mighty pleased; and, mum, they thank you kindly. They say, the boys do, there ain't such a mascot as theirs in five hundred miles; they see luck comin', chunks of it, pard, already." And the big fellow went out and closed the door gently.

MISTRESS ESTEEM ELLIOTT'S MOLASSES CAKE[3]
The Story of a Postponed Thanksgiving[4]

By Kate Upson Clark.

Older boys and girls who are familiar with "The Courtship of
Miles Standish" will enjoy the colonial flavour of this tale of 1705.

"Obed!" called Mistress Achsah Ely from her front porch, "step thee over to
Squire Belding's, quick! Here's a teacup! Ask Mistress Belding for the loan of some
molasses. Nothing but molasses and hot water helps the baby when he is having
such a turn of colic. Beseems me he will have a fit! Make haste, Obed!"

[Note 3: From **Wideawake**, November, 1891, Lothrop, Lee & Shepard
Company.]

[Note 4: The main facts in this story are strictly historical.]

At that very moment Squire Belding's little daughter Hitty was travelling toward Mistress Ely's for the purpose of borrowing molasses wherewith to sweeten a
ginger cake. Hitty and Obed, who were of an age, met, compared notes, and then
returned to their respective homes. Shortly afterward both of them darted forth
again, bound on the same errands as before, only in different directions.

Mr. Chapin, the storekeeper, hadn't "set eyes on any molasses for a week. The
river's frozen over so mean and solid," he said, "there's no knowing when there'll
be any molasses in town."

There had been very peculiar weather in Colchester during this month of October, 1705. First, on the 13th (Old Style), an unprecedently early date, had come a
"terrible cold snap," lasting three days. This was followed by two days of phenom-
enal mildness. The river had frozen over during the "cold snap," and the ice had
melted during the warm days, until, on the 19th, it was breaking up and preparing to go out to sea. In the night of the 19th had descended a frigid blast, colder
than the original one. This had arrested the broken ice, piled it up in all sorts of
fantastic forms, and congealed it till it looked like a rough Alaskan glacier. After

the cold wind had come a heavy snowstorm. All Colchester lay under three feet of snow. Footpaths and roads were broken out somewhat in the immediate village, but no farther. It was most unusual to have the river closed so early in the season, and consequently the winter supplies, which were secured from New London and Norwich, had not been laid in. Even Mr. Chapin, the storekeeper, was but poorly supplied with staples of which he ordinarily kept an abundance on hand.

Therefore when Obed and Hitty had made the tour of the neighbourhood they found but one family, that of Deacon Esteem Elliott, the richest man in the place, which had any molasses. Mistress Elliott, in spite of her wealth, was said to be "none too free with her stuff," and she was not minded to lend any molasses under the circumstances, for "a trifling foolish" cake. Obed's representation of the distress of the Ely baby, however, appealed even to her, and she lent him a large spoonful of the precious liquid.

That afternoon there was as much visiting about among the Colchester house-wives as the drifts permitted. Such a state of things had never been known since the town was settled. No molasses! And Thanksgiving appointed for the first Thursday in November! Pray what would Thanksgiving amount to, they inquired, with no pumpkin pies, no baked beans, no molasses cake, no proper sweetening for the rum so freely used in those days?

Mistress Esteem Elliott was even more troubled than the rest of Colchester, for was not her buxom daughter, and only child, Prudence Ann, to be married on Thanksgiving Day to the son of a great magnate in the neighbouring town of Hebron? And was it not the intention to invite all of the aristocracy of both towns to be present at the marriage feast?

Mistress Elliott accordingly pursued her way upon this Tuesday afternoon, October 19, 1705, over to Mistress Achsah Ely's. There she found Mistress Belding, who, remembering Mistress Elliott's refusal to lend her molasses, was naturally somewhat chill in her manner.

Mistress Elliott had scarcely pulled off her homespun leggings (made with stout and ample feet) and pulled out her knitting work, when Mistress Camberly, the parson's wife, a lady of robust habit and voluble tongue, came in.

"And what are we going to do, Mistress Ely?" she burst out, as soon as the door was opened at her knock. "Not a drop of molasses to be had for love nor money, and

Thanksgiving Day set for the 4th of November!"

"Mistress Elliott has a-plenty of molasses," affirmed Mistress Belding, with a haughty look at her unaccommodating neighbour.

"I'd have you to know, Mistress Betty Belding," retorted Mistress Elliott, "that I have a bare quart or so in my jug, and, so far as I can learn, that is all that the whole town of Colchester has got to depend upon till the roads or the river can be broken to Norwich."

Mistress Ely well understood this little passage-at-arms, for Obed had told her the whole story; but as her baby had been cured by Mistress Elliott's molasses, she did not think it proper to interfere in the matter. Neither did the good parson's wife, although she could not comprehend the rights of the case. She simply repeated her first question: "What are we going to do about it, I should like to know?"

"I wonder if Thanksgiving Day could not be put off a week," suggested Mistress Belding, who had a good head, and was even reported to give such advice to her husband that he always thought best to heed it.

"Such a thing was never heard of!" cried Mistress Elliott.

"But there's no law against it," insisted Mistress Belding boldly. "By a week from the set day there will surely be some means of getting about the country, and then we can have a Thanksgiving that's worth the setting down to."

After a long talk the good women separated in some doubt, but as Squire Belding and Mr. Ely were two of the three selectmen, they were soon acquainted with the drift of the afternoon's discussion. The result of it all is thus chronicled in the town records of Colchester:

> "At a legal town-meeting held in Colchester, October 29,
> 1705, it was voted that WHEREAS there was a Thanksgiving
> appointed to be held on the first Thursday in November, and
> our present circumstances being such that it cannot with
> convenience be attended on that day, it is therefore voted
> and agreed by the inhabitants as aforesaid (concluding the
> thing will not be otherwise than well resented) that the
> second Thursday of November aforesaid shall be set aside for
> that service."

This proceeding was, on the whole, as the selectmen had hoped that it would be, "well resented" among the Colchester people, but there was one household in which there was rebellion at the mandate. In the great sanded kitchen of Deacon Esteem Elliott pretty, spoilt Prudence Ann was fairly raging over it.

"I had set my heart on being married on Thanksgiving Day," she sobbed, "And here it won't be Thanksgiving Day at all! And as for putting off a wedding, everybody knows there is no surer way of bringing ill luck down than that! I say I won't have it put off! But we can't have any party with no molasses in town! Oh, dear! I might as well be married in the back kitchen with a linsey gown on, as if I were the daughter of old Betty, the pie woman! There!"

Then the proud girl would break into fresh sobs, and vow vengeance upon the selectmen of Colchester. She even sent her father to expostulate with them, but it was of no use. They had known all along that the Elliotts did not want the festival day put off, but nobody in Colchester minded very much if the Elliotts were a little crossed.

Prudence Ann would not face the reality till after the Sabbath was past. On that day the expectant bridegroom managed to break his way through the drifts from Hebron, and he was truly grieved, as he should have been, at the very unhappy state of mind of his betrothed. He avowed himself, however, in a way which augured well for the young people's future, ready to do just what Prudence Ann and her family decided was best.

On Monday morning Mistress Elliott sat down with her unreasonable daughter and had a serious talk with her.

"Now, Prudence Ann," she began, "you must give up crying and fretting. If you are going to be married on Thursday, we have got a great deal of work to do between now and then. If you are going to wait till next week, I want to know it. Of course you can't have a large party, if you choose to be married on the 4th, but we will ask John's folks and Aunt Susanna and Uncle Martin and Parson Camberley and his wife. We can bake enough for them with what's in the house. If you wait another week, you can probably have a better party--and now you have it all in a nutshell."

Prudence Ann was hysterical even yet, but at last her terror of a postponed wedding overcame every other consideration. The day was set for the 4th, and the few guests were bidden accordingly.

On the morning of the wedding, on a neat shelf in the back kitchen of the Elliott residence, various delicacies were resting, which had been baked for the banquet. Mistress Elliott's molasses had sufficed to make a vast cake and several pumpkin pies. These, hot from the oven, had been placed in the coolness of the back kitchen until they should be ready for eating.

It so happened that Miss Hitty Belding's sharp eyes, as she passed Mistress Elliott's back door, bound on an errand to the house of the neighbour living just beyond, fell upon the rich golden brown of this wonderful cake. As such toothsome dainties were rare in Colchester at just this time, it is not strange that her childish soul coveted it, for Hitty was but ten years old. As she walked on she met Obed Ely.

"I tell you what, Obed," said Miss Hitty, "you ought to see the great molasses cake which Mistress Elliott has made for Prudence Ann's wedding. It is in her back kitchen. I saw it right by the door. Mean old thing! She wouldn't lend my mother any molasses to make *us* a cake. I wish I had hers!"

"So do I!" rejoined Obed, with watering lips. "I'm going to peek in and see it."

Obed went and "peeked," while Hitty sauntered slowly on. The contemplation of the cake under the circumstances was too much for even so well-brought-up a boy as Obed. Without stopping to really think what he was doing, he unwound from his neck his great woollen "comforter," wrapped it hastily around the cake, and was walking with it beside Hitty in the lonely, drifted country road five minutes later. The hearts of the two little conspirators--for they felt guilty enough--beat very hard, but they could not help thinking how good that cake would taste. A certain Goodsir Canty's cornhouse stood near them in a clump of trees beside the road, and as the door was open they crept in, gulped down great "chunks" of cake, distributed vast slices of what was left about their persons, Obed taking by far the lion's share, and then they parted, vowing eternal secrecy. Nobody had seen them, and something which happened just after they had left Mistress Elliott's back kitchen directed suspicion to an entirely different quarter.

Not two minutes after Obed's "comforter" had been thrown around the great cake a beautiful calf, the pride of Mistress Elliott's heart, and which was usually kept tied in the barn just beyond the back kitchen, somehow unfastened her rope and came strolling along past the open back door. The odour of the pumpkin pies naturally interested her, and she proceeded to lick up the delicious creamy filling of one after another with great zest.

Just as she was finishing the very last one of the four or five which had stood there, Mistress Elliott appeared upon the scene, to find her precious dainties faded like the baseless fabric of a vision, leaving behind them only a few broken bits of pie crust. A series of "short, sharp shocks" (as described in "The Mikado") then rent the air, summoning Prudence Ann and Delcy, the maid, to the scene of the calamity. Let us draw a veil over the succeeding ten minutes.

At the end of that time Prudence Ann lay upon the sitting-room lounge (or "settle," as they called it then) passing from one fainting fit into another, and Delcy was out in search of the doctor and such family friends as were likely to be of service in this unexpected dilemma. It was, of course, supposed that the calf had devoured the whole of the mighty cake as well as the pies. It was lucky for Obed and Hitty that the poor beast could not speak. As it was, nobody so much as thought of accusing them of the theft, though there were plenty of crumbs in their pockets, while the death of the innocent heifer was loudly demanded by the angry Prudence Ann. It was only by artifice and diplomacy that Mistress Elliott was able to preserve the life of her favourite, which, if it had really eaten the cake, must surely have perished.

The wedding finally came off on the 4th, though there was a pouting bride, and nuts, apples, and cider were said to be the chief refreshments. Prudence Ann, however, probably secured the "good luck" for which she was so anxious, for there is no record nor tradition to the contrary in all Colchester.

Nothing would probably ever have been known of the real fate of the famous cake if the tale had not been told by Mistress Hitty in her old age to her grandchildren, with appropriate warnings to them never to commit similar misdemeanours themselves.

Little Obed Ely, the active agent in the theft, died not long after it. His tombstone, very black and crumbled, stands in one of the old burying grounds of the town, but nothing is carved upon it as to the cause of his early death.

The story of the Colchester molasses famine, and the consequent postponement of their Thanksgiving, naturally spread throughout all the surrounding towns.

It was said that in one of these a party of roguish boys loaded an old cannon with molasses and fired it in the direction of Colchester. How they did this has not been stated, and some irreverent disbelievers in the more uncommon of our grandfathers' stories have profanely declared it a myth.

THE FIRST THANKSGIVING[5]
By Albert F. Blaisdell and Francis K. Ball.

A story of the time long ago when the Pilgrims of Plymouth
invited the Indian chief Massasoit and his followers to
share their feast.

All through the first summer and the early part of autumn the Pilgrims were busy and happy. They had planted and cared for their first fields of corn. They had found wild strawberries in the meadows, raspberries on the hillsides, and wild grapes in the woods.

[Note 5: From "Short Stories from American History," Ginn & Co.]

In the forest just back of the village wild turkeys and deer were easily shot. In the shallow waters of the bay there was plenty of fish, clams, and lobsters.

The summer had been warm, with a good deal of rain and much sunshine; and so when the autumn came there was a fine crop of corn.

"Let us gather the fruits of our first labours and rejoice together," said Governor Bradford.

"Yes," said Elder Brewster, "let us take a day upon which we may thank God for all our blessings, and invite to it our Indian friends who have been so kind to us."

The Pilgrims said that one day was not enough; so they planned to have a celebration for a whole week. This took place most likely in October.

The great Indian chief, Massasoit, came with ninety of his bravest warriors, all gayly dressed in deerskins, feathers, and foxtails, with their faces smeared with red, white, and yellow paint.

As a sign of rank, Massasoit wore round his neck a string of bones and a bag of tobacco. In his belt he carried a long knife. His face was painted red, and his hair was so daubed with oil that Governor Bradford said he "looked greasily."

Now there were only eleven buildings in the whole of Plymouth village, four log storehouses and seven little log dwelling-houses; so the Indian guests ate and slept out of doors. This was no matter, for it was one of those warm weeks in the season we call Indian summer.

To supply meat for the occasion four men had already been sent out to hunt wild turkeys. They killed enough in one day to last the whole company almost a week.

Massasoit helped the feast along by sending some of his best hunters into the woods. They killed five deer, which they gave to their paleface friends, that all might have enough to eat.

Under the trees were built long, rude tables on which were piled baked clams, broiled fish, roast turkey, and deer meat.

The young Pilgrim women helped serve the food to the hungry redskins.

Let us remember two of the fair girls who waited on the tables. One was Mary Chilton, who leaped from the boat at Plymouth Rock; the other was Mary Allerton. She lived for seventy-eight years after this first Thanksgiving, and of those who came over in the *Mayflower* she was the last to die.

What a merry time everybody had during that week! It may be they joked Governor Bradford about stepping into a deer trap set by the Indians and being jerked up by the leg.

How the women must have laughed as they told about the first Monday morning at Cape Cod, when they all went ashore to wash their clothes!

It must have been a big washing, for there had been no chance to do it at sea, so stormy had been the long voyage of sixty-three days. They little thought that Monday would afterward be kept as washday.

Then there was young John Howland, who in mid-ocean fell overboard but was quick enough to catch hold of a trailing rope. Perhaps after dinner he invited Elizabeth Tilley, whom he afterward married, to sail over to Clarke's Island and return by moonlight.

With them, it may be, went John Alden and Priscilla Mullins, whose love story is so sweetly told by Longfellow.

One proud mother, we may be sure, showed her bright-eyed boy, Peregrine White.

And so the fun went on. In the daytime the young men ran races, played games, and had a shooting match. Every night the Indians sang and danced for their friends; and to make things still more lively they gave every now and then a shrill war whoop that made the woods echo in the still night air.

The Indians had already learned to love and fear Captain Miles Standish. Some of them called him "Boiling Water" because he was easily made angry. Others called him "Captain Shrimp," on account of his small size.

Every morning the shrewd captain put on his armour and paraded his little company of a dozen or more soldiers; and when he fired off the cannon on Burial Hill the Indians must have felt that the English were men of might thus to harness up thunder and lightning.

During this week of fun and frolic it was a wonder if young Jack Billington did not play some prank on the Indians. He was the boy who fired off his father's gun one day, close to a keg of gunpowder, in the crowded cabin of the *Mayflower*.

The third day came. Massasoit had been well treated, and no doubt would have liked to stay longer, but he had said he could stay only three days. So the pipe of peace was silently passed around.

Then, taking their presents of glass beads and trinkets, the Indian king and his warriors said farewell to their English friends and began their long tramp through the woods to their wigwams on Mount Hope Bay.

On the last day of this Thanksgiving party the Pilgrims had a service of prayer and praise. Elder Brewster preached the first Thanksgiving sermon. After thanking God for all his goodness, he did not forget the many loved ones sleeping on the hillside.

He spoke of noble John Carver, the first governor, who had died of worry and overwork.

Nor was Rose Standish forgotten, the lovely young wife of Captain Miles Standish, whose death was caused by cold and lack of good food.

And then there was gentle Dorothy, wife of Governor Bradford, who had fallen overboard from the *Mayflower* in Provincetown harbour while her husband was coasting along the bleak shore in search of a place for a home.

The first Thanksgiving took place nearly three hundred years ago. Since that time, almost without interruption, Thanksgiving has been kept by the people of New England as the great family festival of the year. At this time children and grandchildren return to the old home, the long table is spread, and brothers and sisters, separated often by many miles, again sit side by side.

To-day Thanksgiving is observed in nearly all the states of the Union, a season of sweet and blessed memories.

THANKSGIVING AT TODD'S ASYLUM[6]
By Winthrop Packard.

Many a chuckle lies in wait for the reader in the pages of this story. And the humour is of the sweet, mellow sort that sometimes brings moisture to the eyes as well as laughter to the lips.

People said that if it had not been for that annuity Eph Todd would have been at the poor farm himself instead of setting up a rival to it; but there *was* the annuity, and that was the beginning of Todd's asylum.

[Note 6: From the *Outlook*, November 19, 1898.]

No matter who or what you were, if you were in hard luck, Todd's asylum was open to you. The No. 4 district schoolhouse clock was a sample. For thirty years it had smiled from the wall upon successive generations of scholars, until, one day, bowed with years and infirmities, it had ceased to tick. It had been taken gently down, laid out on a desk in state for a day or two, and finally was in funeral procession to the rubbish heap when Eph Todd appeared.

"You're not going to throw that good old clock away?" Eph had asked of the committeeman who acted as bearer.

"Guess I'll have to," replied the other. "I've wound it up tight, put 'most a pint of kerosene in it, and shook it till I'm dizzy, and it won't tick a bit. Guess the old clock's done for."

"Now see here," said Eph; "you just let me have a try at it. Let me take it home a spell."

"Oh, for that matter I'll give it to you," the committeeman replied. "We've bought another for the schoolhouse."

A day or two after the old clock ticked away as soberly as ever on the wall of the Todd kitchen.

"Took it home and boiled it in potash," Eph used to say; "and there it is, just as good as it was thirty years ago."

This was true, with restrictions, for enough enamel was gone from the face to make the exact location of the hour an uncertain thing; and there were days, when the wind was in the east, when the hour hand needed periodical assistance.

"It wasn't much of a job," as Eph said, "to reach up once an hour and send the hand along one space, and Aunt Tildy had to have something to look forward to."

Aunt Tildy was the first inmate at Todd's, and if Eph had possessed no other recommendation to eternal beatitude, surely Aunt Tildy's prayers had been sufficient. She passed his house on her way to the poor farm on the very day that news of the legacy arrived, and Eph had stopped the carriage and begged the overseer to leave her with him.

"Are you sure you can take care of her?" asked the overseer, doubtfully.

"Sure?" echoed Eph with delight. "Of course I'm sure. Ain't I got four hundred dollars a year for the rest of my natural born days?"

"He's a good fellow, Eph Todd," mused the overseer as he drove away, "but I never heard of his having any money."

Next day the news of the legacy was common property, and Aunt Tildy had been an inmate at Todd's ever since. Her gratitude knew no bounds, and she really managed to keep the house after a fashion, her chief care being the clock.

Then there was the heaven-born inventor. He had dissipated his substance in inventing an incubator that worked with wonderful success till the day the chickens were to come out, when it took fire and burned up, taking with it chickens, barn, house, and furniture, leaving the heaven-born inventor standing in the field, thinly clad, and with nothing left in the world but another incubator.

With this he had shown up promptly at Todd's, and there he had dwelt thenceforth, using a pretty fair portion of the annuity in further incubator experiments.

With excellent sagacity, for him, Eph had obliged the heaven-born inventor to keep his machine in a little shed behind the barn, so that when this one burned up there was time to get the horse and cow out before the barn burned, and the village fire department managed to save the house. Repairing this loss made quite a hole in the annuity, and all the heaven-born inventor had to show for it was Miltiades. He had put a single turkey's egg in with a previous hatch, and though he had raised nary chicken, and it was contrary to all rhyme and reason, the turkey's egg had hatched and the chick had grown up to be Miltiades.

Miltiades was a big gobbler now, and had a right to be named Ishmael, for his hand was against all men. He took care of himself, was never shut up nor handled, and led a wild, nomadic life.

Last of all came Fisherman Jones. He was old now and couldn't see very well, unable to go to the brook or pond to fish, but he still started out daily with the fine new rod and reel which the annuity had bought for him, and would sit out in the sun, joint his rod together, and fish in the dry pasture with perfect contentment.

You would not think Fisherman Jones of much use, but it was he who caught Miltiades and made the Thanksgiving dinner possible.

The new barn had exhausted the revenues completely, and there would be no more income until January 1st; but one must have a turkey for Thanksgiving, and there was Miltiades. To catch Miltiades became the household problem, and the heaven-born inventor set wonderful traps for him, which caught almost everything but Miltiades, who easily avoided them. Eph used to go out daily before breakfast and chase Miltiades, but he might as well have chased a government position. The turkey scorned him, and grew only wilder and tougher, till he had a lean and hungry look that would have shamed Cassius.

The day before Thanksgiving it looked as if there would be no turkey dinner at Todd's, but here Fisherman Jones stepped into the breach. It was a beautiful Indian-summer day, and he hobbled out into the field for an afternoon's fishing. Here he sat on a log, and began to make casts in the open. Nearby, under a savin bush, lurked Miltiades, and viewed these actions with the scorn of long familiarity. By and by Fisherman Jones kicked up a loose bit of bark, and disclosed beneath it a fine fat white grub, of the sort which blossoms into June beetles with the coming of spring. He was not so blind but that he saw this, and with a chuckle at the thoughts it called up, he baited his hook with it.

A moment after, Eph Todd, coming out of the new barn, heard the click of a reel, and was astonished to see Fisherman Jones standing almost erect, his eyes blazing with the old-time fire, his rod bent, his reel buzzing, while at the end of a good forty feet of line was Miltiades rushing in frantic strides for the woods.

"Good land!" said Eph; "it's the turkey! Snub him," he yelled. "Don't let him get all the line on you! He's hooked! Snub him! snub him!"

The whir of the reel deadened now, and the stride of Miltiades was perceptibly lessened and then became but a vigorous up-and-down hop, while the tense line sang in the gentle autumn breeze.

"Eph Todd!" gasped Fisherman Jones, "this is the whoppingest old bass I ever hooked onto yet. Beeswax, how he does pull!" And with the words Fisherman Jones went backward over the log, waving the pole and a pair of stiff legs in air. The turkey had suddenly slackened the line.

"Give him the butt! Give him the butt!" roared Eph, rushing up. Even where he lay the fisherman blood in Fisherman Jones responded to this stirring appeal, and as the rod bent in a tense half circle a race began such as no elderly fisherman was ever the centre of before.

Round and round went Miltiades, with the white grub in his crop, and the line above it gripped tightly in his strong beak; and round and round went Eph Todd, his outstretched arms waving like the turkey's wings, and his big boots denting the soft pasture turf with the vigour of his gallop. In the centre Fisherman Jones, too nearsighted to see what he had hooked, had risen on one knee, and revolved with the coursing bird, his soul wrapped in one idea: to keep the butt of his rod aimed at the whirling game.

"Hang to him! Reel him in! We'll get him!" shouted Eph; and, with the word, he caught his toe and vanished into the prickly depths of the savin bush, just as the heaven-born inventor came over the hill. It would be interesting to know just what scheme the heaven-born inventor would have put in motion for the capture of Miltiades, but just then he stepped into one of his own extraordinary traps, set for the turkey of course, and, with one foot held fast, began to flounder about with cries of rage and dismay.

This brought Eph's head above the fringe of savin bush again, and now he beheld a wonderful sight. Fisherman Jones was again on his feet, staring in wild surprise at Miltiades, whom he sighted for the first time, within ten feet of him. There was no pressure on the reel, and Miltiades was swallowing the line in big gulps, evidently determined to have not only the white grub, but all that went with it.

Fisherman Jones's cry of dismay was almost as bitter as that of the heaven-born inventor, who still writhed in his own trap.

"Oh, Eph! Eph!" he whimpered, "he's eating up my tackle! He's eating up my tackle!"

"Never mind!" shouted Eph. "Don't be afraid! I reckon he'll stop when he gets to the pole!"

Those of us who knew Miltiades at his best have doubts as to this, but, fortunately, it was not put to the test. Eph scrambled out of his bush, and, taking up the chase once more, soon brought it to an end, for Fisherman Jones, his nerve completely gone, could only stand and mumble sadly to himself, "He's eating up my tackle! He's eating up my tackle!" and the line, wrapping about his motionless form, led Eph and the turkey in a brief spiral which ended in the conjunction of the three.

It was not until the turkey was decapitated that Eph remembered the heaven-born inventor and hastened to his rescue. He was still in the trap, but he was quite content, for he was figuring out a plan for an automatic release from the same, something which should hold the captive so long and then let him go in the interests of humanity. He found the trap from the captive's point of view very interesting and instructive.

The tenacity of Miltiades's make-up was further shown by the difficulty Eph and Fisherman Jones had in separating him from his feathers that evening; and Aunt Tildy was so interested in the project of the heaven-born inventor to raise featherless turkeys that she forgot the yeast cake she had put to soak until it had been boiling merrily for some time. Everything seemed to go wrong-end-to, and they all sat up so late that Mrs. Simpkins, across the way, was led to observe that "Either some one was dead over at Todd's or else they were having a family party"; and in a certain sense she was right both ways.

The crowning misadventure came next morning. Eph started for the village with his mind full of commissions from Aunt Tildy, some of which he was sure to forget, and in a great hurry lest he forget them all. He threw the harness hastily upon Dobbin, hitched him into the wagon which had stood out on the soft ground overnight, and with an eager "Get up, there!" gave him a slap with the reins.

Next moment there was a ripping sound, and the heaven-born inventor came to the door just in time to see the horse going out of the yard on a run, with Eph following, still clinging to the reins, and taking strides much like those of Baron Munchausen's courier.

"Here, here!" called the inventor, "you've forgot the wagon. Come back, Eph! You've forgot the wagon!"

"Jeddediah Jodkins!" said Eph, as he swung an eccentric curve about the gate-post; "do you--whoa!--suppose I'm such a--whoa! whoa!--fool that I don't know that I'm not riding--whoa! in a--whoa! whoa!--wagon?" And with this Eph vanished up street in the wake of the galloping horse, still clinging valiantly to the reins.

"I believe he did forget that wagon," said the heaven-born inventor; "he's perfectly capable of it." But when he reached the barn he saw the trouble. The ground had frozen hard overnight, and the wagon wheels sunken in it were held as in a vise. Eph had started the horse suddenly, and the obedient animal had walked right out of the shafts, harness and all.

A half hour later Eph was back with Dobbin, unharmed but a trifle weary. It took an hour more and all Aunt Tildy's hot water to thaw out the wheels, and when it was done Eph was so confused that he drove to the village and back and forgot every one of his commissions. And in the midst of all this the clock stopped. That settled the matter for Aunt Tildy. She neglected the pudding, she forgot the pies, and she let the turkey bake and bake in the overheated oven while she fretted about that clock; and when it was finally set going, after long and careful investigation by Eph, and frantic but successful attempts on the part of Aunt Tildy to keep the heaven-born inventor from ruining it forever, it was the dinner hour.

Poor Aunt Tildy! That dinner was the crowning sorrow of her life. The vegetables were cooked to rags, the pies were charcoal shells, and the pudding had not been made. As for Miltiades, he was ten times tougher than in life, and Eph's carving knife slipped from his form without making a dent. Aunt Tildy wept at this, and Fisherman Jones and the inventor looked blank enough, but there was no sorrow in the countenance of Eph. He cheered Aunt Tildy, and he cracked jokes that made even Fisherman Jones laugh.

"Why, bless you!" he said, "ever since I was a boy I've been looking for a chance to make a Thanksgiving dinner out of bread and milk. And now I've got it. Why, I wouldn't have missed this for anything!" And there came a knock at the door.

Even Eph looked a trifle blank at this. If it should be company! "Come in!" he called.

The door was pushed aside and a big, steaming platter entered. It was upheld by a small boy, who stammered diffidently, "My moth-moth-mother thaid she wanted you to try thum of her nith turkey."

"Well, well!" said Eph; "Aunt Tildy has cooked a turkey for us to-day, and she's a main good cook"--Eph did not appear to see the signs the heaven-born inventor was making to him--"but I've heard that your mother does things pretty well, too. We're greatly obliged." And Eph put the steaming platter on the table.

"She thays you c-c-can thend the platter home to-morrow," stammered the boy, and stammering himself out, he ran into another. The other held high a big dish of plum pudding, from which a spicy aroma filled the room. Again the heaven-born inventor made signs to Eph.

"Our folks told me to ask if you wouldn't try this plum pudding," said the new-comer. "They made an extra one, and the cousins we expected didn't come, so we can spare it just as well as not."

It seemed as if Eph hesitated a moment, and the inventor's face became a panorama. Then he took the boy by the hand, and there was an odd shake in his voice as he said:

"I'm greatly obliged to you. We all are. Something happened to our plum pudding, and we didn't have any. Tell your ma we send our thanks."

There was a sound of voices greeting in the hallway, and two young girls entered, each laden with a basket.

"Oh, Mr. Todd," they both said at once, "we couldn't wait to knock. We want you to try some of our Thanksgiving. It was mother's birthday, and we cooked extra for that, and we've got so much. We can't get all ours onto the table. She'll feel real hurt if you don't."

Somehow Eph couldn't say a word, but there was nothing the matter with the heaven-born inventor. His speech of delighted acceptance was such a good one that before he was half done the girls had loaded the table with good things, and, with smiles and nods and "good-byes," slipped out as rapidly and as gayly as they had come in. It was like a gust of wind from a summer garden.

The table, but now so bare, fairly sagged and steamed with offerings of Thanksgiving. Somehow the steam got into Eph's eyes and made them wet, till all he could do was to say whimsically:

"There goes my last chance at a bread-and-milk Thanksgiving."

But now Aunt Tildy had the floor, with her faded face all alight.

"Eph Todd," she said, "you needn't look so flustrated. It's nothing more than you deserve and not half so much either. Ain't you the kindest man yourself that ever lived? Ain't you always doing something for everybody, and helping every one of these neighbours in all sorts of ways? I'd like to know what the whole place would do without you! And now, just because they remember you on Thanksgiving Day, you look like--"

The steam had got into Aunt Tildy's eyes now, and she sat down again just as there came another knock at the door, a timid sort of knock this time.

The heaven-born inventor's face widened in beatified smiles of expectation at this, but Eph looked him sternly in the eye.

"Jeddediah Jodkins!" he said; "if that is any more people bringing things to eat to this house, they'll have to go away. We can't have it. We've got enough here now to feed a--a boarding school."

The heaven-born inventor sprang eagerly to his feet. "Don't you do it, Eph," he said, "don't you do it. I've just thought of a way to can it."

A thinly clad man and woman stood at the door which Eph opened. Both looked pale and tired, and the woman shivered.

"Can you tell me where I can get work," asked the man, doggedly, "so that I can earn a little something to eat? We are not beggars"--he flushed a little through his pallor--"but I have had no work lately, and we have eaten nothing since yesterday. We are looking--"

The man stopped, and well he might, for Eph was dancing wildly about the two, and hustling them into the house.

"Come in!" he shouted. "Come in! Come in! You're the folks we are waiting for! Eat? Why, goodness gra-cious! We've got so much to eat we don't know what to do with it."

He had them in chairs in a moment and was piling steaming roast turkey on their plates. "There!" he said, "don't you say another word till you have filled up on that. Folks"--and he returned to the others--"here's two friends that have come to stay a week with us and help eat turkey. Fall to! This is going to be the pleasantest Thanksgiving we've had yet."

And thus two new inmates were added to Todd's asylum.

HOW WE KEPT THANKSGIVING AT OLDTOWN[7] BY HARRIET BEECHER STOWE.

The old-time New England Thanksgiving has been described many times, but never better then by the author of "Uncle Tom's Cabin" in her less successful but more artistic novel, "Oldtown Folks," from which book the following narrative has been adapted.

When the apples were all gathered and the cider was all made, and the yellow pumpkins were rolled in from many a hill in billows of gold, and the corn was husked, and the labours of the season were done, and the warm, late days of Indian summer came in, dreamy and calm and still, with just frost enough to crisp the ground of a morning, but with warm trances of benignant, sunny hours at noon, there came over the community a sort of genial repose of spirit--a sense of something accomplished, and of a new golden mark made in advance on the calendar of life--and the deacon began to say to the minister, of a Sunday, "I suppose it's about time for the Thanksgiving proclamation."

[Note 7: Adapted from "Oldtown Folks," Houghton, Mifflin Co.]

Conversation at this time began to turn on high and solemn culinary mysteries and receipts of wondrous power and virtue. New modes of elaborating squash pies and quince tarts were now ofttimes carefully discussed at the evening firesides by Aunt Lois and Aunt Keziah, and notes seriously compared with the experiences of certain other aunties of high repute in such matters. I noticed that on these occasions their voices often fell into mysterious whispers, and that receipts of especial power and sanctity were communicated in tones so low as entirely to escape the vulgar ear. I still remember the solemn shake of the head with which my Aunt Lois conveyed to Miss Mehitable Rossiter the critical properties of *mace*, in relation to its powers of producing in corn fritters a suggestive resemblance to oysters. As ours was an oyster-getting district, and as that charming bivalve was perfectly easy to come at, the interest of such an imitation can be accounted for only by the fondness of the human mind for works of art.

For as much as a week beforehand, "we children" were employed in chopping mince for pies to a most wearisome fineness, and in pounding cinnamon, all-spice, and cloves in a great lignum-vitae mortar; and the sound of this pounding and chopping reechoed through all the rafters of the old house with a hearty and vigorous cheer most refreshing to our spirits.

In those days there were none of the thousand ameliorations of the labours of housekeeping which have since arisen--no ground and prepared spices and sweet herbs; everything came into our hands in the rough, and in bulk, and the reducing of it into a state for use was deemed one of the appropriate labours of childhood. Even the very salt that we used in cooking was rock salt, which we were required to wash and dry and pound and sift before it became fit for use.

At other times of the year we sometimes murmured at these labours, but those that were supposed to usher in the great Thanksgiving festival were always entered into with enthusiasm. There were signs of richness all around us--stoning of raisins, cutting of citron, slicing of candied orange peel. Yet all these were only dawnings and intimations of what was coming during the week of real preparation, after the Governor's proclamation had been read.

The glories of that proclamation! We knew beforehand the Sunday it was to be read, and walked to church with alacrity, filled with gorgeous and vague expectations.

The cheering anticipation sustained us through what seemed to us the long waste of the sermon and prayers; and when at last the auspicious moment approached--when the last quaver of the last hymn had died out--the whole house rippled with a general movement of complacency, and a satisfied smile of pleased expectation might be seen gleaming on the faces of all the young people, like a ray of sunshine through a garden of flowers.

Thanksgiving now was dawning! We children poked one another, and fairly giggled with unreproved delight as we listened to the crackle of the slowly unfolding document. That great sheet of paper impressed us as something supernatural, by reason of its mighty size and by the broad seal of the State affixed thereto; and when the minister read therefrom, "By his Excellency, the Governor of the Commonwealth of Massachusetts, a Proclamation," our mirth was with difficulty repressed by admonitory glances from our sympathetic elders. Then, after a solemn enumeration of the benefits which the Commonwealth had that year received at the hands of Divine Providence, came at last the naming of the eventful day, and, at the end of all, the imposing heraldic words, "God save the Commonwealth of Massachusetts." And then, as the congregation broke up and dispersed, all went their several ways with schemes of mirth and feasting in their heads.

And now came on the week in earnest. In the very watches of the night preceding Monday morning a preternatural stir below stairs and the thunder of the pounding barrel announced that the washing was to be got out of the way before daylight, so as to give "ample scope and room enough" for the more pleasing duties of the season.

The making of *pies* at this period assumed vast proportions that verged upon the sublime. Pies were made by forties and fifties and hundreds, and made of everything on the earth and under the earth.

The pie is an English institution, which, planted on American soil, forthwith ran rampant and burst forth into an untold variety of genera and species. Not merely the old traditional mince pie, but a thousand strictly American seedlings from that main stock, evinced the power of American housewives to adapt old institutions to new uses. Pumpkin pies, cranberry pies, huckleberry pies, cherry pies, green-currant pies, peach, pear, and plum pies, custard pies, apple pies, Marlborough-pudding pies--pies with top crusts and pies without--pies adorned with all sorts of fanciful flutings and architectural strips laid across and around, and otherwise varied, attested the boundless fertility of the feminine mind when once let loose in a given direction.

Fancy the heat and vigour of the great pan formation, when Aunt Lois and

Aunt Keziah, and my mother and grandmother, all in ecstasies of creative inspiration, ran, bustled, and hurried--mixing, rolling, tasting, consulting--alternately setting us children to work when anything could be made of us, and then chasing us all out of the kitchen when our misinformed childhood ventured to take too many liberties with sacred mysteries. Then out we would all fly at the kitchen door, like sparks from a blacksmith's window.

On these occasions, as there was a great looseness in the police department over us children, we usually found a ready refuge at Miss Mehitable's with Tina,[8] who, confident of the strength of her position with Polly, invited us into the kitchen, and with the air of a mistress led us around to view the proceedings there.

> [Note 8: Tina was Miss Mehitable's adopted child; Polly her faithful old maid-servant.]

A genius for entertaining was one of Tina's principal characteristics; and she did not fail to make free with raisins, or citrons, or whatever came to hand, in a spirit of hospitality at which Polly seriously demurred. That worthy woman occasionally felt the inconvenience of the state of subjugation to which the little elf had somehow or other reduced her, and sometimes rattled her chains fiercely, scolding with a vigour which rather alarmed us, but which Tina minded not a whit. Confident of her own powers, she would, in the very midst of her wrath, mimic her to her face with such irresistible drollery as to cause the torrent of reproof to end in a dissonant laugh, accompanied by a submissive cry for quarter.

"I declare, Tina Percival," she said to her one day, "you're saucy enough to physic a horn bug! I never did see the beater of you! If Miss Mehitable don't keep you in better order, I don't see what's to become of any of us!"

"Why, what did 'come of you before I came?" was the undismayed reply. "You know, Polly, you and Aunty both were just as lonesome as you could be till I came here, and you never had such pleasant times in your life as you've had since I've been here. You're a couple of old beauties, both of you, and know just how to get along with me. But come, boys, let's take our raisins and go up into the garret and play Thanksgiving."

In the corner of the great kitchen, during all these days, the jolly old oven roared and crackled in great volcanic billows of flame, snapping and gurgling as if the old fellow entered with joyful sympathy into the frolic of the hour; and then, his great heart being once warmed up, he brooded over successive generations of pies and cakes, which went in raw and came out cooked, till buteries and dressers and shelves and pantries were literally crowded with a jostling abundance.

A great cold northern chamber, where the sun never shone, and where in winter the snow sifted in at the window cracks, and ice and frost reigned with undisputed sway, was fitted up to be the storehouse of these surplus treasures. There, frozen solid, and thus well preserved in their icy fetters, they formed a great repository for all the winter months; and the pies baked at Thanksgiving often came out fresh and good with the violets of April.

During this eventful preparation week all the female part of my grandmother's household, as I have before remarked, were at a height above any ordinary state of mind; they moved about the house rapt in a species of prophetic frenzy. It seemed to be considered a necessary feature of such festivals that everybody should be in a hurry, and everything in the house should be turned bottom upwards with enthusiasm--so at least we children understood it, and we certainly did our part to keep the ball rolling.

At this period the constitutional activity of Uncle Fliakim increased to a degree that might fairly be called preternatural. Thanksgiving time was the time for errands of mercy and beneficence through the country; and Uncle Fliakim's immortal old rubber horse and rattling wagon were on the full jump in tours of investigation into everybody's affairs in the region around. On returning, he would fly through our kitchen like the wind, leaving open the doors, upsetting whatever came in his way--now a pan of milk, and now a basin of mince--talking rapidly, and forgetting only the point in every case that gave it significance, or enabled any one to put it to any sort of use. When Aunt Lois checked his benevolent effusions by putting the test questions of practical efficiency, Uncle Fliakim always remembered that he'd "forgotten to inquire about that," and skipping through the kitchen, and springing into his old wagon, would rattle off again on a full tilt to correct and amend his investigations.

Moreover, my grandmother's kitchen at this time began to be haunted by those occasional hangers-on and retainers, of uncertain fortunes, whom a full experience of her bountiful habits led to expect something at her hand at this time of the year. All the poor, loafing tribes, Indian and half-Indian, who at other times wandered, selling baskets and other light wares, were sure to come back to Oldtown a little before Thanksgiving time, and report themselves in my grandmother's kitchen.

The great hogshead of cider in the cellar, which my grandfather called the Indian hogshead, was on tap at all hours of the day; and many a mugful did I draw and dispense to the tribes that basked in the sunshine at our door.

Aunt Lois never had a hearty conviction of the propriety of these arrangements; but my grandmother, who had a prodigious verbal memory, bore down upon her with such strings of quotations from the Old Testament that she was utterly routed.

"Now," says my Aunt Lois, "I s'pose we've got to have Betty Poganut and Sally Wonsamug, and old Obscue and his wife, and the whole tribe down, roosting around our doors till we give 'em something. That's just mother's way; she always keeps a whole generation at her heels."

"How many times must I tell you, Lois, to read your Bible?" was my grandmother's rejoinder; and loud over the sound of pounding and chopping in the kitchen could be heard the voice of her quotations: "If there be among you a poor man in any of the gates of the land which the Lord thy God giveth thee, thou shalt not harden thy heart, nor shut thy hand, from thy poor brother. Thou shalt surely give him; and thy heart shall not be grieved when thou givest to him, because that for this thing the Lord thy God shall bless thee in all thy works; for the poor shall never cease from out of the land."

These words seemed to resound like a sort of heraldic proclamation to call around us all that softly shiftless class, who, for some reason or other, are never to be found with anything in hand at the moment that it is wanted.

"There, to be sure," said Aunt Lois, one day when our preparations were in full blast; "there comes Sam Lawson down the hill, limpsy as ever; now he'll have his doleful story to tell, and mother'll give him one of the turkeys."

And so, of course, it fell out.

Sam came in with his usual air of plaintive assurance, and seated himself a contemplative spectator in the chimney corner, regardless of the looks and signs of unwelcome on the part of Aunt Lois.

"Lordy massy, how prosperous everything does seem here!" he said in musing tones, over his inevitable mug of cider; "so different from what 'tis t' our house.

There's Hepsey, she's all in a stew, an' I've just been an' got her thirty-seven cents' wuth o' nutmegs, yet she says she's sure she don't see how she's to keep Thanksgiving, an' she's down on me about it, just as ef 'twas my fault. Yeh see, last winter our old gobbler got froze. You know, Mis' Badger, that 'ere cold night we hed last winter. Wal, I was off with Jake Marshall that night; ye see, Jake, he had to take old General Dearborn's corpse into Boston, to the family vault, and Jake, he kind o' hated to go alone; 'twas a drefful cold time, and he ses to me,' Sam, you jes' go 'long with me'; so I was sort o' sorry for him, and I kind o' thought I'd go 'long. Wal, come 'long to Josh Bissel's tahvern, there at the Halfway House, you know, 'twas so swingeing cold we stopped to take a little suthin' warmin', an' we sort o' sot an' sot over the fire, till, fust we knew, we kind o' got asleep; an' when we woke up we found we'd left the old General hitched up t' th' post pretty much all night. Wal, didn't hurt him none, poor man; 'twas allers a favourite spot o' his'n. But, takin' one thing with another, I didn't get home till about noon next day, an' I tell you, Hepsey she was right down on me. She said the baby was sick, and there hadn't been no wood split, nor the barn fastened up, nor nuthin'. Lordy massy, I didn't mean no harm; I thought there was wood enough, and I thought likely Hepsey'd git out an' fasten up the barn. But Hepsey, she was in one o' her contrary streaks, an' she wouldn't do a thing; an' when I went out to look, why, sure 'nuff, there was our old tom-turkey froze as stiff as a stake--his claws jist a stickin' right straight up like this." Here Sam struck an expressive attitude, and looked so much like a frozen turkey as to give a pathetic reality to the picture.

"Well, now, Sam, why need you be off on things that's none of your business?" said my grandmother. "I've talked to you plainly about that a great many times, Sam," she continued, in tones of severe admonition. "Hepsey is a hard-working woman, but she can't be expected to see to everything, and you oughter 'ave been at home that night to fasten up your own barn and look after your own creeturs."

Sam took the rebuke all the more meekly as he perceived the stiff black legs of a turkey poking out from under my grandmother's apron while she was delivering it. To be exhorted and told of his shortcomings, and then furnished with a turkey at Thanksgiving, was a yearly part of his family program. In time he departed, not only with the turkey, but with us boys in procession after him, bearing a mince and a pumpkin pie for Hepsey's children.

"Poor things!" my grandmother remarked; "they ought to have something good to eat Thanksgiving Day; 'tain't their fault that they've got a shiftless father."

Sam, in his turn, moralized to us children, as we walked beside him: "A body'd think that Hepsey'd learn to trust in Providence," he said, "but she don't. She allers has a Thanksgiving dinner pervided; but that 'ere woman ain't grateful for it, by no manner o' means. Now she'll be jest as cross as she can be, 'cause this 'ere ain't *our* turkey, and these 'ere ain't our pies. Folks doos lose so much that hes sech dispositions."

A multitude of similar dispensations during the course of the week materially reduced the great pile of chickens and turkeys which black Caesar's efforts in slaughtering, picking, and dressing kept daily supplied....

*   *   *   *   *

Great as the preparations were for the dinner, everything was so contrived that not a soul in the house should be kept from the morning service of Thanksgiving in the church, and from listening to the Thanksgiving sermon, in which the minister was expected to express his views freely concerning the politics of the country and the state of things in society generally, in a somewhat more secular vein of thought than was deemed exactly appropriate to the Lord's day. But it is to be confessed that, when the good man got carried away by the enthusiasm of his subject to extend these exercises beyond a certain length, anxious glances, exchanged between good wives, sometimes indicated a weakness of the flesh, having a tender reference to the turkeys and chickens and chicken pies which might possibly be overdoing in the ovens at home. But your old brick oven was a true Puritan institution, and backed up the devotional habits of good housewives by the capital care which he took of whatever was committed to his capacious bosom. A truly well-bred oven would have been ashamed of himself all his days and blushed redder than his own fires, if a God-fearing house matron, away at the temple of the Lord, should come home and find her pie crust either burned or underdone by his over or under zeal; so the old fellow generally managed to bring things out exactly right.

When sermons and prayers were all over, we children rushed home to see the great feast of the year spread.

What chitterings and chatterings there were all over the house, as all the aunties and uncles and cousins came pouring in, taking off their things, looking at one another's bonnets and dresses, and mingling their comments on the morning sermon with various opinions on the new millinery outfits, and with bits of home news and kindly neighbourhood gossip.

Uncle Bill, whom the Cambridge college authorities released, as they did all the other youngsters of the land, for Thanksgiving Day, made a breezy stir among them all, especially with the young cousins of the feminine gender.

The best room on this occasion was thrown wide open, and its habitual coldness had been warmed by the burning down of a great stack of hickory logs, which had been heaped up unsparingly since morning. It takes some hours to get a room warm where a family never sits, and which therefore has not in its walls one particle of the genial vitality which comes from the indwelling of human beings. But on Thanksgiving Day, at least, every year this marvel was effected in our best room.

Although all servile labour and vain recreation on this day were by law forbidden, according to the terms of the proclamation, it was not held to be a violation of the precept that all the nice old aunties should bring their knitting work and sit gently trotting their needles around the fire; nor that Uncle Bill should start a full-fledged romp among the girls and children, while the dinner was being set on the long table in the neighbouring kitchen. Certain of the good elderly female relatives, of serious and discreet demeanour, assisted at this operation.

But who shall do justice to the dinner, and describe the turkey, and chickens, and chicken pies, with all that endless variety of vegetables which the American soil and climate have contributed to the table, and which, without regard to the French doctrine of courses, were all piled together in jovial abundance upon the smoking board? There was much carving and laughing and talking and eating, and all showed that cheerful ability to despatch the provisions which was the ruling spirit of the hour. After the meat came the plum puddings, and then the endless array of pies, till human nature was actually bewildered and overpowered by the tempting variety; and even we children turned from the profusion offered to us, and wondered what was the matter that we could eat no more.

When all was over, my grandfather rose at the head of the table, and a fine venerable picture he made as he stood there, his silver hair flowing in curls down each side of his clear, calm face, while, in conformity to the old Puritan custom, he called their attention to a recital of the mercies of God in His dealings with their family.

It was a sort of family history, going over and touching upon the various events which had happened. He spoke of my father's death, and gave a tribute to his memory; and closed all with the application of a time-honoured text, expressing the hope that as years passed by we might "so number our days as to apply our hearts unto wisdom"; and then he gave out that psalm which in those days might be called the national hymn of the Puritans.

"Let children hear the mighty deeds
Which God performed of old,
Which in our younger years we saw,
And which our fathers told.

"He bids us make his glories known,
His works of power and grace.
And we'll convey his wonders down
Through every rising race.

"Our lips shall tell them to our sons,
And they again to theirs;
That generations yet unborn
May teach them to their heirs.

"Thus shall they learn in God alone Their hope securely stands; That they may ne'er forget his works, But practise his commands."

This we all united in singing to the venerable tune of St. Martin's, an air which, the reader will perceive, by its multiplicity of quavers and inflections gave the greatest possible scope to the cracked and trembling voices of the ancients, who united in it with even more zeal than the younger part of the community.

Uncle Fliakim Sheril, furbished up in a new crisp black suit, and with his spindleshanks trimly incased in the smoothest of black silk stockings, looking for all the world just like an alert and spirited black cricket, outdid himself on this occasion in singing *counter*, in that high, weird voice that he must have learned from the wintry winds that usually piped around the corners of the old house. But any one who looked at him, as he sat with his eyes closed, beating time with head and hand, and, in short, with every limb of his body, must have perceived the exquisite satisfaction which he derived from this mode of expressing himself. I much regret to be obliged to state that my graceless Uncle Bill, taking advantage of the fact that the eyes of all his elders were devotionally closed, stationing himself a little in the rear of my Uncle Fliakim, performed an exact imitation of his **counter** with such a killing facility that all the younger part of the audience were nearly dead with suppressed laughter. Aunt Lois, who never shut her eyes a moment on any occasion, discerned this from a distant part of the room, and in vain endeavoured to stop it by vigorously shaking her head at the offender. She might as well have shaken it at a bobolink tilting on a clover top. In fact, Uncle Bill was Aunt Lois's weak point, and the corners of her own mouth were observed to twitch in such a suspicious manner that the whole moral force of her admonition was destroyed.

And now, the dinner being cleared away, we youngsters, already excited to a tumult of laughter, tumbled into the best room, under the supervision of Uncle Bill, to relieve ourselves with a game of "blindman's bluff," while the elderly women washed up the dishes and got the house in order, and the men folks went out to the barn to look at the cattle, and walked over the farm and talked of the crops.

In the evening the house was all open and lighted with the best of tallow candles, which Aunt Lois herself had made with especial care for this illumination. It was understood that we were to have a dance, and black Caesar, full of turkey and pumpkin pie, and giggling in the very jollity of his heart, had that afternoon rosined his bow, and tuned his fiddle, and practised jigs and Virginia reels, in a way that made us children think him a perfect Orpheus....

You may imagine the astounding wassail among the young people.... My Uncle Bill related the story of "the Wry-mouth Family," with such twists and contortions and killing extremes of the ludicrous as perfectly overcame even the minister; and he was to be seen, at one period of the evening, with a face purple with laughter and the tears actually rolling down over his well-formed cheeks, while some of the more excitable young people almost fell in trances and rolled on the floor in the extreme of their merriment. In fact, the assemblage was becoming so tumultuous, that the scrape of Caesar's violin and the forming of sets for a dance seemed necessary to restore the peace....

Uncle Bill would insist on leading out Aunt Lois, and the bright colour rising to her thin cheeks brought back a fluttering image of what might have been beauty in some fresh, early day. Ellery Davenport insisted upon leading forth Miss Deborah Kittery, notwithstanding her oft-repeated refusals and earnest protestations to the contrary. As to Uncle Fliakim, he jumped and frisked and gyrated among the single sisters and maiden aunts, whirling them into the dance as if he had been the little black gentleman himself. With that true spirit of Christian charity which marked all his actions, he invariably chose out the homeliest and most neglected, and thus worthy Aunt Keziah, dear old soul, was for a time made quite prominent by his attentions....

Grandmother's face was radiant with satisfaction, as the wave of joyousness crept up higher and higher round her, till the elders, who stood keeping time with their heads and feet, began to tell one another how they had danced with their sweethearts in good old days gone by, and the elder women began to blush and bridle, and boast of steps that they could take in their youth, till the music finally subdued them, and into the dance they went.

"Well, well!" quoth my grandmother; "they're all at it so hearty I don't see why I shouldn't try it myself." And into the Virginia reel she went, amid screams of laughter from all the younger members of the company.

But I assure you my grandmother was not a woman to be laughed at; for whatever she once set on foot she "put through" with a sturdy energy befitting a daughter of the Puritans.

"Why shouldn't I dance?" she said, when she arrived red and resplendent at the bottom of the set. "Didn't Mr. Despondency and Miss Muchafraid and Mr. Readytohalt all dance together in the 'Pilgrim's Progress?'" And the minister in his ample flowing wig, and my lady in her stiff brocade, gave to my grandmother a solemn twinkle of approbation.

As nine o'clock struck, the whole scene dissolved and melted; for what well-regulated village would think of carrying festivities beyond that hour?

And so ended our Thanksgiving at Oldtown.

WISHBONE VALLEY[9]
BY R. K. MUNKITTRICK.

A Thanksgiving ghost story about a boy who dined not wisely but too well.

The Thanksgiving feast had just ended, and only Donald and his little sister Grace remained at the table, looking drowsily at the plum-pudding that they couldn't finish, but which they disliked to leave on their plates.

[Note 9: From **Harper's Young People**, November 21, 1893.]

When the plates had been removed, and the plum-pudding taken to the kitchen and placed beside the well-carved gobbler, Donald and Grace were too tired to rise from their chairs to have their faces washed. They seemed lost in a roseate repose, until Grace finally thought of the wishbone that they intended to break after dinner.

"Come, now, Donald," she said, "let's break the old gobbler's wishbone."

"All right," replied Donald, opening his eyes slowly, and unwrapping the draperies of his sweet plum-pudding dreams from about him, "let's do it now." So he held up the wishbone, and Grace took hold of the other end of it with a merry laugh.

"Here, you must not take hold so far from the end, because I have a fine wish to make, and want to get the big half if possible."

"So have I a nice wish to make," replied Grace, with a sigh, "and I also want the big end."

And so they argued for a few minutes, until their mother entered the room and told them that if they could not stop quarrelling over the wishbone she would take it from them and throw it into the fire. So they lost no time in taking it by the ends and snapping it asunder.

"Hurrah!" exclaimed Donald, observing Grace's expression of disappointment.

"I've got it!"

"Well, I've made a wish, too," said Grace.

"But it won't come true," replied Donald, "because you have the little end."

And then Donald thought he would go out in the air and play, because his great dinner made him feel very uncomfortable. When he was out in the barnyard it was just growing dusk, and Donald, through his half-closed eyes, observed a gobbler strutting about. To his great surprise the gobbler approached him instead of running away.

"I thought we had you for dinner to-day," said Donald.

"You did," replied the gobbler coldly, "and you had a fine old time, didn't you?"

"Yes," said Donald, "you made a splendid dinner, and you ought to be pleased to think you made us all so happy. Your second joints were very sweet and juicy, and your drumsticks were like sticks of candy."

"And you broke my poor old wishbone with your little sister, didn't you?"

"I did."

"And what did you wish?" asked the gobbler.

"You mustn't ask me that," replied Donald, "because, you know, if I tell you the wish I made it would not come true."

"But it was my wishbone," persisted the gobbler, "and I think I ought to know something about it."

"You have rights, I suppose, and your argument is not without force," replied Donald, with calm dignity.

The gobbler was puzzled at so lofty a reply, and not understanding it, said:

"I am only the ghost, or spirit, of the gobbler you ate to-day, but still I remember how one day last summer you threw a pan of water on me, and alluded to my wattles as a red necktie, and called me 'Old Harvard,' Now, come along!"

"Where?" asked Donald.

"To Wishbone Valley, where you will see the spirits of my ancestors eaten by your family."

It was now dusk, and Donald didn't like the idea of going to such a place. He was a brave, courageous boy, on most occasions, but the idea of going to Wishbone Valley when the stars were appearing filled him with a dread that he didn't like to acknowledge even to the ghost of a gobbler.

"I can't go with you now, Mr. Gobbler," he said, "because I have a lot of lessons to study for next Monday; wait until to-morrow, and I will gladly go with you."

"Come along," replied the gobbler, with a provoked air, "and let your lessons go until to-morrow, when you will have plenty of light."

Thereupon the gobbler extended his wing and took Donald by the hand, and started on a trot.

"Not so fast," protested Donald.

"Why not?" demanded the gobbler in surprise.

"Because," replied Donald, with a groan, "I have just had my dinner, and I'm too full of you to run."

So the gobbler kindly and considerately slackened his pace to a walk, and the two proceeded out of the barnyard and across a wide meadow to a little valley surrounded by a dense thicket. The moon was just rising and the thicket was silvered by its light, while the dry leaves rustled weirdly in the cold crisp air.

"This," said the gobbler, "is Wishbone Valley. Look and see."

Donald strained his eyes, and, sure enough, there were wishbones sticking out of the ground in every direction. He thought they looked like little croquet hoops, but he made no comments, for fear of offending the old gobbler. But he felt that he must say something to make the gobbler think that he was not frightened, so he remarked, in an offhand way:

"Let's break one and make a wish."

The ghost of the old gobbler frowned, drew himself up, and uttered a ghostly whistle that seemed to cut the air. As he did so, the ghosts of the other turkeys long since eaten popped out of the thickets with a great flapping of wings, and each one perched upon a wishbone and gazed upon poor Donald, who was so frightened that his collar flew into a standing position, while he stood upon his toes, with his knees knocking together at a great rate.

Every turkey fixed its eyes upon the trembling boy, who was beside himself with fear.

"What shall we do with him, grandpapa?" asked the gobbler of an ancient bird that could scarcely contain itself and remain on its wishbone.

"I cannot think of anything terrible enough, Willie," replied the grandparent.

"It almost makes my ghost-ship boil when I think of the way in which he used to amuse himself by making me a target for his bean shooter. Often when I was asleep in the button-ball he would fetch me one on the side of the head that would give me an earache for a week. But now it is our turn."

Here the other turkeys broke into a wild chorus of approval.

"Take his bean shooter from his pocket," suggested another bird, "and let's have a shot at him."

Donald was compelled to hand out his bean shooter, and the grandparent took it, lay on his back, and with the handle of the bean shooter in one claw and the missile end in the other began to send pebbles at Donald at a great rate. He could hear them whistling past his ears, but could not see them to dodge. Fortunately none struck him, and when the turkeys felt that they had had fun enough of that kind at his expense the bean shooter was returned to him.

"Now, then," said the gobbler's Aunt Fanny, "he once gave me a string of yellow beads for corn."

"What shall we do to him for that?" asked the gobbler.

"Make him eat a lot of yellow beads," said the chorus.

"But we have no beads," said the gobbler sadly.

"Then let's poke him with a stick," suggested the gobbler's Granduncle Sylvester; "he used to do that to us."

So they all took up their wishbones and poked Donald until he was sore. Sometimes they would hit him in a ticklish spot, and throw him into such a fit of laughter that they thought he was enjoying it all and chaffing them. So they stuck their wishbones into the ground, and took their positions on them once more, to take a needed rest, for the poor ghosts were greatly exhausted.

There was one quiet turkey who had taken no part in the proceedings.

"Why don't you suggest something?" demanded Uncle Sylvester.

"Because," replied the quiet turkey, "Donald never did anything to me, and I must treat him accordingly. I was raised and killed a long way from here, and canned. Donald's father bought me at a store. To be a ghost in good standing I should be on the farm where I was killed, and really I don't know why I should be here."

"Then you should be an impartial judge," said Aunt Fanny. "Now what shall we do with him?"

"Tell them to let me go home," protested Donald, "and I'll agree never to molest or eat turkey again; I will give them all the angleworms I can dig every day, and on Thanksgiving Day I'll ask my father to have roast beef."

"I think," replied the impartial canned ghost, "that as all boys delight in chasing turkeys with sticks, it would be eminently just and proper for us, with the exception of myself, to chase this boy and beat him with our' wishbones, to let him learn by experience that which he could scarcely learn by observation."

"What could I do but eat turkey when it was put on the table?" protested Donald.

"But you could help chasing us around with sticks," sang the chorus.

They thereupon descended from the wishbones upon which they had been perching, and flying after him, they darted the wishbones, which they held in their beaks, into his back and neck as hard as they could. Donald ran up and down Wishbone Valley, calling upon them to stop, and declaring that if turkey should ever be put upon the table again he would eat nothing but the stuffing. When Donald found that the wishbones were sticking into his neck like so many hornet stings, he made up his mind that he would run for the house. Finally the wishbone tattoo stopped, and when he looked around, the gobbler, who was twenty feet away, said: "When a Thanksgiving turkey dies, his ghost comes down here to Wishbone Valley to join his ancestors, and it never after leaves the valley. You will now know why every spring the turkeys steal down here to hatch their little ones. As you are now over the boundary line you are safe."

"Thank you," said Donald gratefully.

"Good-bye," sang all the ghosts in chorus.

There was then a great ghostly flapping and whistling, and the turkeys and wishbones all vanished from sight.

Donald ran home as fast as his trembling legs could carry him, and he fancied that the surviving turkeys on the place made fun of him as he passed on his way.

When he reached the house he was very happy, but made no allusion to his experience in Wishbone Valley, for fear of being laughed at.

"Come, Donald," said his mother, shortly after his arrival, "it is almost bedtime; you had better eat that drumstick and retire."

"I think I have had turkey enough for to-day," replied Donald, with a shudder, "and if it is just the same, I would rather have a nice thick piece of pumpkin pie."

So the girl placed a large piece of pie before him; and while he was eating with the keen appetite given him by the crisp air of Wishbone Valley, he heard a great clattering of hoofs coming down the road. These sounds did not stop until the express wagon drew up in front of the house, and the driver brought in a large package for Donald.

"Hurrah!" shouted Donald, in boundless glee. "Uncle Arthur has sent me a nice bicycle! Wasn't it good of him?"

"Didn't you wish for a bicycle to-day, when you got the big end of the wishbone?" asked his little sister Grace.

"What makes you think so?" asked Donald, with a laugh.

"Oh, I knew it all the time; and my wish came true, too."

"How could your wish come true?" asked Donald, with a puzzled look, "when you got the little half of the wishbone?"

"I don't know," replied Grace, "but my wish did come true."

"And what did you wish?"

"Why," said Grace, running up and kissing her little brother affectionately, "I wished your wish would come true, of course."

PATEM'S SALMAGUNDI[10]
BY E. S. BROOKS.

New York boys, especially, will enjoy this tale of the doings of a group of Dutch schoolboys in old New Amsterdam.

Little Patem Onderdonk meant mischief. There was a snap in his eyes and a look on his face that were certain proof of this. I am bound to say, however, that there was nothing new or strange in this, for little Patem Onderdonk generally did mean mischief. Whenever any one's cow was found astray beyond the limits, or any one's bark gutter laid askew so that the roof-water dripped on the passer's head, or whenever the dominie's dog ran howling down the Heeren Graaft with a battered pypken cover tied to his suffering tail, the goode vrouws in the neighbourhood did not stop to wonder who could have done it; they simply raised both hands in a sort of injured resignation and exclaimed:

"***Ach so***; what's gone of Patem's Elishamet's Patem?"

So you see little Patem Onderdonk was generally at the bottom of whatever mischief was afoot in those last Dutch days of New Amsterdam on the island of Manhattan.

[Note 10: From "Storied Holidays," Lothrop, Lee & Shepard Company.]

But this time he was conjuring a more serious bit of mischief than even he usually attempted. This was plain from the appearance of the startled but deeply interested faces of the half-dozen boys gathered around him on the bridge.

"But I say, Patem," queried young Teuny Vanderbreets, who was always ready to second any of Patem's plans, "how can we come it over the dominie as you would have us?"

"So then, Teuny," cried Patem, in his highest key of contempt, "did your wits blow away with your hat out of Heer Snediker's nut tree yesterday? Do not you know that the Heer Governor is at royal odds with Dominie Curtius because the skinflint old dominie will not pay the taxes due the town? Why, lad, the Heer Governor will back us up!"

"And why will he not pay the taxes, Patem?" asked Jan Hooglant, the tanner's son.

"Because he's a skinflint, I tell you," asserted Patem, "though I do believe he says that he was brought here from Holland as one of the Company's men, and ought not therefore pay taxes to the Company. That's what I did hear them say at the Stadt Huys this morning, and Heer Vanderveer, the schepen, said there, too, that Dominie Curtius was not worth one of the five hundred guilders which he doth receive for our teaching. And sure, if the burgomaster and schepens will have none of the old dominie, why then no more will we who know how stupid are his lessons, and how his switch doth sting. So, hoy, lads, let's turn him out."

And with that little Patem Onderdonk gave Teuny Vanderbreets' broad back a sounding slap with his battered horn book and crying, "Come on, lads," headed his mutinous companions on a race for the rickety little schoolhouse near the fort.

It was hard lines for Dominie Curtius all that day at school. The boys had never been so unruly; the girls never so inattentive. Rebellion seemed in the air, and the dominie, never a patient or gentle-mannered man, grew harsher and more exacting as the session advanced. His reign as master of the Latin School of New Amsterdam had not been a successful one, and his dispute with the town officers as to his payment of taxes had so angered him that, as Patem declared, "he seemed moved to avenge himself upon the town's children."

This being the state of affairs, Dominie Curtius's mood this day was not a pleasant one, and the school exercises had more to do with the whipping horse and the birch twigs than with the horn book and the Latin conjugations.

The boys, I regret to say, were hardened to this, because of much practice, but when the dominie, enraged at some fresh breach of rigid discipline, glared savagely over his big spectacles and then swooped down upon pretty little Antje Adrianse who had done nothing whatever, the whole school broke into open rebellion. Horn books, and every possible missile that the boys had at hand, went flying at the master's head, and the young rebels, led on by Patem and Teuny, charged down upon the unprepared dominie, rescued trembling little Antje from his clutch, and then one and all rushed pell-mell from the school with shouts of triumph and derision.

But when the first flush of their victory was over, the boys realized that they had done a very daring and risky thing. It was no small matter in those days of stern authority and strict home government for girls and boys to resist the commands of their elders; and to run away from school was one of the greatest of crimes. So they all looked at Patem in much anxiety.

"Well," cried several of the boys almost in a breath, "and now what shall we do, Patem? You have us in a pretty fix."

Patem waved his hand like a young Napoleon.

"***Ach***! ye are all cowards," he cried shrilly. "What will we ***do***? Why, then we will but do as if we were burgomasters and schepens--as we will be some day. We will to the Heer Governor straight, and lay our demands before him."

Well, well; this ***was*** bold talk! The Heer Governor! Not a boy in all New Amsterdam but would sooner face a gray wolf in the Sapokanican woods than the Heer Governor Stuyvesant.

"So then, Patem Onderdonk," they cried, "you may do it yourself, for, good faith, we will not."

"Why," said Jan Hooglant, "why, Patem, the Heer Governor will have us rated soundly over the ears for daring such a thing; and we will all catch more of it when we get home. Demand of the Heer Governor indeed! Why, boy, you must be crazy!"

But Patem was not crazy. He was simply determined; and at last, by threats and arguments and coaxing words, he gradually won over a half-dozen of the boldest spirits to his side and, without more ado, started with them to interview the Heer Governor.

But, quickly as they acted, the schoolmaster was still more prompt in action. Defeated and deserted by his scholars, Dominie Curtius had raged about the schoolroom for a while, spluttering angrily in mingled Dutch and Polish, and then, clapping his broad black hat upon his head, marched straight to the fort to lay his grievance before the Heer Governor.

The Heer Petrus Stuyvesant, Director General for the Dutch West India Company in their colony of New Netherlands, walked up and down the Governor's chamber in the fort at New Amsterdam woefully perplexed. The Heer Governor was not a patient man, and a combination of annoyances was hedging him about and making his government of his island province anything but pleasant work.

The "malignant English" of the Massachusetts and Hartford colonies were pressing their claim to the ownership of the New Netherlands, just as, to the south, the settlers on Lord De La Ware's patent were also doing; the "people called Quakers," whom the Heer Governor had publicly whipped for heresy and sent a-packing, were spreading their "pernicious doctrine" through Long Island and other outer edges of the colony, and the Indians around Esopus, the little settlement which the province had planted midway on the Hudson between New Amsterdam and Beaverwyck (now Albany), were growing restless and defiant. Thump, thump, thump, across the floor went the wooden leg with its silver bands, and with every thump the Heer Governor grew still more puzzled and angered. For the Heer Governor could not bear to have things go wrong.

Suddenly, with scant ceremony and but the apology of a request for admittance, there came into the Heer Governor's presence the Dominie Doctor Alexander Carolus Curtius, master of the Latin School.

"Here is a pretty pass, Heer Governor!" he cried excitedly. "My pupils of the Latin School have turned upon me in revolt and have deserted me in a body."

"*Ach*; then you are rightly served for a craven and a miser, sir!" burst out the angry Governor, turning savagely upon the surprised schoolmaster.

This was a most unexpected reception for Doctor and Dominie Curtius. But, as it happened, the Heer Governor Stuyvesant was just now particularly vexed with the objectionable Dominie. At much trouble and after much solicitation on his part the Heer Governor had prevailed upon his superiors and the proprietors of the province, the Dutch West India Company, to send from Holland a schoolmaster or "rector" for the children of their town of New Amsterdam, and the Company had sent over Dominie Curtius.

The Heer Governor had entertained great hopes of what the new schoolmaster was to do, and now to find him a subject of complaint from both the parents of the scholars and the officials of the town made the hasty Governor doubly dissatisfied. The Dominie's intrusion, therefore, at just this stage of all his perplexities gave the Heer Governor a most convenient person on whom to vent his bad feelings.

"Yes, sirrah, a craven and a miser!" continued the angry Governor, stamping upon the floor with both wooden leg and massive cane. "You, who can neither govern our children nor pay your just dues to the town, can be no fit master for our youth. No words, sirrah, no words," he added, as the poor dominie tried to put in a word in his defence, "no words, sir; you are discharged from further labour in this province. I will see that one who can ride wisely and pay his just dues shall be placed here in your stead."

Protests and appeals, explanations and arguments, were of no avail. When the Heer Governor Stuyvesant said a thing, he meant it, and it was useless for any one to hope for a change. The unpopular Dominie Curtius must go--and go he did.

But, as he left, the delegation of boys, headed by young Patem Onderdonk, came into the fort and sought to interview the Heer Governor.

The sentry at the door would have sent them off without further ado, but, hearing their noise, the Heer Governor came to the door.

"So, so, young rapscallions," he cried, "you, too, must needs disturb the peace and push yourself forward into public quarrels! Get you gone! I will have none of your words. Is it not enough that I must needs send the schoolmaster a-packing, without being worried by graceless young varlets as you?"

"And hath the Dominie Curtius gone indeed, Heer Governor?" Patem dared to ask.

"Hath he, hath he, boy?" echoed the Governor, turning upon his audacious young questioner with uplifted cane. "Said I not so, and will you dare doubt my word, rascal? Begone from the fort, all of you, ere I do put you all in limbo, or send word to your good folk to give you the floggings you do no doubt all so richly deserve."

Discretion is the better part of valour, and the boyish delegation hastily withdrew. But when once they were safely out of hearing of the Heer Governor, beyond the Land Gate at the Broad Way, they took breath and indulged in a succession of boyish shouts.

"And that doth mean no school, too!" cried young Patem Onderdonk, flinging his cap in air. "Huzzoy for that, lads; huzzoy for that!"

And the "huzzoys" came with right good-will from every boy of the group.

Within less than a week the whole complexion of affairs in that little island city was entirely changed. Both the Massachusetts and the Maryland claimants ceased, for a time at least, their unfounded demands. A treaty at Hartford settled the disputed question of boundary-lines, and the Maryland governor declared "that he had not intended to meddle with the government of Manhattan." Added to this, Sewackenamo, chief of the Esopus Indians, came to the fort at New Amsterdam and "gave the right hand of friendship" to the Heer Governor, and by the interchange of presents a treaty of peace was ratified. So, one by one, the troubles of the Heer Governor melted away, his brow became clear and, "partaking of the universal satisfaction," so says the historian, "he proclaimed a day of general thanksgiving."

Thanksgiving in the colonies was a matter of almost yearly occurrence. Since the first Thanksgiving Day on American shores, when, in 1621, the Massachusetts colony, at the request of Governor Bradford, rejoiced, "after a special manner after we had gathered the fruit of our labours," the observance of days of thanksgiving for mercies and benefits had been frequent. But the day itself dates still further back. The States of Holland after establishing their freedom from Spain had, in the year 1609, celebrated their deliverance from tyranny "by thanksgiving and hearty prayers," and had thus really first instituted the custom of an official thanksgiving.

And the Dutch colonists in America followed the customs of the Fatherland quite as piously and fervently as did the English colonists.

So, when the proclamation of the Heer Governor Stuyvesant for a day of thanksgiving was made known, in this year of mercies, 1659, all the townfolk of New Amsterdam made ready to keep it.

But young people are often apt to think that the world moves for them alone. The boys of this little Dutch town at the mouth of the Hudson were no different from other boys, and cared less for treaties and Indians and boundary questions than for their own matters. They, therefore, concluded that the Heer Governor had proclaimed a thanksgiving because, as young Patem Onderdonk declared, "he had gotten well rid of Dominie Curtius and would have no more schoolmasters in the colony."

"And so, lads," cried the exuberant young Knickerbocker, "let us wisely celebrate the Thanksgiving. I will even ask the mother to make for me a rare salmagundi which we lads, who were so rated by the Heer Governor, will ourselves give to him as our Thanksgiving offering, for the Heer Governor, so folk do say, doth rarely like the salmagundi."

Now the salmagundi was (to some palates) a most appetizing mixture, compounded of salted mackerel, or sometimes of chopped meat, seasoned with oil and vinegar, pepper and raw onions--not an altogether attractive dish to read of, but welcome to and dearly loved by many an old Knickerbocker even up to a recent date. Its name, too, as most of you bright boys and girls doubtless know, furnished the title for one of the works of Washington Irving, best loved of all the Knickerbockers.

Thanksgiving Day came around, and so did Patem's salmagundi, as highly seasoned and appetizing a one as the Goode Vrouw Onderdonk could make.

The lengthy prayers and lengthier sermon of good Dominie Megapolensis in the Fort Church were over and the Thanksgiving dinners were very nearly ready when up to the Heer Governor's house came a half-dozen boys, with Patem Onderdonk at their head bearing a neatly covered dish.

Patem had well considered and formed in his mind what he deemed just the speech of presentation to please the Heer Governor, but when the time came to face that awful personage his valour and his eloquence alike began to ooze away.

And, it must be confessed, the Heer Governor Stuyvesant did not understand boys, nor did he particularly favour them. He was hasty and overbearing though high-minded, loyal, and brave, but he never could "get on" with the ways and pranks of boys.

And as for the boys themselves, when once they stood in the presence of the greatest dignitary in the province, Patem's ready tongue seemed to cleave to the roof of his mouth, and he hummed and hawed and hesitated until the worthy Heer Governor lost patience and broke in:

"Well, well, boys; what is the stir? Speak quick if at all, for when a man's dinner waiteth he hath scant time for stammering boys."

Then Patem spoke up.

"Heer Governor," he said, "the boys hereabout, remembering your goodness in sending away our most pestilential master, the Dominie Curtius, and in proclaiming a Thanksgiving for his departure and for the ending of our schooling--"

"What, what, boy!" cried the Heer Governor, "art crazy then, or would you seek to make sport of me, your governor? Thanksgiving for the breaking up of school! Out on you for a set of malapert young knaves! Do you think the world goeth but for your pleasures alone? Why, this is ribald talk! I made no Thanksgiving for your convenience, rascals, but because that the Lord in His grace hath relieved the town from danger--"

"Of which, Heer Governor," broke in the most impolitic Patem, "we did think the Dominie Curtius and his school were part. And so we have brought to you this salmagundi as our Thanksgiving offering to you for thus freeing us of a pest and a sorrow--"

"How now, how now, sirrah!" again came the interruption from the scandalized Heer Governor when he could recover from his surprise, "do you then dare to call your schooling a pest and a sorrow? Why, you graceless young varlets, I do not seek to free you from schooling. I do even now seek to bring you speedily the teaching you do so much stand in need of. Even now, within the week forthcoming, the good Dominie Luyck, the tutor of mine own household, will see to the training and teaching of this town, and so I will warrant to the flogging, too, of all you sad young rapscallions who even now by this your wicked talk do show your need both of teaching and of flogging."

And then, forgetful of the boys' Thanksgiving offering and in high displeasure at what he deemed their wilful and deliberate ignorance, the Heer Governor turned the delegation into the street and hastened back to his waiting dinner.

"*Ach, so,*" cried young Teuny Vanderbreets, as the disgusted and disconsolate six gathered in the roadway and looked at one another ruefully. "Here is a fine mix-up--a regular salmagundi, Patem Onderdonk, and no question. And you did say that this Thanksgiving was all our work. Out upon you, say I! Here are we to be saddled with a worse master than before. Hermanus Smeeman did tell me that Nick Stuyvesant did tell him that Dominie Luyck is a most hard and worry-ful master."

There was a universal groan of disappointment and disgust, and then Patem said philosophically:

"Well, lads, what's done is done and what is to be will be. Let us eat the salmagundi anyhow and cry, 'Confusion to Dominie Luyck.'"

And they did eat it, then and there, for indigestion had no terror to those lads of hardy stomachs.

But as for the toast of "Confusion to Dominie Luyck," that came to naught. For Dominie Aegidius Luyck proved a most efficient and skilful teacher. Under his rule the Latin School of New Amsterdam became famous throughout the colonies, so that scholars came to it for instruction from Beaverwyck and South River and even from distant Virginia.

So the Thanksgiving of the boys of New Amsterdam became a day of mourning, and Patem's influence as a leader and an oracle suffered sadly for a while.

Five years after, on a sad Monday morning in September, 1664, the little city was lost to the Dutch West India Company and, spite of the efforts and protests of its sturdy Governor, the red, white, and blue banner of the Netherlands gave place to the flag of England. And when that day came the young fellows who then saw the defeat and disappointment of the Heer Governor Stuyvesant were not so certain that Patem Onderdonk was wrong when he claimed that it was all a just and righteous judgment on the Heer Governor for his refusal of the boys' request for no school, and for his treatment of them on that sad Thanksgiving Day when he so harshly rebuked their display of gratitude and lost forever his chance to partake of Patem's Salmagundi.

MRS. NOVEMBER'S DINNER PARTY[11]
BY AGNES CARR.

An amusing allegorical fantasy. All the most interesting
Days, grandchildren of Mother Year, came to Mrs. November's
dinner party, to honour the birthday of her daughter,
Thanksgiving.

The widow November was very busy indeed this year. What with elections
and harvest homes, her hands were full to overflowing; for she takes great interest
in politics, besides being a social body, without whom no apple bee or corn husking
is complete.

[Note 11: From **Harper's Young People**, November 23, 1880.]

Still, worn out as she was, when her thirty sons and daughters clustered round,
and begged that they might have their usual family dinner on Thanksgiving Day,
she could not find it in her hospitable heart to refuse, and immediately invitations
were sent to her eleven brothers and sisters, old Father Time, and Mother Year, to
come with all their families and celebrate the great American holiday.

Then what a busy time ensued! What a slaughter of unhappy barnyard families-
-turkeys, ducks, and chickens! What a chopping of apples and boiling of doughnuts!
What a picking of raisins and rolling of pie crust, until every nook and corner of
the immense storeroom was stocked with "savoury mince and toothsome pumpkin
pies," while so great was the confusion that even the stolid red-hued servant, Indian
Summer, lost his head, and smoked so continually he always appeared surrounded
by a blue mist, as he piled logs upon the great bonfires in the yard, until they lighted
up the whole country for miles around.

But at length all was ready; the happy day had come, and all the little Novembers, in their best "bib and tucker," were seated in a row, awaiting the arrival of their
uncles, aunts, and cousins, while their mother, in russet-brown silk trimmed with

misty lace, looked them over, straightening Guy Fawkes's collar, tying Thanksgiving's neck ribbon, and settling a dispute between two little presidential candidates as to which should sit at the head of the table.

Soon a merry clashing of bells, blowing of horns, and mingling of voices were heard outside, sleighs and carriages dashed up to the door, and in came, "just in season," Grandpa Time, with Grandma Year leaning on his arm, followed by all their children and grandchildren, and were warmly welcomed by the hostess and her family.

"Oh, how glad I am we could all come to-day!" said Mr. January, in his crisp, clear tones, throwing off his great fur coat, and rushing to the blazing fire. "There is nothing like the happy returns of these days."

"Nothing, indeed," simpered Mrs. February, the poetess. "If I had had time I should have composed some verses for the occasion; but my son Valentine has brought a sugar heart, with a sweet sentiment on it, to his cousin Thanksgiving. I, too, have taken the liberty of bringing a sort of adopted child of mine, young Leap Year, who makes us a visit every four years."

"He is very welcome, I am sure," said Mrs. November, patting Leap Year kindly on the head. "And, Sister March, how have you been since we last met?"

"Oh! we have had the North, South, East, and West Winds all at our house, and they have kept things breezy, I assure you. But I really feared we should not get here to-day; for when we came to dress I found nearly everything we had was lent; so that must account for our shabby appearance."

"He! he! he!" tittered little April Fool. "What a sell!" And he shook until the bells on his cap rang; at which his father ceased for a moment showering kisses on his nieces and nephews, and boxed his ears for his rudeness.

"Oh, Aunt May! do tell us a story," clamoured the younger children, and dragging her into a corner she was soon deep in such a moving tale that they were all melted to tears, especially the little Aprils, who cry very easily.

Meanwhile, Mrs. June, assisted by her youngest daughter, a "sweet girl graduate," just from school, was engaged in decking the apartment with roses and lilies and other fragrant flowers that she had brought from her extensive gardens and conservatories, until the room was a perfect bower of sweetness and beauty; while Mr. July draped the walls with flags and banners, lighted the candles, and showed off the tricks of his pet eagle, Yankee Doodle, to the great delight of the little ones.

Madam August, who suffers a great deal with the heat, found a seat on a comfortable sofa, as far from the fire as possible, and waved a huge feather fan back and forth, while her thirty-one boys and girls, led by the two oldest, Holiday and Vacation, ran riot through the long rooms, picking at their Aunt June's flowers, and playing all sorts of pranks, regardless of tumbled hair and torn clothes, while they shouted, "Hurrah for fun!" and behaved like a pack of wild colts let loose in a green pasture, until their Uncle September called them, together with his own children, into the library, and persuaded them to read some of the books with which the shelves were filled, or play quietly with the game of Authors and the Dissected Maps.

"For," said Mr. September to Mrs. October, "I think Sister August lets her children romp too much. I always like improving games for mine, although I have great trouble to make Equinox toe the line as he should."

"That is because you are a schoolmaster," laughed Mrs. October, shaking her head, adorned with a wreath of gayly tinted leaves; "but where is my baby?"

At that moment a cry was heard without, and Indian Summer came running in to say that little All Hallows had fallen into a tub of water while trying to catch an apple that was floating on top, and Mrs. October, rushing off to the kitchen, returned with her youngest in a very wet and dripping condition, and screaming at the top of his lusty little lungs, and could only be consoled by a handful of chestnuts, which his nurse, Miss Frost, cracked open for him.

The little Novembers, meanwhile, were having a charming time with their favourite cousins, the Decembers, who were always so gay and jolly, and had such a delightful papa. He came with his pockets stuffed full of toys and sugarplums, which he drew out from time to time, and gave to his best-loved child, Merry Christmas, to distribute amongst the children, who gathered eagerly around their little cousin, saying:

"Christmas comes but once a year, But when she comes she brings good cheer."

At which Merry laughed gayly, and tossed her golden curls, in which were twined sprays of holly and clusters of brilliant scarlet berries.

At last the great folding-doors were thrown open. Indian Summer announced that dinner was served, and a long procession of old and young being quickly formed, led by Mrs. November and her daughter Thanksgiving, whose birthday it was, they filed into the spacious dining-room, where stood the long table groaning beneath its weight of good things, while four servants ran continually in and out bringing more substantials and delicacies to grace the board and please the appetite. Winter staggered beneath great trenchers of meat and poultry, pies and puddings; Spring brought the earliest and freshest vegetables; Summer, the richest creams and ices; while Autumn served the guests with fruit, and poured the sparkling wine.

All were gay and jolly, and many a joke was cracked as the contents of each plate and dish melted away like snow before the sun; and the great fires roared in the wide chimneys as though singing a glad Thanksgiving song.

New Year drank everybody's health, and wished them "many happy returns of the day," while Twelfth Night ate so much cake he made himself quite ill, and had to be put to bed.

Valentine sent mottoes to all the little girls, and praised their bright eyes and glossy curls. "For," said his mother, "he is a sad flatterer, and not nearly so truthful, I am sorry to say, as his brother, George Washington, who never told a lie."

At which Grandfather Time gave George a quarter, and said he should always remember what a good boy he was.

After dinner the fun increased, all trying to do something for the general amusement. Mrs. March persuaded her son, St. Patrick, to dance an Irish Jig, which he did to the tune of the "Wearing of the Green," which his brothers, Windy and Gusty, blew and whistled on their fingers.

Easter sang a beautiful song, the little Mays "tripped the light fantastic toe" in a pretty fancy dance, while the Junes sat by so smiling and sweet it was a pleasure to look at them.

Independence, the fourth child of Mr. July, who is a bold little fellow, and a fine speaker, gave them an oration he had learned at school; and the Augusts suggested games of tag and blindman's buff, which they all enjoyed heartily.

Mr. September tried to read an instructive story aloud, but was interrupted by Equinox, April Fool, and little All Hallows, who pinned streamers to his coat tails, covered him with flour, and would not let him get through a line; at which Mrs. October hugged her tricksy baby, and laughed until she cried, and Mr. September retired in disgust.

"That is almost too bad," said Mrs. November, as she shook the popper vigorously in which the corn was popping and snapping merrily; "but, Thanksgiving, you must not forget to thank your cousins for all they have done to honour your birthday."

At which the demure little maiden went round to each one, and returned her thanks in such a charming way it was quite captivating.

Grandmother Year at last began to nod over her teacup in the chimney corner.

"It is growing late," said Grandpa Time.

"But we must have a Virginia Reel before we go," said Mr. December.

"Oh, yes, yes!" cried all the children.

Merry Christmas played a lively air on the piano, and old and young took their positions on the polished floor with grandpa and grandma at the head.

Midsummer danced with Happy New Year, June's Commencement with August's Holiday, Leap Year with May Day, and all "went merry as a marriage bell."

The fun was at its height when suddenly the clock in the corner struck twelve. Grandma Year motioned all to stop, and Grandfather Time, bowing his head, said softly, "Hark! my children, Thanksgiving Day is ended."

THE VISIT[12]
A STORY OF THE CHILDREN OF THE TOWER
BY MAUD LINDSAY.

The children went back to spend Thanksgiving at grandfather's farm. They got into some trouble and were afraid that they would miss their dinner.

Early one morning Grandmother Grey got up, opened the windows and doors of the farmhouse, and soon everybody on the place was stirring. The cook hurried breakfast, and no sooner was it over than Grandfather Grey went out to the barn and hitched the two horses to the wagon.

[Note 12: From "More Mother Stories," Milton Bradley Company.]

"Get up, Robin and Dobbin!" he said, as he drove through the big gate. "If you knew who were coming back in this wagon you would not be stepping so slowly."

The old horses pricked up their ears when they heard this, and trotted away as fast as they could down the country road until they came to town. Just as they got to the railway station the train came whizzing in.

"All off!" cried the conductor, as the train stopped; and out came a group of children who were, every one of them, Grandfather and Grandmother Grey's grandchildren. They had come to spend Thanksgiving Day on the farm.

There was John, who was named for grandfather and looked just like him, and the twins, Teddie and Pat, who looked like nobody but each other; their papa was grandfather's oldest son. Then there was Louisa, who had a baby sister at home, and then Mary Virginia Martin, who was her mamma's only child.

"I tell you," said grandfather, as he helped them into the wagon, "your grandmother will be glad to see you!"

And so she was. She was watching at the window for them when they drove up, and when the children spied her they could scarcely wait for grandfather to stop the wagon before they scrambled out.

"Dear me, dear me!" said grandmother, as they all tried to kiss her at the same time, "how you have grown."

"I am in the first grade," said John, hugging her with all his might.

"So am I," cried Louisa.

"We are going to be," chimed in the twins; and then they all talked at once, till grandmother could not hear herself speak.

Then, after they had told her all about their mammas and papas, and homes, and cats and dogs, they wanted to go and say "how do you do" to everything on the place.

"Take care of yourselves," called grandmother, "for I don't want to send any broken bones home to your mothers."

"I can take care of myself," said John.

"So can we," said the rest; and off they ran.

First they went to the kitchen where Mammy 'Ria was getting ready to cook the Thanksgiving dinner; then out to the barnyard, where there were two new red calves, and five little puppies belonging to Juno, the dog, for them to see. Then they climbed the barnyard fence and made haste to the pasture where grandfather kept his woolly sheep. "Baa-a!" said the sheep when they saw the children; but then, they always said that, no matter what happened.

There were cows in this pasture, too, and Mary Virginia was afraid of them, even though she knew that they were the mothers of the calves she had seen in the barnyard.

"Silly Mary Virginia!" said John, and Mary Virginia began to cry.

"Don't cry," said Louisa. "Let's go to the hickory-nut tree."

This pleased them all, and they hurried off; but on the way they came to the big shed where grandfather kept his plows and reaper and threshing machine and all his garden tools.

The shed had a long, wide roof, and there was a ladder leaning against it. When John saw that, he thought he must go up on the roof; and then, of course, the twins went, too. Then Louisa and Mary Virginia wanted to go, and although John insisted that girls could not climb, they managed to scramble up the ladder to where the boys were. And there they all sat in a row on the roof.

"Grandmother doesn't know how well we can take care of ourselves," said John. "But I am such a big boy that I can do anything. I can ride a bicycle and go on errands--"

"So can I," said Louisa.

"We can ride on the trolley!" cried the twins.

"Mamma and I go anywhere by ourselves," said Mary Virginia.

"Moo!" said something down below; and when they looked, there was one of the cows rubbing her head against the ladder.

"Don't be afraid, Mary Virginia," said Louisa. "Cows can't climb ladders."

"Don't be afraid, Mary Virginia," said John. "I'll drive her away."

So he kicked his feet against the shed roof and called, "Go away! go away!" The twins kicked their feet, too, and called, "Go away! go away!" and somebody, I don't know who, kicked the ladder and it fell down and lay in the dry grass. And the cow walked peacefully on, thinking about her little calf.

"There, now!" exclaimed Louisa, "how shall we ever get down?"

"Oh, that's nothing," said John. "All I'll have to do is to stand up on the roof and call grandfather. Just watch me do it."

So he stood up and called, "Grandfather! Grandfather! Grandfather!" till he was tired; but no grandfather answered.

Then the twins called, "Grandfather! Grandmother!"

"Baa," said the sheep, as if beginning to think that somebody ought to answer all that calling.

Then they all called together: "Grandfather! Grandfather! Grandfather!" and when nobody heard that, they began to feel frightened and lonely.

"I want to go home to my mother! I wish I hadn't come!" wailed Mary Virginia.

"It's Thanksgiving dinner time, too," said John, "and there's turkey for dinner, for I saw it in the oven."

"Pie, too," said Louisa.

"Dear, dear!" cried the twins.

And then they all called together once more, but this time with such a weak little cry that not even the sheep heard it.

The sun grew warmer and the shadows straighter as they sat there, and grandmother's house seemed miles away when John stood up to look at it.

"They've eaten dinner by this time, I know," he said as he sat down again; "and grandfather and grandmother have forgotten all about us."

But grandfather and grandmother had not forgotten them, for just about then grandmother was saying to grandfather: "You had better see where the children are, for Thanksgiving dinner will soon be ready and I know that they are hungry."

So grandfather went out to look for them. He did not find them in the kitchen nor the barnyard, so he called, "Johnnie! Johnnie!" and when nobody answered he made haste to the pasture.

The children saw him coming, and long before he had reached the gate they began to call with all their might. This time grandfather answered, "I'm coming!" and I cannot tell you how glad they were.

In another minute he had set the ladder up again and they all came down. Mary Virginia came first because she was the youngest girl, and John came last because he was the biggest boy. Grandfather put his arms around each one as he helped them down, and carried Mary Virginia home on his back. When they got to the house dinner was just ready.

The turkey was brown, the potatoes were sweet,
The sauce was so spicy, the biscuits were beat,
The great pumpkin pie was as yellow as gold,
And the apples were red as the roses, I'm told.
It was such a good dinner that I had to tell you about it in rhyme!

And I'm sure you'll agree,
With the children and me,
That there's never a visit so pleasant to pay
As a visit to grandma on Thanksgiving Day.

THE STORY OF RUTH AND NAOMI[13]
ADAPTED FROM THE BIBLE
BY C. S. BAILEY AND C. M. LEWIS.

Ruth's story is one of the most beautiful ones to be found in the Old Book. As a tale of the harvest, it deserves to be included in this collection.

Now it came to pass, many hundreds of years ago, that there was a good woman named Naomi who lived in the land of the Moabites. She had once been very rich and happy, but now her husband was dead and her two sons also, and she had left only Orpah and Ruth, the wives of her sons. There was a famine in the land. Naomi could find no grain in the fields to beat into flour. She and Orpah and Ruth were lonely and sad and very hungry.

[Note 13: From "For the Children's Hour," Milton Bradley Company.]

But Naomi heard there was a land where the Lord had visited His people and given them bread; so she went forth from the place where she was, and her two daughters with her, to the land called Judah. It was a long, hard way to go. There were rough roads to travel and steep hills to climb. Their feet grew so weary they could scarcely walk, and at last Naomi said:

"Go, return each to your father's house. The Lord deal kindly with you as you have dealt with me. The Lord grant you that you may find rest."

Then she kissed them, and Orpah kissed her and left her, but Ruth would not leave Naomi. And Naomi said to Ruth:

"Behold, thy sister is gone back unto her own people; return thou!"

But Ruth clung to Naomi more closely, as she said:

"Entreat me not to leave thee, or to return from following after thee: for whither thou goest, there will I go; and where thou lodgest, there will I lodge. Thy people shall be my people, and thy God my God."

When Naomi saw that Ruth loved her so much, she forgot how tired and hungry she was, and the two journeyed on together until they came to Bethlehem in Judah in the beginning of the barley harvest. There was no famine in Bethlehem. The fields were full of waving grain, and busy servants were reaping it and gathering it up to bind into sheaves. Above all were the fields of the rich man, Boaz, shining with barley and corn.

Naomi and Ruth came to the edge of the fields and watched the busy reapers. They saw that after each sheaf was bound, and each pile of corn was stacked, a little grain fell, unnoticed, to the ground. Ruth said to Naomi: "Let me go to the field and glean the ears of corn after them." And Naomi said to her, "Go, my daughter." And she went, and came and gleaned in the field after the reapers.

And Boaz came from Bethlehem, and said to his reapers: "Whose damsel is this?" for he saw how very beautiful Ruth was, and how busily she was gleaning. The reapers said: "It is the damsel that came back with Naomi out of the land of the Moabites."

And Ruth ran up to Boaz, crying: "I pray you, let me glean and gather after the reapers among the sheaves."

And Boaz, who was good and kind, said to Ruth:

"Hearest thou not, my daughter? Go not to glean in any other field, but abide here."

Then Ruth bowed herself to the ground, and said: "Why have I found such favour in thine eyes, seeing I am a stranger?"

And Boaz answered her: "It hath been showed me all that thou hast done to thy mother."

So, all day, Ruth gleaned in Boaz's fields. At noon she ate bread and parched corn with the others. Boaz commanded his reapers to let fall large handfuls of grain, as they worked, for Ruth to gather, and at night she took it all home to Naomi.

"Where hast thou gleaned to-day?" asked Naomi, when she saw the food that Ruth had brought to her.

"The man's name with whom I wrought to-day is Boaz," said Ruth. And Naomi said: "Blessed be he of the Lord--the man is near of kin unto us."

So Ruth gleaned daily, and at the end of the barley harvest the good man Boaz took Ruth and Naomi to live with him in his own house forever.

BERT'S THANKSGIVING[14]
BY J. T. TROWBRIDGE.

Bert is a manly, generous, warm-hearted fellow. Other boys will like to read how good luck began to come his way on acertain memorable Thanksgiving Day.

At noon, on a dreary November day, a lonesome little fellow, looking very red about the ears and very blue about the mouth, stood kicking his heels at the door of a cheap eating house in Boston, and offering a solitary copy of a morning paper for sale to the people passing.

[Note 14: From "Young Joe," Lothrop, Lee & Shepard Company.]

But there were really not many people passing, for it was Thanksgiving Day, and the shops were shut, and everybody who had a home to go to and a dinner to eat seemed to have gone home to eat that dinner, while Bert Hampton, the news-boy, stood trying in vain to sell the last "extry" left on his hands by the dull business of the morning.

An old man, with a face that looked pinched, and who was dressed in a seedy black coat and a much-battered stovepipe hat, stopped at the same doorway, and, with one hand on the latch, appeared to hesitate between hunger and a sense of poverty before going in.

It was possible, however, that he was considering whether he could afford himself the indulgence of a morning paper (seeing it was Thanksgiving Day); so, at least, Bert thought, and accosted him accordingly.

"Buy a paper, sir? All about the fire in East Boston, and arrest of safe-burglars in Springfield. Only two cents!"

The little old man looked at the boy with keen gray eyes, which seemed to light up the pinched and skinny face, and answered in a shrill voice that whistled through white front teeth:

"You ought to come down in your price this time of day. You can't expect to sell a morning paper at twelve o'clock for full price."

"Well, give me a cent then," said Bert. "That's less'n cost; but never mind; I'm bound to sell out anyhow."

"You look cold," said the old man.

"Cold?" replied Bert; "I'm froze. And I want my dinner. And I'm going to have a big dinner, too, seeing it's Thanksgiving Day."

"Ah! lucky for you, my boy!" said the old man. "You've a home to go to, and friends, too, I hope?"

"No, *sir*; nary home, and nary friend; only my mother"--Bert hesitated, and grew serious; then suddenly changed his tone--"and Hop Houghton. I told him to meet me here, and we'd have a first-rate Thanksgiving dinner together; for it's no fun to be eatin' alone Thanksgiving Day! It sets a feller thinking of everything, if he ever had a home and then hain't got a home any more."

"It's more lonesome not to eat at all," said the old man, his gray eyes twinkling. "And what can a boy like you have to think of? Here, I guess I can find one cent for you, though there's nothing in the paper, I know."

The old man spoke with some feeling, his fingers trembled, and somehow he dropped two cents instead of one into Bert's hand.

"Here! You've made a mistake!" cried Bert. "A bargain's a bargain. You've given me a cent too much."

"No, I didn't. I never give anybody a cent too much."

"But, see here!" And Bert showed the two cents, offering to return one.

"No matter," said the old man, "it will be so much less for *my* dinner, that's all."

Bert had instinctively pocketed the pennies when, on a moment's reflection, his sympathies were excited.

"Poor old man!" he thought; "he's seen better days I guess. Perhaps he's no home. A boy like me can stand it, but I guess it must be hard for *him*. He *meant* to give me the odd cent all the while; and I don't believe he has had a decent dinner for many a day."

All this, which I have been obliged to write out slowly in words, went through Bert's mind like a flash. He was a generous little fellow, and any kindness shown him, no matter how trifling, made his heart overflow.

"Look here!" he cried, "where are *you* going to get your dinner to-day?"

"I can get a bite here as well as anywhere. It don't matter much to me," replied the old man.

"Dine with *me*," said Bert, laughing. "I'd like to have you."

"I'm afraid I couldn't afford to dine as you are going to," said the man, with a smile, his eyes twinkling again and his white front teeth shining.

"I'll pay for your dinner!" Bert exclaimed. "Come! We don't have a Thanksgiving but once a year, and a feller wants a good time then."

"But you are waiting for another boy."

"Oh, Hop Houghton! He won't come now, it's so late. He's gone to a place down in North Street, I guess--a place I don't like: there's so much tobacco smoked and so much beer drank there." Bert cast a final glance up the street. "No, he won't come now. So much the worse for him! He likes the men down there; I don't."

"Ah!" said the man, taking off his hat, and giving it a brush with his elbow, as they entered the restaurant, as if trying to appear as respectable as he could in the eyes of a newsboy of such fastidious tastes.

To make him feel quite comfortable in his mind on that point, Bert hastened to say:

"I mean rowdies, and such. Poor people, if they behave themselves, are just as respectable to me as rich folks. I ain't the least mite aristocratic."

"Ah, indeed!" And the old man smiled again, and seemed to look relieved. "I'm very glad to hear it."

He placed his hat on the floor and took a seat opposite Bert at a little table, which they had all to themselves.

Bert offered him the bill of fare.

"No, I must ask you to choose for me; but nothing very extravagant, you know. I'm used to plain fare."

"So am I. But I'm going to have a good dinner for once in my life, and so shall you!" cried Bert, generously. "What do you say to chicken soup, and then wind up with a thumping big piece of squash pie? How's that for a Thanksgiving dinner?"

"Sumptuous!" said the old man, appearing to glow with the warmth of the room and the prospect of a good dinner. "But won't it cost you too much?"

"Too much? No, *sir*!" laughed Bert. "Chicken soup, fifteen cents; pie--they give tremendous pieces here; thick, I tell you--ten cents. That's twenty-five cents; half a dollar for two. Of course, I don't do this way every day in the year. But mother's glad to have me, once in a while. Here, waiter!" And Bert gave his princely order as if it were no very great thing for a liberal young fellow like him, after all.

"Where is your mother? Why don't you dine with her?" the little man asked.

Bert's face grew sober in a moment.

"That's the question: why don't I? I'll tell you why I don't. I've got the best mother in the world. What I'm trying to do is to make a home for her, so we can live together and eat our Thanksgiving dinners together some time. Some boys want one thing, some another. There's one goes in for good times; another's in such a hurry to get rich he don't care much how he does it; but what I want most of anything is to be with my mother and my two sisters again, and I ain't ashamed to say so."

Bert's eyes grew very tender, and he went on, while his companion across the table watched him with a very gentle, searching look.

"I haven't been with her now for two years, hardly at all since father died. When his business was settled up--he kept a little grocery store on Hanover Street--it was found he hadn't left us anything. We had lived pretty well up to that time, and I and my two sisters had been to school; but then mother had to do something, and her friends got her places to go out nursing, and she's a nurse now. Everybody likes her, and she has enough to do. We couldn't be with her, of course. She got us boarded at a good place, but I saw how hard it was going to be for her to support us, so I said, 'I'm a boy; *I* can do something for *myself*. You just pay their board, and keep 'em to school, and I'll go to work, and maybe help you a little, besides taking care of myself.'"

"What could *you* do?" said the little old man.

"That's it. I was only 'leven years old, and what could I? What I should have liked would have been some nice place where I could do light work, and stand a chance of learning a good business. But beggars mustn't be choosers. I couldn't find such a place; and I wasn't going to be loafing about the streets, so I went to selling newspapers. I've sold newspapers ever since, and I shall be twelve years old next month."

"You like it?" said the old man.

"I like to get my own living," replied Bert, proudly, "but what I want is to learn some trade, or regular business, and settle down, and make a home for--But there's no use talking about that. Make the best of things, that's my motto. Don't this soup smell good? And don't it taste good, too? They haven't put so much chicken in yours as they have in mine. If you don't mind my having tasted it, we'll change."

The old man declined this liberal offer, took Bert's advice to help himself freely to bread, which "didn't cost anything," and ate his soup with prodigious relish, as it seemed to Bert, who grew more and more hospitable and patronizing as the repast proceeded.

"Come, now, won't you have something between the soup and the pie? Don't be afraid: I'll pay for it. Thanksgiving don't come but once a year. You won't? A cup of tea, then, to go with your pie?"

"I think I *will* have a cup of tea; you are *so* kind," said the old man.

"All right! Here, waiter! Two pieces of your fattest and biggest squash pie; and a cup of tea, strong, for this gentleman."

"I've told you about myself," added Bert; "suppose, now, *you* tell *me* something."

"About myself?"

"Yes. I think that would go pretty well with the pie."

But the man shook his head. "I could go back and tell about my plans and hopes when I was a lad of your age, but it would be too much like your own story over again. Life isn't what we think it will be when we are young. You'll find that out soon enough. I am all alone in the world now, and I am sixty-seven years old."

"Have some cheese with your pie, won't you? It must be so lonely at your age! What do you do for a living?"

"I have a little place in Devonshire Street. My name is Crooker. You'll find me up two flights of stairs, back room, at the right. Come and see me, and I'll tell you all about my business, and perhaps help you to such a place as you want, for I know several business men. Now don't fail."

And Mr. Crooker wrote his address with a little stub of a pencil on a corner of the newspaper which had led to their acquaintance, tore it off carefully, and gave it to Bert.

Thereupon the latter took a card from his pocket, not a very clean one, I must say (I am speaking of the card, though the remark will apply equally well to the pocket) and handed it across the table to his new friend.

"*Herbert Hampton, Dealer in Newspapers*," the old man read, with his sharp gray eyes, which glanced up funnily at Bert, seeming to say, "Isn't this rather aristocratic for a twelve-year-old newsboy?"

Bert blushed, and explained: "Got up for me by a printer's boy I know. I'd done some favours for him, so he made me a few cards. Handy to have sometimes, you know."

"Well, Herbert," said the little old man, "I'm glad to have made your acquaintance. The pie was excellent--not any more, thank you--and I hope you'll come and see me. You'll find me in very humble quarters; but you are not aristocratic, you say. Now won't you let me pay for my dinner? I believe I have money enough. Let me see."

Bert would not hear of such a thing, but walked up to the desk and settled the bill with the air of a person who did not regard a trifling expense.

When he looked around again the little old man was gone.

"Never mind, I'll go and see him the first chance I have," said Bert, as he looked at the pencilled strip of newspaper margin again before putting it into his pocket.

He then went round to his miserable quarters, in the top of a cheap lodging-house, where he made himself ready, by means of soap and water and a broken comb, to walk five miles into the suburbs and get a sight, if only for five minutes, of his mother.

On the following Monday Bert, having a leisure hour, went to call on his new acquaintance in Devonshire Street.

Having climbed the two flights, he found the door of the back room at the right ajar, and looking in, saw Mr. Crooker at a desk, in the act of receiving a roll of money from a well-dressed visitor.

Bert entered unnoticed and waited till the money was counted and a receipt signed. Then, as the visitor departed, old Mr. Crooker looked round and saw Bert. He offered him a chair, then turned to lock up the money in a safe.

"So this is your place of business?" said Bert, glancing about the plain office room. "What do you do here?"

"I buy real estate sometimes--sell--rent--and so forth."

"Who for?" asked Bert.

"For myself," said little old Mr. Crooker, with a smile.

Bert stared, perfectly aghast at the situation. This, then, was the man whom he had invited to dinner, and treated so patronizingly the preceding Thursday!

"I--I thought--you was a poor man."

"I *am* a poor man," said Mr. Crooker, locking his safe. "Money doesn't make a man rich. I've money enough. I own houses in the city. They give me something to think of, and so keep me alive. I had truer riches once, but I lost them long ago."

From the way the old man's voice trembled and eyes glistened, Bert thought he must have meant by these riches friends he had lost--wife and children, perhaps.

"To think of *me* inviting *you* to dinner!" the boy cried, abashed and ashamed.

"It *was* odd." And Mr. Crooker showed his white front teeth with a smile. "But it may turn out to have been a lucky circumstance for both of us. I like you; I believe in you; and I've an offer to make to you: I want a trusty, bright boy in this office, somebody I can bring up to my business, and leave it with, as I get too old to attend to it myself. What do you say?"

What *could* Bert say?

Again that afternoon he walked--or rather, ran--to his mother, and after consulting with her, joyfully accepted Mr. Crooker's offer.

Interviews between his mother and his employer soon followed, resulting in something for which at first the boy had not dared to hope. The lonely, childless old man, who owned so many houses, wanted a home; and one of these houses he offered to Mrs. Hampton, with ample support for herself and her children, if she would also make it a home for him.

Of course this proposition was accepted; and Bert soon had the satisfaction of seeing the great ambition of his youth accomplished. He had employment which promised to become a profitable business (as indeed it did in a few years, he and the old man proved so useful to each other); and, more than that, he was united once more with his mother and sisters in a happy home where he has since had a good many Thanksgiving dinners.

A THANKSGIVING STORY[15]
BY MISS L. B. PINGREE.

A three-minute story for the littlest boys and girls.

It was nearly time for Thanksgiving Day. The rosy apples and golden pumpkins were ripe, and the farmers were bringing them into the markets.

[Note 15: From "Boston Collection of Kindergarten Stories," J. L. Hammett Company.]

One day when two little children, named John and Minnie, were going to school, they saw the turkeys and chickens and pumpkins in the window of a market, and they exclaimed, "Oh, Thanksgiving Day! Oh, Thanksgiving Day!" After school was over, they ran home to their mother, and asked her when Thanksgiving Day would be. She told them in about two weeks; then they began to talk about what they wanted for dinner, and asked their mother a great many questions. She told them she hoped they would have turkey and even the pumpkin pie they wanted so much, but that Thanksgiving Day was not given us so that we might have a good dinner, but that God had been a great many days and weeks preparing for Thanksgiving. He had sent the sunshine and the rain and caused the grains and fruits and vegetables to grow. And Thanksgiving Day was for glad and happy thoughts about God, as well as for good things to eat.

Not long after, when John and Minnie were playing, John said to Minnie, "I wish I could do something to tell God how glad I am about Thanksgiving." "I wish so, too," said Minnie. Just then some little birds came flying down to the ground, and Minnie said: "Oh, I know." Then she told John, but they agreed to keep it a se-cret till the day came. Now what do you think they did? Well, I will tell you.

They saved their pennies, and bought some corn, and early Thanksgiving Day, before they had their dinner, they went out into the street near their home, and scattered corn in a great many places. What for? Why, for the birds. While they were doing it, John said, "I know, Minnie, why you thought of the birds: because they do not have any papas and mammas after they are grown up to get a dinner for them on Thanksgiving Day." "Yes, that is why," said Minnie.

By and by the birds came and found such a feast, and perhaps they knew some-thing about Thanksgiving Day and must have sung and chirped happily all day.

JOHN INGLEFIELD'S THANKSGIVING BY NATHANIEL HAWTHORNE.

A sad Thanksgiving story is a rarity indeed. But the one which follows reminds us that the Puritans, although they originated our Thanksgiving festival, were after all a sombre people, seldom free from a realizing sense of the   imminence of sin. Nathaniel Hawthorne, a genuine product of Puritanism, inherited a full share of his forefathers' constitu-tional melancholy and preoccupation with the darker aspects of life--as this story bears witness.

On the evening of Thanksgiving Day, John Inglefield, the blacksmith, sat in his elbow-chair among those who had been keeping festival at his board. Being the central figure of the domestic circle, the fire threw its strongest light on his massive and sturdy frame, reddening his rough visage so that it looked like the head of an iron statue, all aglow, from his own forge, and with its features rudely fashioned on his own anvil. At John Inglefield's right hand was an empty chair. The other places round the hearth were filled by the members of the family, who all sat qui-etly, while, with a semblance of fantastic merriment, their shadows danced on the wall behind them. One of the group was John Inglefield's son, who had been bred at college, and was now a student of theology at Andover. There was also a daughter of sixteen, whom nobody could look at without thinking of a rosebud almost blossomed. The only other person at the fireside was Robert Moore, formerly an apprentice of the blacksmith, but now his journeyman, and who seemed more like an own son of John Inglefield than did the pale and slender student.

Only these four had kept New England's festival beneath that roof. The vacant chair at John Inglefield's right hand was in memory of his wife, whom death had snatched from him since the previous Thanksgiving. With a feeling that few would have looked for in his rough nature, the bereaved husband had himself set the chair in its place next his own; and often did his eye glance hitherward, as if he deemed it possible that the cold grave might send back its tenant to the cheerful fireside, at least for that one evening. Thus did he cherish the grief that was dear to him. But there was another grief which he would fain have torn from his heart; or, since that could never be, have buried it too deep for others to behold, or for his own remembrance. Within the past year another member of his household had gone from him, but not to the grave. Yet they kept no vacant chair for her.

While John Inglefield and his family were sitting round the hearth with the shadows dancing behind them on the wall, the outer door was opened, and a light footstep came along the passage. The latch of the inner door was lifted by some familiar hand, and a young girl came in, wearing a cloak and hood, which she took off and laid on the table beneath the looking-glass. Then, after gazing a moment at the fireside circle, she approached, and took the seat at John Inglefield's right hand, as if it had been reserved on purpose for her.

"Here I am, at last, father," said she. "You ate your Thanksgiving dinner without me, but I have come back to spend the evening with you."

Yes, it was Prudence Inglefield. She wore the same neat and maidenly attire which she had been accustomed to put on when the household work was over for the day, and her hair was parted from her brow in the simple and modest fashion that became her best of all. If her cheek might otherwise have been pale, yet the glow of the fire suffused it with a healthful bloom. If she had spent the many months of her absence in guilt and infamy, yet they seemed to have left no traces on her gentle aspect. She could not have looked less altered had she merely stepped away from her father's fireside for half an hour, and returned while the blaze was quivering upward from the same brands that were burning at her departure. And to John Inglefield she was the very image of his buried wife, such as he remembered on the first Thanksgiving which they had passed under their own roof. Therefore, though naturally a stern and rugged man, he could not speak unkindly to his sinful child, nor yet could he take her to his bosom.

"You are welcome home, Prudence," said he, glancing sideways at her, and his voice faltered. "Your mother would have rejoiced to see you, but she has been gone from us these four months."

"I know, father, I know it," replied Prudence quickly. "And yet, when I first came in, my eyes were so dazzled by the firelight that she seemed to be sitting in this very chair!"

By this time, the other members of the family had begun to recover from their surprise, and became sensible that it was no ghost from the grave, nor vision of their vivid recollections, but Prudence, her own self. Her brother was the next that greeted her. He advanced and held out his hand affectionately, as a brother should; yet not entirely like a brother, for, with all his kindness, he was still a clergyman and speaking to a child of sin.

"Sister Prudence," said he, earnestly, "I rejoice that a merciful Providence hath turned your steps homeward in time for me to bid you a last farewell. In a few weeks, sister, I am to sail as a missionary to the far islands of the Pacific. There is not one of these beloved faces that I shall ever hope to behold again on this earth. Oh, may I see all of them--yours and all--beyond the grave!"

A shadow flitted across the girl's countenance.

"The grave is very dark, brother," answered she, withdrawing her hand some-what hastily from his grasp. "You must look your last at me by the light of this fire."

While this was passing, the twin girl--the rosebud that had grown on the same stem with the castaway--stood gazing at her sister, longing to fling herself upon her bosom, so that the tendrils of their hearts might intertwine again. At first she was restrained by mingled grief and shame, and by a dread that Prudence was too much changed to respond to her affection, or that her own purity would be felt as a reproach by the lost one. But, as she listened to the familiar voice, while the face grew more and more familiar, she forgot everything save that Prudence had come back. Springing forward she would have clasped her in a close embrace. At that very instant, however, Prudence started from her chair and held out both her hands with a warning gesture.

"No, Mary, no, my sister," cried she, "do not you touch me! Your bosom must not be pressed to mine!"

Mary shuddered and stood still, for she felt that something darker than the grave was between Prudence and herself, though they seemed so near each other in the light of their father's hearth, where they had grown up together. Meanwhile Prudence threw her eyes around the room in search of one who had not yet bidden her welcome. He had withdrawn from his seat by the fireside and was standing near the door, with his face averted so that his features could be discerned only by the flickering shadow of the profile upon the wall. But Prudence called to him in a cheerful and kindly tone:

"Come, Robert," said she, "won't you shake hands with your old friend?"

Robert Moore held back for a moment, but affection struggled powerfully and overcame his pride and resentment; he rushed toward Prudence, seized her hand, and pressed it to his bosom.

"There, there, Robert," said she, smiling sadly, as she withdrew her hand, "you must not give me too warm a welcome."

And now, having exchanged greetings with each member of the family, Prudence again seated herself in the chair at John Inglefield's right hand. She was naturally a girl of quick and tender sensibilities, gladsome in her general mood, but with a bewitching pathos interfused among her merriest words and deeds. It was remarked of her, too, that she had a faculty, even from childhood, of throwing her own feelings like a spell over her companions. Such as she had been in her days of innocence, so did she appear this evening. Her friends, in the surprise and bewilderment of her return, almost forgot that she had ever left them, or that she had forfeited any of her claims to their affection. In the morning, perhaps, they might have looked at her with altered eyes, but by the Thanksgiving fireside they felt only that their own Prudence had come back to them, and were thankful. John Inglefield's rough visage brightened with the glow of his heart, as it grew warm and merry within him; once or twice, even, he laughed till the room rang again, yet seemed startled by the echo of his own mirth. The brave young minister became as frolicsome as a schoolboy. Mary, too, the rosebud, forgot that her twin-blossom had ever been torn from the stem and trampled in the dust. And as for Robert Moore, he gazed at Prudence with the bashful earnestness of love new-born, while she, with sweet maiden coquetry, half smiled upon and half discouraged him.

In short, it was one of those intervals when sorrow vanishes in its own depth of shadow, and joy starts forth in transitory brightness. When the clock struck eight, Prudence poured out her father's customary draught of herb tea, which had been steeping by the fireside ever since twilight.

"God bless you, child," said John Inglefield, as he took the cup from her hand; "you have made your old father happy again. But we miss your mother sadly, Prudence, sadly. It seems as if she ought to be here now."

"Now, father, or never," replied Prudence.

It was now the hour for domestic worship. But while the family were making preparations for this duty, they suddenly perceived that Prudence had put on her cloak and hood, and was lifting the latch of the door.

"Prudence, Prudence! where are you going?" cried they all with one voice.

As Prudence passed out of the door, she turned toward them and flung back her hand with a gesture of farewell. But her face was so changed that they hardly recognized it. Sin and evil passions glowed through its comeliness, and wrought a horrible deformity; a smile gleamed in her eyes, as of triumphant mockery, at their surprise and grief.

"Daughter," cried John Inglefield, between wrath and sorrow, "stay and be your father's blessing, or take his curse with you!"

For an instant Prudence lingered and looked back into the fire-lighted room, while her countenance wore almost the expression as if she were struggling with a fiend who had power to seize his victim even within the hallowed precincts of her father's hearth. The fiend prevailed, and Prudence vanished into the outer darkness. When the family rushed to the door, they could see nothing, but heard the sound of wheels rattling over the frozen ground.

That same night, among the painted beauties at the theatre of a neighbouring city, there was one whose dissolute mirth seemed inconsistent with any sympathy for pure affections, and for the joys and griefs which are hallowed by them. Yet this was Prudence Inglefield. Her visit to the Thanksgiving fireside was the realization of one of those waking dreams in which the guilty soul will sometimes stray back to its innocence. But Sin, alas! is careful of her bondslaves; they hear her voice, perhaps, at the holiest moment, and are constrained to go whither she summons them. The same dark power that drew Prudence Inglefield from her father's hearth--the same in its nature, though heightened then to a dread necessity--would snatch a guilty soul from the gate of heaven, and make its sin and its punishment alike eternal.

HOW OBADIAH BROUGHT ABOUT A THANKSGIVING[16] BY EMILY HEWITT LELAND.

The Waddle family had very bad luck on their farm in the West. And they certainly were homesick! But Obadiah and his uncle, between them, found means to mend matters.

That an innocent and helpless baby should be named Obadiah Waddle was an outrage which the infant unceasingly resented from the time he got old enough to realize the awful gulf that lay between his name and those of his more fortunate mates. The experiences of his first day at school were branded into his soul; and although he made friends by his bright face and kind and honest nature, scarcely a day passed during his six years of village schooling without his absurd name flying out at him from some unsuspected ambush and making him wince.

[Note 16: From the *Youth's Companion*, November 26, 1903.]

It was bad enough when the guying came from a boy, but when a girl took to punning, jeering, or giggling at him it seemed as if his burden was greater than he could bear. Then he would go home through the woods and fields to avoid human beings, so hurt and unhappy that nothing but his mother's greeting and the smell of a good supper could cheer him.

At home he had no trouble. His mother and his baby sister called him Obie, and sweet was his name on their lips. His father, who had objected to "Obadiah" from the first, called him Bub or Bubby; but one can bear almost any name when it comes with a loving smile or a pat on the shoulder, which was Mr. Waddle's way of addressing his only son.

Very early in life it had been explained to Obadiah that he was named for his mother's favourite brother, who went to California to live, after hanging a silver dollar on a black silk cord round the neck of his little namesake.

Obadiah often looked at this dollar, which was kept in a little box with a broken earring, a hair chain, a glass breastpin, and an ancient "copper"; and sometimes on circus days or on the Fourth of July he wished there was no hole in it that he might expend it on side-shows and lemonade or on monstrous firecrackers.

But he knew that his mother valued it highly because Uncle Obie gave it to him and because there were little dents in it made by his vigorous first teeth; so he always returned it to the box with a sigh of resignation, and made the most of the twenty-five cents given him by his father on the great days of the year.

When he was eleven years old the Waddle family moved West, and the last thing Obadiah heard as the train pulled away from the little station of his native town was this verse, lustily shouted from a group of schoolmates assembled to bid him good-bye:

"Oh, Obadiah, you're going West,   Where the prairie winds don't have no rest,   You'll have to waddle your level best.   Good-bye, my lover, good-bye!"

Ill-fortune attended the Waddles in their western home. To be sure, they had their rich, broad acres, with never a stone or a stump to hinder the smooth cutting plow, but a frightful midsummer storm in the second year literally wiped out crops and cattle, and left them with their bare lives in their lowly sod house.

"Drought first year, tornado second. If next year's a failure, we'll go back--if we can raise money enough to go with. Three times and then out!" said Mr. Waddle.

Mrs. Waddle broke down and wept. It scared the children to learn that their mother could cry--their mother, who was always so bright and cheerful and who always laughed away their griefs!

Mr. Waddle was scared, too. He bent down and patted her shoulder--his favourite way of soothing beast or human being.

"Now, Mary, Mary! Don't you go back on us. We can stand everything as long as you are all right. Don't feel bad! We'll pick up again. There's time enough yet to grow turnips and fodder corn."

"But what will we fodder it to?" wailed Mrs. Waddle.

Mr. Waddle could not answer, thinking of his splendid horses, and of his pure Jersey cows that would never answer to his call again.

"Well, I am ashamed of myself!" said Mrs. Waddle, after a few moments, bravely drying her eyes. "And I'm wicked, too! I've just wished that something would happen so we'd have to go back East, and it's happened; and we might have all been killed. And I'm going to stop just where I am. I don't care where we live--or how we live--so long as we are all together--and well--and there's a crust in the house and water to drink."

Rising, she seized the broom and began vigorously to sweep together the leaves and grass which the cyclone had cast in through the open door.

"I declare, Mary!" said Mr. Waddle. "Do you mean to say you've been homesick all this time?"

"I'd give more for the north side of one of those old Vermont hills than I would for the whole prairie!" was the emphatic reply. "But I'm not going to say another single word."

Mr. Waddle felt a thrill of comfort in knowing he was not alone in his yearning for the old home. It was singular that these two, who loved each other so truly, could so hide their inmost feelings. Each had feared to appear weak to the other.

Mr. Waddle looked at his wife with almost a radiant smile. "Well, Mary, we'll go back in the fall--if we can sell. I guess we can hire the Deacon Elbridge place I see by last week's paper it's still for sale or rent, and carpenter work in old Hartbridge is about as profitable for me as farming out West."

"I'm glad you wouldn't mind going back, Homer," said Mrs. Waddle, and they looked at each other as in the days of their courtship.

But selling the farm was not easy, and October found the Waddles in painful straits.

"What will we have for Thanksgiving, Ma?" asked Obadiah.

"Oh, a pair of nice prairie chickens, mashed turnips, hot biscuits, and melted sugar," cheerfully replied Mrs. Waddle.

"That sounds pretty good," said Obadiah; but when he got out of doors he said to himself that you could not shoot prairie chickens without ammunition, and that he had no bait even if he tried to use his quail traps. He also reflected that his mother looked thin and pale, that sister Ellie needed shoes, and that plum pudding and mince pie used to be on Thanksgiving tables. But this was the day for his story paper--post-office day--which seemed to cheer things up somehow.

When he went to town for the mail he would see if his father, who was at work carpentering on a barn, could not spare a dime for a little powder and shot. So the boy trudged away on his long walk, with his empty gun on his shoulder and the hope of youth in his heart.

His father, busy at work, greeted him cheerily, but had no dime for powder and shot. Pay for the work was not to be had until the first of December, and meanwhile every penny must be saved--for coal and for Ellie's shoes.

"It leaves Thanksgiving out in the cold, doesn't it, Bub? But we'll make it up at Christmas, maybe," said Mr. Waddle, as Obadiah turned to go. "Here's three cents for a bite of candy for Sis, and take good care of mother. I'll be home day after to-morrow, likely."

Obadiah jingled the three pennies in his pocket as he walked to the combined store and post-office. Three cents! They would buy a charge or two of powder and shot, and he still had a few caps. And candy was not good for people anyhow! He wished he had asked his father if he might buy ammunition instead.

"But I'll not bother him again," he decided, "and Sis will be glad enough of the candy."

He would not buy rashly. He looked over the jars of striped sticks, peppermint drops, chocolate mice, and mixed varieties. Then he sat down on a nail keg to await the distribution of the mail. He watched the people standing by for the opening of the delivery window. It was a rare thing for his family to get a letter, but then they seldom sent one.

Once in a while a newspaper came from Uncle Obadiah, but only one letter in two years. Perhaps if he knew what hard luck they were having he would write oftener. The boy had heard his mother say only the week before that she wanted to write to Brother Obie, but was no hand at letters, especially when there was no good news to write.

A thought now came to young Obadiah. He would write to his Uncle to-morrow, and his brain began fairly to hum with what he would say. When his time came he invested one cent in a clean white stick of candy and the remaining two in a postage stamp. "I'll pay two cents back to pa as soon as I get the answer," he said confidently to his questioning conscience.

His walk home abounded in exasperations. Never had game appeared so plentiful. Three separate flocks of prairie chickens flew directly over his head, a rabbit scurried across his path, and in the stubble of the ruined grainfields rose and fell little clouds of quail.

"They just know it ain't loaded!" grumbled Obadiah, trudging with his empty gun.

That night, after Sis had gone to sleep, and his mother had lain down beside her, cheerfully remarking that bed was cheaper than fire, and that she was glad there was a good wood lot on the Elbridge place, Obadiah, behind the sheltering canvas partition that separated the kitchen from the bedrooms, wrote the following letter:

DEAR UNCLE:--Last year our crops were burned up by the
drought and this year they were swept away by a cyclone and
all the stock was killed, and father will not get his pay
for carpenter work until December. If there was no hole in
the dollar you gave me when I was a baby I would take it and
buy something for Thanksgiving. I wish you would send me a
dollar without a hole in it as soon as you can and I will
send you the one with a hole in it. I would send it now but
I have not got stamps enough. I hope you are well. We are
all well, only ma is homesick. Your sincere nephew,
OBADIAH WADDLE.

P. S.--Please send your answer right to me, because I want
to surprise ma with some things for Thanksgiving.

The next morning he set off to look at his most distant quail traps, found them empty, and circled round to the village, where he posted his letter.

The days crept slowly by, and times grew more and more uncomfortable in the little sod house. Often when Obadiah was doing his "sums" his pencil would shy off to a corner of his slate and scribble a list of items something like this:

2 cents to Pa
$.02 Stamps and paper (to send the D)
.06 Powder and shot
.10 Tea and sugar for Ma
.30 1 lb. raisens
.15 6 eggs
.08 1 lb. butter
.20

.91 More powder
.09

$1.00

Sometimes he would set down half a pound of "raisens" and add "candy for Sis, .05," but this was in his reckless moments. Sober second thought always convinced him that "raisens" would bring the greatest good to the greatest number about Thanksgiving time.

He casually asked his mother how long it took people to go to California.

"Well, Uncle Obie's newspapers always get here about four or five days after they are printed. Dear me! I must write to your Uncle Obie just as soon as we can spare the money for paper and stamps. He'll be glad to know we are all alive and well, and that's about all I can tell him."

Obadiah smiled broadly behind his geography and began reckoning the days. The answer might arrive about the 18th, but he heroically waited until the 21st before going to ask for it. He reached the village long before mail time, but saw so many things to consider in the grocery and provision line that he was almost surprised when the rattle of the "mail rig" and an in-gathering of people told that the important time had arrived.

The Waddles had given up their box, so he could not expect to see his letter until it should be handed out to him from the general "W" pile. He waited patiently.

The fortunate owners of lock boxes took out their letters with a proud air while the distributing was still going on. Others, who had mere open boxes, drew close and tried to read inverted superscriptions with poor success. Others who never had either letters or papers, but who came in at this hour from force of habit, stood near the stove or leaned on the counters and spoke of the weather and swapped feeble jokes. Finally the small wooden window was flung open. The little group got its papers and letters and gradually retired.

"Any letter for me?" cried Obadiah, his heart jumping.

"Nope; your pa got your papers last Saturday."

"But--ain't there a letter--for me?"

The man hastily ran over the half-dozen "W" missives. "Nope."

Obadiah's heart was heavy as lead now. He went out into the sleety weather and faced the long walk home. His eyes were so blurred with tears he could hardly see and his feet came near slipping.

A derisive shout came from across the street: "Hallo! Pretty bad 'waddling' this weather!"

Obadiah pulled his hat over his eyes and tramped on in scornful silence.

And now another voice called out to him, a voice from the rear: "Oh, say! Waddle! Come back here--package for ye!" Obadiah hastily went back, his heart leaping.

"Registered package," explained the postmaster. "'Most forgot it. Sign your name on that line. Odd name you've got. No danger your mail going to some other fellow."

Obadiah laughed and said he guessed not, and hardly believing his senses, again started for home, and soon struck out upon the far-stretching road. In the privacy of the great prairie he looked at the package again. How heavy it was for such a small one, and how important looked the long row of stamps; and there was Uncle Obadiah's name in one corner, proving that it was truly the answer!

There must be a jackknife in it, or something besides the dollar. He cut the stout twine, removed the wrapper, and lifted the cover of a strong paper box. There was something wrapped in neat white paper and feeling very solid.

Obadiah removed the paper, and a heavy, handsome and very fat leather purse slipped into his hand. He opened it. It had several compartments, and in each one were three or more hard, flat, round objects wrapped in more white paper to keep them from jingling, very likely.

Obadiah unwrapped one of these round, flat objects, and even in the dull light of the drizzling and fading November day he could see that it was a bright, clean, shining silver dollar--and had no hole in it.

With hands fairly shaking with joy, he returned the purse to the box and sped homeward. He ran all the way, only slowing up for breath now and then, but it was dark, and the poor little supper was waiting when he reached the house. The small lamp did not shed a very brilliant light, but a mother does not need an electric glare in order to read her child's face.

"Well, Obie, what's happened?" asked his mother as soon as he was inside the door. "Have you caught a whole flock of quails?"

"Something better'n quails! Guess again, Ma!"

"Three nice fat prairie hens then."

"Something better'n prairie hens." And then Obie could wait no longer. He pulled the package from under his coat and tossed it down beside the poor old tea-pot, which had known little but hot water these many weeks.

"Why, it's from Brother Obie--to *you*!" exclaimed his mother, while his father drew near and said, "Well, well!"

"And look inside! I haven't half looked yet," said Obie, "but *you* look, Ma! I just want you to look!"

Ma opened the box, and then the purse, and then the fourteen round objects wrapped in white paper. And they made a fine glitter on the red tablecloth.

"Well, *well*!" repeated Mr. Waddle.

"And here's something written," said Mrs. Waddle, taking a paper from a pocket at the back of the purse.

"Read it, Ma--out loud! *I* don't care," said Obie generously.

So Ma read it in a voice that trembled a little:

MY DEAR NEPHEW:--If I count rightly, it is thirteen years since your good mother labelled you Obadiah. I'm not near enough to give you thirteen slaps--I wish I were--so I send you thirteen dollars, and one to grow on. Never mind returning the dollar with the hole in it--keep it for your grandchildren to cut their teeth on. Give my love to your parents and little sister; and if you look the purse through closely, I think you will find something of interest to your mother. It is about time she paid our old Vermont a visit.

Be a good boy.

Your affectionate uncle,

OBADIAH BROWN.

"Oh, that blessed brother!" cried Mrs. Waddle, wiping her eyes with her apron.

Obie seized the purse and examined it on all sides. It was a very wizard of a purse, for another little flat pocket was found in its inmost centre, and from it Obie drew out another bit of folded paper and opened it.

"Why, it's a check!" shouted Mr. Waddle. "A check for you, Mary, for--two--hundred--dollars! My! There's a brother for you!"

"Oh, not two ***hundred***--it must be twenty--it can't be--" faltered Mrs. Waddle, wiping her eyes to look at the paper.

Then she gave a little cry and fell to hugging all her family. "We can all go back--we can go next week!" and she almost danced up and down on the unresponsive clay floor.

"I owe you two cents, Pa, and I'll pay it back to you just as soon as I can get a dollar changed," said Obadiah proudly, fingering the shining coins.

"How's that, Bubby?"

Then Obadiah explained.

"I hope you didn't complain, Obie," said his mother, her happy face clouding.

"Well, I told him about the drought and the cyclone. I guess if I was a near relation I wouldn't call that complaining. And then I asked him if he wouldn't swap dollars with me, so I could have one without a hole in it to get something for Thanks--"

Mr. Waddle broke in with a shout of laughter, and Mrs. Waddle kissed her son once more, and laughed, too, although her eyes were full of tears. And then Obadiah knew everything was all right.

"We can have Thanksgiving now, can't we, Ma?" he asked. "It's so near; and I'm going to get all the things. We'll have chicken pie--*tame* chicken pie--and plum pudding--and butter--and cream for the coffee--and cranberries--and lump sugar--and pumpkin pie--and--"

"Oh, me wants supper!" exclaimed Sis. And then they laughed again, and fell upon the cooling corn-bread and molasses and melancholy bits of fried pork and the thin ghost of tea as if they were already engaged in a feast of Thanksgiving. And so they were.

THE WHITE TURKEY'S WING[17]
BY SOPHIE SWETT.

Priscilla, the big white hen turkey, deserved a better fate than to be eaten on Thanksgiving Day, and Minty and Jason contrived to save her.

Mary Ellen was coming home from her school teaching at the Falls, and Nahum from 'tending in Blodgett's store at Edom Four Corners, and Uncle and Aunt Piper with Mirandy and Augustus and the twins were coming from Juniper Hill, and there was every prospect of as merry a Thanksgiving as one could wish to see. And Thanksgivings were always merry at the Kittredge farm on Red Hill. Uncle Kittredge might be a trifle over thrifty--a leetle nigh, his neighbours called him--but there was no stinting at Thanksgiving, and when a boy is accustomed to perpetual corn-bread and sausages, he knows how to appreciate unlimited turkey and plum pudding; and when he is used to gloomy evenings, in which Uncle Kittredge holds the one feeble kerosene lamp between himself and a newspaper, Aunt Kittredge knits in silent meditation on blue yarn stockings, he knows how good it is to have the house filled with lights and people, jolly games going on in the parlour, and candy-pulling in the kitchen. All these delights were directly before Jason Kittredge as he dangled his legs from the stone wall and whittled away at the skewers which Clorinda, the "hired girl," had demanded of him, and yet his heart was as heavy as lead.

[Note 17: From ***Harper's Young People***, November 22, 1892.]

He did not even look up when his sister Minty came up the hill toward him. He knew it was Minty, because she was hop-skipping and humming, and he knew that Aunt Kittredge had sent her to Mrs. Deacon Preble's to get a recipe for snow pudding; she had said she "must have something real stylish, because she had invited the new minister and his daughter to dinner."

"Oh, Jason, don't you wish it was always going to be Thanksgiving Day after to-morrow?" Minty continued her hop-skipping; she went to and fro before the dejected figure on the wall. Minty was tall for twelve, and she had a very high forehead, which made Aunt Kittredge think that she was going to be "smart." Aunt Kittredge made her comb her hair straight back from the high forehead, and fasten it with a round comb; not a vestige of hair showed under Minty's blue hood, and her forehead looked bleak and cold, and her pale blue eyes were watery, and her new teeth were large and overlapped each other; but Aunt Kittredge said it was no matter, if she was only good and "smart."

"Why, Jason, is anything the matter?" Minty stopped, breathless, and the joy faded out of her face. Jason continued to whittle in gloomy silence. His hands were almost purple with cold, and the wind flapped his large pantaloons--they were Uncle Kittredge's old ones, and Aunt Kittredge never thought it worth the while to consider the fit if they were turned up so that he could walk in them.

"You don't care because the new minister and his daughter are coming?" pursued Minty. Jason's tastes, as she well knew, did not incline to ministers and schoolmasters as companions in merrymaking. "She's a big girl, almost sixteen, and she will go with Mary Ellen, and we shall have Mirandy and Augustus and the twins, and the Sedgell girls and Nehemiah Ham are coming in the evening, and we shall have such fun, and such lots to eat!"

"That's just like you. You're friv'lous. You don't know what an awful hard world it is. You haven't got a realizing sense," said Jason crushingly.

This last accusation was one with which Aunt Kittredge was accustomed to overwhelm Clorinda when she burned the pies or wore her best bonnet to evening meeting. Minty's face grew so long that it looked like the reflection of a face in a spoon, and the tears came into her eyes. It must be a hard world, since Jason found it so. He was much stouter-hearted than she; his round, snub-nosed, freckled face was generally as cheerful as the sunshine. Jason had his troubles--Minty well knew what they were--but he bore them manfully. He didn't like to have Clorinda use his hens' eggs when he was saving them to sell, and perhaps it was even more trying to be at school when the eggs man came around, and have Aunt Kittredge sell his eggs and put the money into her pocket. Jason wished to go into business for himself, and he had a high opinion of the poultry business for a beginning. Cyrus, their "hired man," had once lived with a man at North Edom who made fabulous sums by raising poultry. But Aunt Kittredge's peculiar views of the rights of boys interfered with his accumulation of the necessary capital. All these troubles Jason bore bravely. It must be some great misfortune that caused him to look so utterly despairing, and to accuse her of such dreadful things, thought poor Minty.

Jason took pity on her woful face. "P'raps you're not so much to blame, Mint. You don't know," he said, in a somewhat softened tone. "It's Aunt Kittredge."

Minty heaved a long, long sigh. It generally *was* Aunt Kittredge.

"She's told Cyrus to kill the--the white turkey!" continued Jason, with almost a break in his voice.

"To kill Priscilla!" gasped Minty. "She couldn't--she wouldn't! Oh, Jason, Cyrus won't do it, will he?"

"Hasn't he got to if she says so?" demanded Jason grimly.

"But Priscilla is yours," said Minty stoutly.

"She says she only let me call her mine. Just as if I didn't save her out of that weak brood when all the rest were killed by the thunderstorm! And brought her up in cotton behind the kitchen stove, no matter how much Clorinda scolded! And found her nest with thirty-one eggs in it in the old pine stump! And she knows me and follows me round."

"I shouldn't think Aunt Kittredge would want to," said Minty reflectively.

"She wants a big turkey, because the minister and his daughter are coming to dinner, and she doesn't want to have one of the young ones killed, because she is too stin--"

"I wouldn't care if I were you. After all, Priscilla is only a turkey," said Minty, attempting to be cheerful.

But this well-meant effort at consolation aroused Jason's wrath. "That's just like a girl!" he cried. "What do you care if you only have blue beads and lots of candy?"

Poor Minty's face lengthened again, and her jaw fell. "There's my two dollars and thirty cents, Jason," she said anxiously.

Jason started; a ray of hope flushed his freckled face.

"We can buy a big turkey over at Jonas Hicks's for all that money," continued Minty. And then she drew nearer to Jason, and added a thrilling whisper, "And we can hide Priscilla!"

Jason stared at her in amazement. He had never expected Minty to come to the front in an emergency. Perhaps the high forehead meant something after all. "***She***'ll be after you about the money, you know," he said, with a significant nod toward the house.

"It's my own. I earned it picking berries and weeding old Mrs. Jackman's garden. It's in my bank, and the bank won't open till there's five dollars in it."

Jason's face darkened.

"But we can smash it," said Minty calmly.

Certainly the high forehead meant something.

Priscilla was hidden. The "smashing" was done in extreme privacy behind the stone wall of the pasture. Cyrus was bound over to secrecy, as was also Jonas Hicks, who, after some haggling, sold them his finest turkey for two dollars and thirty cents.

"Cyrus is gettin' real handy and accommodatin'," said Clorinda the next morning, when they were all in the kitchen, and Jason, ignobly arrayed in Clorinda's kitchen-belle apron, was chopping, and Minty was seeding raisins. "I expected nothin' but what I'd got to pick the white turkey, and he's fetched her in all picked and drawed."

"She don't weigh quite so much as I expected," said Uncle Kittredge, as he suspended the turkey on the hook of the old steelyards.

Jason and Minty slyly exchanged anxious glances. Neither of them had looked at the turkey, and Minty's face was suffused with red even to the roots of her tow-coloured hair.

Mary Ellen and Nahum came that night, and bright and early on the morning of Thanksgiving Day came Uncle and Aunt Piper with Mirandy and Augustus and the twins, and the house was full of noise and jollity. Jason was obliged to go to church in the morning with the grown people, but Minty stayed at home to help Clorinda, and after much manoeuvring she found an opportunity to run down to the shanty in the logging road and feed the white turkey. The new minister and his daughter came to dinner, and Jason and Minty were glad that the children had seats at the far end of the table. The minister's daughter was sixteen, and looked very stylish, and Aunt Kittredge said she was glad enough that they had the snow pudding, and that she had asked Aunt Piper to bring her sauce dishes.

It had begun to be very merry at the far end of the table, in a quiet way, for Aunt Kittredge's stern eye wandered constantly in that direction, and Jason and Minty had almost forgotten that there were trials and difficulties in life, when suddenly Aunt Piper's loud voice sounded across the table, striking terror to their souls:

"You don't say that this is the white turkey? Seems kind of a pity to kill her, she was so handsome. But she eats real well. Now, you mustn't forget to let me take a wing home to Sabriny. You know you always promised her a wing for her hat when the white turkey was killed."

Sabriny was Aunt Piper's niece, who had been left at home to keep house.

"Sure enough I did," said Aunt Kittredge. "Jason, you go out to the barn and get Cyrus to give you one of the white turkey's wings; and Minty, you wrap it up nice, so it will be handy for your aunt to carry. Go as soon as you've ate your dinner, so's to have it ready, for Uncle Piper has got to get home before sundown."

"Yes'm," answered Jason hoarsely, without lifting his eyes from his plate. He could scarcely eat another mouthful, and Minty found it unexpectedly easy to obey Aunt Kittredge's injunction to decline snow pudding lest there should not be "enough to go round."

"What are you going to do?" asked Minty, overtaking Jason, as he walked dejectedly through the woodshed as soon as dinner was over.

"I don't know; run away and be a cowboy like Hiram Trickey, I guess."

Minty's heart gave a great throb. Hiram Trickey had sent home a photograph, which showed him to have become very like the picture of a pirate in Cyrus's old book, with pistols and a dirk at his belt.

"Jason, the new minister's daughter has got a white gull's wing on her hat, and--it's up in the spare chamber on the bed, and I don't think Sabriny would ever know the difference."

Jason stared in mild-eyed speechless wonder. Minty had never shown herself a leading spirit before.

"It will be dark before the minister's daughter goes, and there's a veil over the hat, and if we put a little something white on it I'm sure she won't notice. And when she does notice she won't know what became of it. And we can save up and buy her another gull's wing."

"Sabriny'll know," said Jason, but there was an accent of hope in his voice.

"They don't have turkeys, and they know that Priscilla wasn't a common turkey; perhaps they won't know the difference," said Minty. "Anyway, it will give us time to get Priscilla out of the way. If Aunt Kittredge finds out, she will have her killed right away."

"You go and get the wing off the minister's daughter's hat, Mint," directed Jason firmly.

Minty worked with trembling fingers in the chilly seclusion of the spare chamber, but she made a neat package. And she stuck on to the hat in place of the wing some feathers from the white rooster.

There was an awful moment as Uncle and Aunt Piper were leaving.

"Just let me see whether he's got a real handsome wing," said Aunt Kittredge, taking the package which Minty had put into Aunt Piper's hand.

"Malachi is in considerable of a hurry, and they've done it up so nice," said Aunt Piper. "There! I 'most forgot my sauce dishes, and Sabriny's going to have company to-morrow!"

Minty drew a long breath of relief as the carriage disappeared down the lane, and Jason privately confided to her his opinion that she was "an orfle smart girl."

There was another dreadful moment when the minister's daughter went home. They had played games until a very late hour, for Corinna, and she dressed so hurriedly that she did not observe that anything had happened to her hat, but as she went down the garden walk Jason and Minty saw in the moonlight the rooster's feathers blowing from it.

The next morning, in the privacy afforded by the great woodpile, to which Jason had gone to chop his daily stint, the children debated the advisability of committing the white turkey to the care of Lot Rankin, who lived with his widowed mother on the edge of the woods.

"It's hard to get a chance to feed her," said Jason, "and she may squawk."

"Lot Rankin may tell," suggested Minty. And she heaved a great sigh. Conspiracy came hard to Minty.

Just then the voice of the new minister's daughter came to their ears. She was talking with Aunt Kittredge on the other side of the woodpile.

"There was a high wind last night when I went home, and I suppose it blew away. I am very sorry to lose it, because it was so pretty, and it was a present, too," she said.

"Maybe the children have found it; they're round everywhere," said Aunt Kittredge. And then she called shrilly to Jason.

Minty shrank down in a little heap behind a huge log as Jason stepped bravely out from behind the woodpile, and answered promptly that he had not seen the gull's wing. That was literally true; but how *she* was going to answer, Minty did not know.

It was so great a relief that tears sprang to Minty's eyes when, after a little more conversation, the minister's daughter went away. Aunt Kittredge had taken it for granted that, as she remarked, "if one of them young ones didn't know anything about it the other didn't."

Minty felt her burden of guilt to be greater than she could bear. And there was no way in which she could earn money enough to buy the minister's daughter a new feather until berries were ripe and the weeds grew in old Mrs. Jackman's garden. Minty racked her brains to think of something she could give the minister's daughter to ease her troubled conscience. There was her Bunker Hill monument, made of shells, her most precious treasure; she would gladly have parted with even that, but it stood upon the table in the parlour, and Aunt Kittredge would discover so soon that it had gone. And Aunt Kittredge was quite capable of asking the minister's daughter to return it. Minty felt, despairingly, that this atonement was impossible.

But suddenly a bright idea struck her. The feather on her summer Sunday hat! It was blue--it had been white originally, but Aunt Kittredge had thriftily had it dyed when it became soiled. Blue would be very becoming to the minister's daughter, and perhaps she would like it as well as her gull's wing. There was another sly visit to the chilly spare chamber. Minty took the summer Sunday hat from its bandbox in the closet, and carefully abstracted the blue feather. It was slightly faded, and there were some traces of the wetting it had received in a thunderstorm in spite of the handkerchief which Aunt Kittredge carefully pinned over it; but Minty thought it still a very beautiful feather. She put it into a little pasteboard box, wrote the minister's daughter's name on it, placed it on her doorstep at dusk, rang the bell, and ran away.

It was nearly a week before she could find this opportunity to present the feather, for Aunt Kittredge didn't allow her to go out after dark; and in all that time they had not been able to negotiate with Lot Rankin, for Lot had the mumps on both sides at once, and could not be seen. But the very next day after the minister's daughter received her feather--as if things were all coming right, thought Minty hopefully--Uncle Kittredge sent her down to Lot Rankin's to find out when he would be strong enough to help Cyrus in the logging camp; and Jason gave her many charges concerning the contract she was to make with Lot. But as she was going out of the house, there stood the minister's daughter in the doorway, talking with Aunt Kittredge.

"I shouldn't have known where it came from if Miss Plympton, the milliner, hadn't happened to come in," the young girl was saying. "She said at once, 'It's Minty Kittredge's feather. I had it dyed for her last summer, and there's the little tag from the dye-house on it now.' I can't think why she sent it to me."

Aunt Kittredge turned to the shrinking figure behind her, holding the blue feather accusingly in her hand.

"Araminta Kittredge, what does this mean?" she demanded sternly.

"I--I--she felt so bad about her gull's wing, and--and--" A rising sob fairly choked Minty.

"Please don't scold her. I'm sure she can explain," pleaded the minister's daughter.

"It's my duty to find out just what this means," said Aunt Kittredge severely. "I never heard of a child doing such a high-handed thing! You can do your errand now, because your uncle wants you to, but when you come back I shall have a settlement with you."

Poor Minty! She ran fast, never looking back, although the minister's daughter called to her in kindliest tones.

There was no hope of keeping a secret from Aunt Kittredge when once she had discovered that there was one. The only chance of saving Priscilla's life lay in persuading Lot Rankin to care for and conceal her.

But, alas! she found that Lot was not to be persuaded. He was going into the woods to work, and his mother was "set against turkeys." Moreover, she was "so lonesome most of the time that when folks *did* come along she told 'em all she knew."

Jason, who had been very anxious, met her at the corner. Perhaps it was not to be wondered at that Jason was somewhat cross and unreasonable. He said only a girl would be so foolish as to send that feather to the minister's daughter. Girls were all silly, even those who had high foreheads, and he would never trust one again. He hoped she was going to have sense enough not to tell, no matter what Aunt Kittredge did.

Poor Minty felt herself to be quite unequal to resisting Aunt Kittredge, but she swallowed a lump in her throat and said firmly that she would try to have sense enough.

As they passed the blacksmith's shop, Liphlet, Uncle Piper's man, called out to them: "Mebbe I shan't have time to go up to your house. The blacksmith is sick, so I had to come over here to get the mare shod, and I wish you'd tell your aunt that Sabriny says 'twan't no turkey's wing that she sent her: 'twas some kind of a sea-bird's wing, and it come off of somebody's bunnit, and she's a-goin' to fetch it back!"

Minty and Jason answered not a word, but as they went on they looked at each other despairingly.

"We should have been found out anyway," said Minty.

Her pitifully white face seemed to touch Jason and arouse a spark of manly courage in his bosom.

"I'll stand by you, Mint, feather and all. You can't help being a girl," he said magnanimously. "And I won't run away to be a cowboy like Hiram Trickey."

Minty gave him a little grateful glance, but she could not speak. It did not seem so dreadful now about Hiram Trickey. She wished that a girl could run away to be a cowboy.

As they slowly and dejectedly drew near the house, they saw a horse and a farm wagon at the door, and through the window they discovered that Uncle and

Aunt Kittredge, Clorinda, and Cyrus were all in the kitchen. There was a visitor. Here was at least a slight reprieve. They went around through the woodshed; it seemed advisable to approach Aunt Kittredge with caution, even in the presence of a visitor.

"Well, I must say I'm consid'able disappointed," the visitor was saying, as they softly opened the door. He was a bluff, burly man, who sat with his tall whip between his knees. "I ought to 'a' stopped when I see her out there top of the stone wall the last time I come by--the handsomest turkey cretur I ever did see, and I've been in the poultry business this twenty years. I knew in a minute she belonged to that breed that old Mis' Joskins had; she fetched 'em from York State. She moved away before I knew it, and carried 'em all with her."

"I bought some eggs of her, and 'most all of 'em hatched, but that white turkey was the only one that lived," said Aunt Kittredge. "I declare if I'd known she was anything more'n common, and worthy of havin' her picture in a book--"

"You'd ought to have known it, Maria!" said Uncle Kittredge testily. "I wa'n't for havin' her killed, and you'd ought to have heard to me!"

"I was calc'latin' to hev her picter right in the front of my new poultry book," continued the visitor, whom the children now recognized as the distinguished poultry dealer of North Edom for whom Cyrus had once worked. "And I was going to have printed under it, 'From the farm of Abner Kittredge, Esq., Corinna.' Be kind of a boom for you 'n' Corinna, too--see? And if you didn't want to sell her right out, I was calc'latin' to make you a handsome offer for all the eggs she laid."

"There! Now you see what you've done, Maria! I declare I wouldn't gredge givin' a twenty dollar bill to fetch that white turkey back!" exclaimed Uncle Kittredge.

"Oh, oh! Uncle Kittredge!" Minty broke away from Jason, who would have held her back, not feeling sure that it was quite time to speak, and rushed into the room. "You needn't give twenty dollars! Priscilla is down in the little shanty in the logging wood! We saved her--Jason and I--and we bought a turkey of Jonas Hicks instead. I paid with my own money, Aunt Kittredge! And then I--I took the gull's wing off the minister's daughter's hat to send to Sabriny, and--and so that's why I sent her the blue feather, and--and Sabriny's going to send the gull's wing back--"

"Jason, you go and fetch that turkey home!" said Uncle Kittredge. "And, Maria, don't you blame them children one mite!"

"I never heard of such high-handed doin's!" gasped Aunt Kittredge.

"I expect I shall have to send you children each a copy of my book with the picter of that turkey in it," said the poultry dealer. "And maybe the boy and I can make kind of a contract about eggs and chickens."

The minister's daughter wore her gull's wing to church the next Sunday, and she privately confided to Minty that she "didn't blame her one bit." Aunt Kittredge looked at Minty somewhat severely for several days but only as she looked at her when she turned around in church or fidgeted in the long prayer. And after the poultry book came out with Priscilla's photograph as a frontispiece, and people began to make pilgrimages to the Red Hill farm to see the poultry, she was heard to say several times that "it was wonderful to see how a smart boy like Jason could make turkey raising pay," and that "as for Minty, she always knew that high forehead of hers wasn't for nothing."

THE THANKSGIVING GOOSE[18]
BY FANNIE WILDER BROWN.

How a little boy learned to be thankful. A charming story even though it *has* a moral.

"But I don't like roast goose," said Guy, pouting. "I'd rather have turkey. Turkey is best for Thanksgiving, anyway. Goose is for Christmas."

[Note 18: From the *Youth's Companion*, November 26, 1908.]

Guy's mother did not answer. He watched her while she carefully wrote G. T. W. on the corner of a pretty new red-bordered handkerchief. Five others, all alike, and all marked alike, lay beside it. The initials were his own.

"Why didn't you buy some blue ones? I'd rather have them different," he said.

Mrs. Wright smiled a queer little smile, but did not answer. She lighted a large lamp and held the marked corner of one of the handkerchiefs against the hot chimney. The heat made the indelible ink turn dark, although the writing had been so faint Guy hardly could see it before.

"Oh, dear," he cried, "there's a little blot at the top of that T! I don't want to carry a handkerchief that has a blot on it."

"Very well," said his mother. "I'll put them away, and you may carry your old ones until you ask me to let you carry this one. I don't care to furnish new things for a boy who doesn't appreciate them."

"I don't like old--"

"That'll do, Guy. Never mind the rest of the things that you don't like. I want you to take this dollar down to Mrs. Burns. Tell her that I shall have a day's work for her on Friday, and I thought she might like to have part of the pay in advance to help make Thanksgiving with. Please go now."

"But a dollar won't help much. She won't like that. She always acts just as if she was as happy as anybody. I don't want to go there on such an errand as that."

Mrs. Wright smiled again, but her tone was very grave.

"Mrs. Burns is 'as happy as anybody,' Guy, and she has the best-behaved children in the neighbourhood. The little ones almost never cry, and I never have seen the older ones quarrel. But there are eight children, and Mr. Burns has only one arm, so he can't earn much money. Mrs. Burns has to turn her hands to all sorts of things to keep the children clothed and fed. She'll be thankful to get the dollar-- you see if she isn't! And tell her if she is making mince pies to sell this year, I'll take three."

Guy walked very slowly down the street until he came to the little house where the Burns family lived.

"I'd hate to live here," he thought. "I don't see where they all sleep. My room isn't big enough, but I don't believe there's a room in this house as big as mine. I shouldn't have a bit of fun, ever, if I lived here. And I'd hate to have my mother make pies and send me about to sell them."

Then he knocked on the front door, for there was no bell. No one came. He could hear people talking in the distance, so he knew some of the family were at home. Some one always was at home here to look after the little children. He walked around to the kitchen door: it stood open. The children were talking so fast they did not hear his knock.

They were very busy. Katie, the eleven-year-old, and Malcolm, ten, Guy's age, were cutting citron into long, thin strips, piling it on a big blue plate. Mary and James, the eight-year-old twins, were paring apples with a paring machine. The long, curling skins fell in a large stone jar standing on a clean paper, spread on the floor. Charlie, who was only four years old, was watching to see that none of the parings fell over the edge of the jar. Susan, who was seven, was putting raisins, a few at a time, into a meat chopper screwed down on the kitchen table. George, three years old, was turning the handle of the chopper to grind the raisins. Baby Joe was creeping about the kitchen floor after a kitten. Mrs. Burns was taking a great piece of meat from a steaming kettle on the back of the stove. Every one was working, except the baby and the kitten, but all seemed to be having a glorious time. What they were saying seemed so funny it was some time before Guy could understand it. At last he was sure it was some kind of a game.

"Mice?" asked Susan. Mary squealed, and they all laughed.

"Because they're small," said Mary. "Snakes?"

"They can't climb trees," Mrs. Burns called out from the pantry. The children fairly roared at that. "A pantry with no window in it?"

"Oh, we've had that before," Katie answered. "I know what you say. It's a good place to ripen pears in when Mrs. Wright gives us some."

Guy knocked very loudly at that. He had not thought that he was listening.

The children started, but did not leave their work. They looked at their mother. "Jamie," she said. Then Jamie came to meet Guy, and invited him to walk in.

"What game is it?" asked Guy, forgetting his errand.

"Making mince pies," said Jamie. "It's lots of fun. Don't you want to play? I'll let you turn the paring machine if you'd like that best."

Guy said "Thank you" and began to turn the parer eagerly.

"But I don't mean what you are doin'," said Guy. "I knew that was mince pies. I thought that was work. I meant what you were saying. It sounds so funny! I never heard it before."

"Mamma made it up," explained Malcolm. "It's great fun. We always play it at Thanksgiving time. You think of something that people don't like, and the one who can think first tells what he is thankful for about it. We call it 'Thanksgiving.'"

Guy stayed for an hour, and played both games. Then, quite to his surprise, the twelve o'clock whistles blew, and he had to go home. But he remembered his errands and did them, to the great pleasure of the whole Burns family.

In the afternoon Guy spent some time writing a note to his mother. It was badly written, but it made his mother happy. It read:

DEAR MOTHER:--I am Thankful the blot isent any bigger. I am
Thankful the hankershefs isent black on the borders. I would
like that one with the Blot on to put in my pocket when you
read this. But my old ones are nice. The Burnses dont have
things to be Thankful for but they are Thankful just the
same.

I am Thankful for the Goose we are going to have. The best
is I am Thankful I am not a Goose myself, for if I was I
wouldent know enough to be Thankful.
Respectfully yours,

GUY THEODORE WRIGHT.
AN ENGLISH DINNER OF THANKSGIVING[19]
BY GEORGE ELIOT.

Americans are not the only people who hold a feast each year
after the crops are gathered into barns.

The older boys and girls who wish to know more of the jolly
English farmer, Martin Poyser, and his household, will enjoy
reading about them in George Eliot's great novel, "Adam
Bede."

It was a goodly sight--that table, with Martin Poyser's round good-humoured
face and large person at the head of it, helping his servants to the fragrant roast beef,
and pleased when the empty plates came again. Martin, though usually blest with
a good appetite, really forgot to finish his own beef to-night--it was so pleasant to
him to look on in the intervals of carving, and see how the others enjoyed their
supper; for were they not men who, on all the days of the year except Christmas

Day and Sundays, ate their cold dinner, in a makeshift manner, under the hedge-rows, and drank their beer out of wooden bottles--with relish certainly, but with their mouths toward the zenith, after a fashion more endurable to ducks than to human bipeds. Martin Poyser had some faint conception of the flavour such men must find in hot roast beef and fresh-drawn ale. He held his head on one side, and screwed up his mouth, as he nudged Bartle Massey, and watched half-witted Tom Tholer, otherwise known as "Tom Saft," receiving his second plateful of beef. A grin of delight broke over Tom's face as the plate was set down before him, between his knife and fork, which he held erect, as if they had been sacred tapers; but the delight was too strong to continue smouldering in a grin--it burst out the next moment in a long-drawn "haw, haw!" followed by a sudden collapse into utter gravity, as the knife and fork darted down on the prey. Martin Poyser's large person shook with his silent unctuous laugh; he turned toward Mrs. Poyser to see if she, too, had been observant of Tom, and the eyes of husband and wife met in a glance of good-natured amusement.

[Note 19: From Chapter LIII of "Adam Bede."]

But *now* the roast beef was finished and the cloth was drawn, leaving a fair large deal table for the bright drinking cans, and the foaming brown jugs, and the bright brass candlesticks, pleasant to behold. *Now* the great ceremony of the evening was to begin--the harvest song, in which every man must join; he might be in tune, if he liked to be singular, but he must not sit with closed lips. The movement was obliged to be in triple time; the rest was *ad libitum*.

As to the origin of this song--whether it came in its actual state from the brain of a single rhapsodist, or was gradually perfected by a school or succession of rhapsodists, I am ignorant. There is a stamp of unity, of individual genius upon it, which inclines me to the former hypothesis, though I am not blind to the consideration that this unity may rather have arisen from that consensus of many minds which was a condition of primitive thought foreign to our modern consciousness. Some will perhaps think that they detect in the first quatrain an indication of a lost line, which later rhapsodists, failing in imaginative vigour, have supplied by the feeble device of iteration; others, however, may rather maintain that this very iteration is an original felicity to which none but the most prosaic minds can be insensible.

The ceremony connected with the song was a drinking ceremony. (That is perhaps a painful fact, but then, you know, we cannot reform our forefathers.) During the first and second quatrain, sung decidedly *forte*, no can was filled:

"Here's a health unto our master,
The founder of the feast;
Here's a health unto our master
And to our mistress!

"And may his doings prosper,
Whate'er he takes in hand,
For we are all his servants,
And are at his command."

But now, immediately before the third quatrain or chorus, sung *fortissimo*, with emphatic raps on the table, which gave the effect of cymbals and drum together. Alick's can was filled, and he was bound to empty it before the chorus ceased.

"Then drink, boys, drink!
And see ye do not spill,
For if ye do, ye shall drink two,
For 'tis our master's will."

When Alick had gone successfully through this test of steady-handed manliness, it was the turn of old Kester, at his right hand--and so on, till every man had drunk his initiatory pint under the stimulus of the chorus. Tom Saft--the rogue--took care to spill a little by accident; but Mrs. Poyser (too officiously, Tom thought) interfered to prevent the exaction of the penalty.

To any listener outside the door it would have been the reverse of obvious why the "Drink, boys, drink!" should have such an immediate and often-repeated encore; but once entered, he would have seen that all faces were at present sober, and most of them serious; it was the regular and respectable thing for those excellent farm-labourers to do, as much as for elegant ladies and gentlemen to smirk and bow over their wine glasses. Bartle Massey, whose ears were rather sensitive, had gone out to see what sort of evening it was at an early stage in the ceremony; and had not finished his contemplation, until a silence of five minutes declared that "Drink, boys, drink!" was not likely to begin again for the next twelve-month. Much to the regret of the boys and Totty; on them the stillness fell rather flat, after that glorious thumping of the table, toward which Totty, seated on her father's knee, contributed with her small might and small fist.

When Bartle reentered, however, there appeared to be a general desire for solo music after the choral. Nancy declared that Tim the wagoner knew a song and was "allays singing like a lark i' the stable"; whereupon Mr. Poyser said encouragingly, "Come, Tim, lad, let's hear it." Tim looked sheepish, tucked down his head, and said he couldn't sing; but this encouraging invitation of the master's was echoed all round the table. It was a conversational opportunity: everybody could say, "Come, Tim"--except Alick, who never relaxed into the frivolity of unnecessary speech. At last Tim's next neighbour, Ben Tholoway, began to give emphasis to his speech by nudges, at which Tim, growing rather savage, said, "Let me alooan, will ye? else I'll ma' ye sing a toon ye wonna like." A good-tempered wagoner's patience has limits, and Tim was not to be urged further.

"Well, then, David, ye're the lad to sing," said Ben, willing to show that he was not discomfited by this check. "Sing 'My loove's a roos wi'out a thorn.'"

The amatory David was a young man of an unconscious abstracted expression, which was due probably to a squint of superior intensity rather than to any mental characteristic; for he was not indifferent to Ben's invitation, but blushed and laughed and rubbed his sleeve over his mouth in a way that was regarded as a symptom of yielding. And for some time the company appeared to be much in earnest about the desire to hear David's song. But in vain. The lyrism of the evening was in the cellar at present, and was not to be drawn from that retreat just yet....

A NOVEL POSTMAN[20]
BY ALICE W. WHEILDON.

A little country girl made known her wants in a decidedly original way. A small boy in the city did his best to satisfy them. This is at once a story of Thanksgiving and of

Christmas.

"Oh, mother! what do you suppose Ellen found in the turkey? You never could guess. It's a letter--yes, a real letter just stuffed inside--see!" And Freddie held before his mother's wondering eyes a soiled and crumpled envelope which seemed to contain a letter.

[Note 20: From *Wideawake*, November, 1889. Lothrop, Lee & Shepard Company.]

Freddie had been in the kitchen all the morning watching the various operations for the Thanksgiving dinner which was "to come off" the next day, when all the "sisters, cousins, and aunts" of the family were to assemble, as was their custom each year, and great was the commotion in the kitchen and much there was for Master Fred to inspect. When Ellen put her hand into the turkey to arrange him for the stuffing, great was her astonishment at finding a piece of paper. Drawing it quickly out she called, "Freddie, Freddie, see here! See what I've found in the turkey! I declare if he isn't a new kind of a postman, for sure as you're born this is a letter, come from somewhere, in the turkey. My! who ever heard of such a thing?"

Freddie, standing with eyes and mouth wide open, finally said, "Why, Ellen, do you believe it is a letter?"

"Why, of course it is! Don't you see it's in a' envelope and all sealed and everything?"

"Yes, but it hasn't any stamp and how could a turkey bring it--how did it get in him?"

"Oh," laughed Ellen, "that's the question! You'd better take it right up to your mother and get her to read it to you and perhaps it will tell."

So Freddie, all excitement, rushed upstairs and into his mother's room, shouting as we have read.

His mother took the letter from him. "Where did you get this, Freddie--what do you mean by finding it in the turkey?"

"Why, Ellen found it in the turkey when she was fixing him, and I don't see how it got there."

Mrs. Page turned the envelope and slowly read, "To the lady who buys this turkey," written with a pencil and in rather crooked letters on the outside; then opening the envelope she found, surely enough, a letter within, also written in pencil, in rather uncertain letters, some large, some quite small, some on the line, others above or below, but all bearing sufficient relation to one another for her finally to decipher the following:

Nov. 20,
Mad River Village, N. H.

dere lady I doo want a dol for Christmas orful and mother
says that Sante Claws is so busy in the city that she gueses
he forgits the cuntry and for me to rite to the city lady
who buys our turkey and ask her if she will pleas to ask
Sante Claws if he could send a dol way up here in the cuntry
to me. I will hang my stockin in the chimly and he cannot
mistake the house becaus it is the only house that is black
in the hole place. I have prayed to him lots of times to
give me a dol but I gues he does not mind prayers much from
a little girl so far away so will you pleas to ask him for
me and oblige
LUCY TILLAGE.

P. S.--I hope the turkey will be good to eat, he is our very
best one and I was sorry to have him killed, but I never had
a dol.

Freddie listened, very much interested, sometimes helping to make out the letters while his mother read this remarkable letter. At its conclusion he dropped upon a chair in deep thought while in his imagination he saw a small black house surrounded by turkeys running wildly about while a little girl tried to catch the largest.

"Oh, mother," at length he sighed, "only think of a girl who never had a doll, and Beth has so many she don't know what to do with them all--shall you ask Santa Claus to send her one?"

"Well," said Mrs. Page, who also had been in deep thought, "do you think we better ask Santa Claus to send her one, or send her one ourselves? You and Beth might send her one for a Christmas present."

At once Freddie became fired with the desire to rush to a store, purchase a doll, and send it off to the little "black house." He seemed to think the house was little because the girl was little.

"No, no, Freddie, not so fast," said Mrs. Page. "I think we better wait till papa comes home and then we will ask his advice about it: first, if he knows of a town in New Hampshire of this name, and then if he thinks there may really be a little girl there who has such an odd name--I shouldn't be surprised if Papa could find out all about her."

Freddie thought it was hard to wait until his father came home before something was done about securing a doll; still he knew his mother was right and tried to be patient, wishing Beth would come home, wondering how the little girl looked, and if she had any brothers who wanted something, and fifty other things, till he heard his father's key in the front door; then down he rushed, flourishing the open sheet in his hand, and gave him a most bewildering and rapid account of the letter and the finding it in the turkey, ending with, "Now, Papa, do you know of any such town, and did you ever hear of Lucy Tillage before, or of anybody's turkey having a letter sent in him, and don't you think we might send her the doll right away so's she might have it for Christmas sure--don't you, Papa? And if we can't get a new one won't you tell Beth to send one of hers? I know she won't want so many and--"

"Oh! stop, my boy," said Mr. Page, laughing heartily; "wait a moment, Fred, I don't half understand what this is all about--a letter and a turkey and a little girl with a doll and a turkey in a black house--"

"Now, Papa, you're getting it all mixed up; you read the letter yourself, please."

So Mr. Page read the letter and heard about finding it in the turkey, and then talked it over with his wife and Freddie and Beth, who had come in from her play, and it was decided that he should write to the postmaster and minister in Mad River Village asking them if they knew of any family in the place of the name of Tillage, and if they did, whether they were a poor family, and how many children they had, and anything else they might know of them.

There was no time to lose if the doll was to be sent for Christmas, so both letters were written that very evening and Freddie begged to put them in the post box himself that there might be no mistake in that.

Then came a long time of waiting for Master Fred. At first he thought one day would be enough for the letter to find its way to Mad River Village; but upon a solemn consultation with the cousins and aunts who came to the Thanksgiving party, it was decided that three days, at least, ought to be allowed for a letter to reach a place that none of them had ever heard of, and perhaps there was not such a village anywhere after all but Freddie had made up his mind that there was somewhere, and so each morning found him watching for the postman and each night he went to bed disappointed, saying, "Oh! I hope there is a truly Mad Village."

Beth was almost as much excited as Fred about Lucy's letter, but still she laughed at him as older sisters sometimes seem to take pleasure in doing, saying, "I guess it's a delicious wonderland kind of a letter, and that the people up there are mad people to be sending letters in turkeys!"

"Well, you just wait, Beth, and see if they are," answered Fred; and sure enough, after ten days of waiting Freddie was rewarded by receiving from the postman a yellow envelope with "Mad River Village" printed in large, clear letters "right side of the stamp." He ran as fast as he could with it to his father, shouting to Beth by the way to "come and see if there isn't a Mad Village and a Lucy Tillage."

Mr. Page was never given so short a time before to open a letter and adjust his glasses, but then a letter had never before been received under such circumstances. It proved to be from the postmaster at Mad River Village, and ran as follows:

Mad River Village, N. H.

MR. PAGE of Boston: I rec. your letter a Day or two since
and hasten to ans. it right away, as you wish, by this
morning's mail which I must put up pretty soon so this
letter must be short. Yes sir I do know a family in this
town by the name of Tillage and they're a good respectable
family too. They live a mile or two out of the village on a
farm his father left him and I guess they have pretty hard
times making both ends meet--there ain't much sale up here
for farm things, you know, and it costs a heap to send them
to Boston but they do say that of late he's raised lots of

chickens and turkeys to send to Boston for Thanksgiving. Last year he and his wife started in on taking summer boarders and I guess they done first rate. They're young folks, got three children, a little girl a small boy and a baby and I guess they'll do as well as any one can on that farm, it's a likely place but his father ain't been dead long and Geo. didn't have no show while the old man was alive. He buys his flour and groceries of me and I call him a honest fellow and I guess you'd like to board with them if you want to try them next summer. I don't think of anything more to say so will close.

Yours respt.

JOSIAH SAFFORD.

P. S.--His name and address are George Tillage, Intervale Farm, Mad River Village, N. H.

This was a highly satisfactory letter, especially to Master Fred who had shouted gleefully to Beth, "I told you so!" "I do know a family of the name of Tillage," and when his father read "three children, a little girl, etc.," he nearly turned a somersault in his excitement, dancing about and saying, "that's Lucy! that's Lucy!"

Mr. Page turned smilingly to his wife, saying, "Well, my dear, this does not sound so much like a fairy tale after all, and I really think you and the children must play Santa Claus and send Lucy a doll."

"Oh, yes, Papa, of course we must! Yes, do, Mamma!" shouted both children at once. "It'll be such fun and she won't know where it comes from."

Mrs. Page was only too willing, so she promised, only adding that she hoped the minister would give an equally good account.

The children, however, were quite satisfied with the postmaster's letter and began preparations the very next morning to secure the doll and her "fit out" as Beth called it. First, Beth's dolls were looked at to see if one of them would do to take a trip into the country, but although there were quite a number of them none seemed to just suit their ideas of what Lucy's doll should be. So Mamma was appealed to and in consequence a visit was paid to Partridge's store by Mrs. Page, accompanied by Beth and Master Fred. Here such a bewildering array of dolls was presented to the children that it was with difficulty they finally decided upon one with blue eyes and short golden hair, and real hair that curled bewitchingly. Then came the selection of the "fit out." Freddie thought she should have skates and a watch and bracelets and one of the cunning waterproof cloaks and a trunk--in fact, everything that could be bought for a doll (and in these days that means all articles of apparel, whether for use or ornament, that could be bought for a real person); but Mrs. Page explained that she would not need so many things in Mad River Village, so he was contented with a trunk which he selected himself, while his mother and Beth bought a little hat and cloak, shoes, stockings, and a pretty sunshade--the dresses and underclothing Beth thought she could make with the aid of her mother's seamstress, and she was very ambitious to try.

Freddie thought the "small boy" and the "baby" ought to have presents sent to them also; so he was allowed to select a drum, which he was sure the boy "would like best of anything," and a pretty rattle and a rubber cow for the baby.

It was a very busy season of the year for the Pages as well as for other people, and Beth had many presents to think about, but she kept the little dresses and clothes for Lucy's doll in mind and worked and planned with a will all the time she could spare for them, and Mary, the seamstress, sewed and sewed, and as she knew how to cut dresses as well as make them, in about two weeks they had, as Beth said, "a lovely fit out," even to a tiny muff and collar made from some bits of fur mamma had and a sweet little hood made just like Beth's own.

Then Miss Doll was dressed in her travelling suit, muff and all, her other dresses and clothing packed in the little trunk, and she herself carefully tucked in on top, then Beth shut the cover and locked it, tying the key to one of the buckles of the side strap--a box had been procured and into it was packed the trunk, the drum, and the presents for the baby, supplemented by Freddie with a ball which he had found among his own playthings and two cornucopias of candy which he had purchased himself, saying that "Christmas won't be Christmas if they don't have some candy." Mrs. Page "filled in the nooks and corners just to steady the whole," as she modestly said, with a pair of strong warm mittens for Mr. Tillage, some magazines and books, several pairs of long thick stockings which Freddie had outgrown but not worn out, and over the whole a beautiful warm shawl.

Then Beth and Fred composed a letter together which Beth wrote and they both signed:

DEAR LUCY TILLAGE:--The turkey brought the letter safely to us and we wanted to be Santa Claus ourselves and so send the doll and the other things for a Christmas present to you and your brother and the baby.

We wish you all a Merry Christmas and a Happy New Year.

BETH PAGE,
FRED PAGE.

This they neatly folded, put in an envelope addressed to Miss Lucy Tillage, Mad River Village, and placed on the shawl where it might be seen the moment the box was opened. They felt very proud and happy when the box was finally nailed up and directed in clear printed letters to

GEORGE TILLAGE,
Intervale Farm,
Mad River Village,
New Hampshire.

Freddie insisted that Lucy's name ought to be put on, too, as she was the one who had written the letter and to whom the box was really sent; so "For Lucy" was printed across one corner and underlined that her father might see it was sent particularly to her. It all seemed so mysterious, sending presents to people they did not know, and so delightful, that they thought this the best Christmas they had ever known and only wished that they could be in the little "black house" when the box was opened, to see Lucy's face as she caught sight of the cunning trunk and then the doll which she had so longed for.

The very day the box was sent on its way there came a letter from a minister in the town in which Mad River Village was located, saying that he "did not know any family of the name of Tillage, but upon inquiry he had found that there was a family of that name living on the other side of the river, but as they did not go to his church he was not acquainted with them; he was sorry, etc., etc."

But the children cared little for this letter; their faith in Lucy was not shaken, and they were very happy that they had answered her letter.

EZRA'S THANKSGIVIN' OUT WEST[21]
BY EUGENE FIELD.

A Kansas settler's recollections of an old-time Thanksgiving in western Massachusetts. Older boys and girls will best appreciate the tender sentiment of the picture which Eugene Field has painted so vividly by his masterly use of homely dialect.

Ezra had written a letter to the home folks, and in it he had complained that never before had he spent such a weary, lonesome day as this Thanksgiving Day had been. Having finished this letter, he sat for a long time gazing idly into the open fire that snapped cinders all over the hearthstone and sent its red forks dancing up the chimney to join the winds that frolicked and gambolled across the Kansas prairies that raw November night. It had rained hard all day, and was cold; and although the open fire made every honest effort to be cheerful, Ezra, as he sat in front of it in the wooden rocker and looked down into the glowing embers, experienced a dreadful feeling of loneliness and homesickness.

[Note 21: From "A Little Book of Profitable Tales," copyright, 1889, published by Charles Scribner's Sons.]

"I'm sick o' Kansas," said Ezra to himself. "Here I've been in this plaguey country for goin' on a year, and--yes, I'm sick of it, powerful sick of it. What a miser'ble Thanksgivin' this has been! They don't know what Thanksgivin' is out this way. I wish I was back in ol' Mass'chusetts--that's the country for *me*, and they hev the kind o' Thanksgivin' I like!"

Musing in this strain, while the rain went patter-patter on the windowpanes, Ezra saw a strange sight in the fireplace--yes, right among the embers and the crackling flames Ezra saw a strange, beautiful picture unfold and spread itself out like a panorama.

"How very wonderful!" murmured the young man. Yet he did not take his eyes away, for the picture soothed him and he loved to look upon it.

"It is a pictur' of long ago," said Ezra softly. "I had like to forgot it, but now it comes back to me as nat'ral-like as an ol' friend. An' I seem to be a part of it, an' the feelin' of that time comes back with the pictur', too."

Ezra did not stir. His head rested upon his hand, and his eyes were fixed upon the shadows in the firelight.

"It is a pictur' of the ol' home," said Ezra to himself. "I am back there in Belchertown, with the Holyoke hills up north an' the Berkshire Mountains a-loomin' up gray an' misty-like in the western horizon. Seems as if it wuz early mornin'; everything is still, and it is so cold when we boys crawl out o' bed that, if it wuzn't Thanksgivin' mornin', we'd crawl back again an' wait for Mother to call us. But it *is* Thanksgivin' mornin', and we're goin' skatin' down on the pond. The squealin' o' the pigs has told us it is five o'clock, and we must hurry; we're goin' to call by for the Dickerson boys an' Hiram Peabody, an' we've got to hyper! Brother Amos gets on about half o' my clothes, and I get on 'bout half o' his, but it's all the same; they are stout, warm clo'es, and they're big enough to fit any of us boys--Mother looked out for that when she made 'em. When we go downstairs, we find the girls there, all bundled up nice an' warm--Mary an' Helen an' Cousin Irene. They're going with us, an' we all start out tiptoe and quiet-like so's not to wake up the ol' folks. The ground is frozen hard; we stub our toes on the frozen ruts in the road. When we come to the minister's house, Laura is standin' on the front stoop a-waitin' for us. Laura is the minister's daughter. She's a friend o' Sister Helen's--pretty as a dagerr'otype, an' gentle-like and tender. Laura lets me carry her skates, an' I'm glad of it, although I have my hands full already with the lantern, the hockies, and the rest. Hiram Peabody keeps us waitin', for he has overslept himself, an' when he comes trottin' out at last the girls make fun of him--all except Sister Mary, an' she sort o' sticks up for Hiram, an' we're all so 'cute we kind o' calc'late we know the reason why.

"And now," said Ezra softly, "the pictur' changes: seems as if I could see the pond. The ice is like a black lookin'-glass, and Hiram Peabody slips up the first thing, an' down he comes, lickety-split, an' we all laugh--except Sister Mary, an' *she* says it is very imp'lite to laugh at other folks' misfortunes. Ough! how cold it is, and how my fingers ache with the frost when I take off my mittens to strap on Laura's skates! But, oh, how my cheeks burn! And how careful I am not to hurt Laura, an' how I ask her if that's 'tight enough,' an' how she tells me 'jist a little tighter' and how we two keep foolin' along till the others hev gone an' we are left alone! An' how quick I get my **own** skates strapped on--none o' your new-fangled skates with springs an' plates an' clamps an' such, but honest, ol'-fashioned wooden ones with steel runners that curl up over my toes an' have a bright brass button on the end! How I strap 'em and lash 'em and buckle 'em on! An' Laura waits for me an' tells me to be sure to get 'em on tight enough--why, bless me! after I once got 'em strapped on, if them skates hed come off, the feet wud ha' come with 'em! An' now away we go--Laura and me. Around the bend--near the medder where Si Barker's dog killed a woodchuck last summer--we meet the rest. We forget all about the cold. We run races an' play snap the whip, an' cut all sorts o' didoes, an' we never mind the pick'rel weed that is froze in on the ice an' trips us up every time we cut the outside edge; an' then we boys jump over the air holes, an' the girls stan' by an' scream an' tell us they know we're agoin' to drownd ourselves. So the hours go, an' it is sun-up at last, an' Sister Helen says we must be gettin' home. When we take our skates off, our feet feel as if they were wood. Laura has lost her tippet; I lend her mine, and she kind o' blushes. The old pond seems glad to have us go, and the fire-hangbird's nest in the willer tree waves us good-bye. Laura promises to come over to our house in the evenin', and so we break up.

"Seems now," continued Ezra musingly, "seems now as if I could see us all at breakfast. The race on the pond has made us hungry, and Mother says she never knew anybody else's boys that had such capac'ties as hers. It is the Yankee Thanks-givin' breakfast--sausages an' fried potatoes, an' buckwheat cakes, an' syrup--maple syrup, mind ye, for Father has his own sugar bush, and there was a big run o' sap last season. Mother says, 'Ezry an' Amos, won't you never get through eatin'? We want to clear off the table, fer there's pies to make, and nuts to crack, and laws sakes alive! The turkey's got to be stuffed yet!' Then how we all fly around! Mother sends Helen up into the attic to get a squash while Mary's makin' the pie crust. Amos an' I crack the walnuts--they call 'em hickory nuts out in this pesky country of sage-brush and pasture land. The walnuts are hard, and it's all we can do to crack 'em. Ev'ry once'n a while one on 'em slips outer our fingers and goes dancin' over the floor or flies into the pan Helen is squeezin' pumpkin into through the col'nder. Helen says we're shif'less an' good for nothin' but frivolin'; but Mother tells us how to crack the walnuts so's not to let 'em fly all over the room, an' so's not to be all jammed to pieces like the walnuts was down at the party at the Peasleys' last winter. An' now here comes Tryphena Foster, with her gingham gown an' muslin apron on; her folks have gone up to Amherst for Thanksgivin', an' Tryphena has come over to help our folks get dinner. She thinks a great deal o' Mother, 'cause Mother teaches her Sunday-school class an' says Tryphena oughter marry a missionary. There is bustle everywhere, the rattle uv pans an' the clatter of dishes; an' the new kitchen stove begins to warm up an' git red, till Helen loses her wits and is flustered, an' sez she never could git the hang o' that stove's dampers.

"An' now," murmured Ezra gently, as a tone of deeper reverence crept into his voice, "I can see Father sittin' all by himself in the parlour. Father's hair is very gray, and there are wrinkles on his honest old face. He is lookin' through the winder at the Holyoke hills over yonder, and I can guess he's thinkin' of the time when he wuz a boy like me an' Amos, an' uster climb over them hills an' kill rattlesnakes an' hunt partridges. Or doesn't his eyes quite reach the Holyoke hills? Do they fall kind o' lovingly but sadly on the little buryin' ground jest beyond the village? Ah, Father knows that spot, an' he loves it, too, for there are treasures there whose memory he wouldn't swap for all the world could give. So, while there is a kind o' mist in Father's eyes, I can see he is dreamin'-like of sweet an' tender things, and a-communin' with memory--hearin' voices I never heard, an' feelin' the tech of hands I never pressed; an' seein' Father's peaceful face I find it hard to think of a Thanksgivin' sweeter than Father's is.

"The pictur' in the firelight changes now," said Ezra, "an' seems as if I wuz in the old frame meetin'-house. The meetin'-house is on the hill, and meetin' begins at half-pas' ten. Our pew is well up in front--seems as if I could see it now. It has a long red cushion on the seat, and in the hymn-book rack there is a Bible an' a couple of Psalmodies. We walk up the aisle slow, and Mother goes in first; then comes Mary, then me, then Helen, then Amos, and then Father. Father thinks it is jest as well to have one o' the girls set in between me an' Amos. The meetin'-house is full, for ev-erybody goes to meetin' Thanksgivin' Day. The minister reads the proclamation an' makes a prayer, an' then he gives out a psalm, an' we all stan' up an' turn 'round an' join the choir. Sam Merritt has come up from Palmer to spend Thanksgivin' with the ol' folks, an' he is singin' tenor to-day in his ol' place in the choir. Some folks say he sings wonderful well, but *I* don't like Sam's voice. Laura sings soprano in the choir, and Sam stands next to her an' holds the book.

"Seems as if I could hear the minister's voice, full of earnestness an' melody, comin' from way up in his little round pulpit. He is tellin' us why we should be thankful, an', as he quotes Scriptur' an' Dr. Watts, we boys wonder how anybody can remember so much of the Bible. Then I get nervous and worried. Seems to me the minister was never comin' to lastly, and I find myself wonderin' whether Laura is listenin' to what the preachin' is about, or is writin' notes to Sam Merritt in the back of the tune book. I get thirsty, too, and I fidget about till Father looks at me, and Mother nudges Helen, and Helen passes it along to me with interest.

"An' then," continues Ezra in his revery, "when the last hymn is given out an' we stan' up agin an' join the choir, I am glad to see that Laura is singin' outer the book with Miss Hubbard, the alto. An' goin' out o' meetin' I kind of edge up to Laura and ask her if I kin have the pleasure of seein' her home.

"An' now we boys all go out on the Common to play ball. The Enfield boys have come over, and, as all the Hampshire county folks know, they are tough fellers to beat. Gorham Polly keeps tally, because he has got the newest jackknife--oh, how slick it whittles the old broom handle Gorham picked up in Packard's store an' brought along jest to keep tally on! It is a great game of ball; the bats are broad and light, and the ball is small and soft. But the Enfield boys beat us at last; leastwise they make 70 tallies to our 58, when Heman Fitts knocks the ball over into Aunt Dorcas Eastman's yard, and Aunt Dorcas comes out an' picks up the ball an' takes it into the house, an' we have to stop playin'. Then Phineas Owen allows he can flop any boy in Belchertown, an' Moses Baker takes him up, an' they wrassle like two tartars, till at last Moses tuckers Phineas out an' downs him as slick as a whistle.

"Then we all go home, for Thanksgivin' dinner is ready. Two long tables have been made into one, and one of the big tablecloths Gran'ma had when she set up housekeepin' is spread over 'em both. We all set round--Father, Mother, Aunt Lydia Holbrook, Uncle Jason, Mary, Helen, Tryphena Foster, Amos, and me. How big an' brown the turkey is, and how good it smells! There are bounteous dishes of mashed potato, turnip, an' squash, and the celery is very white and cold, the biscuits are light and hot, and the stewed cranberries are red as Laura's cheeks. Amos and I get the drumsticks; Mary wants the wishbone to put over the door for Hiram, but Helen gets it. Poor Mary, she always *did* have to give up to 'rushin' Helen,' as we call her. The pies--oh, what pies Mother makes; no dyspepsia in 'em, but good nature an' good health an' hospitality! Pumpkin pies, mince, an' apple, too, and then a big dish of pippins an' russets an' bellflowers, an', last of all, walnuts with cider from the Zebrina Dickerson farm! I tell ye, there's a Thanksgivin' dinner for ye! that's what we get in old Belchertown; an' that's the kind of livin' that makes the Yankees so all-fired good an' smart.

"But the best of all," said Ezra very softly to himself, "oh, yes, the best scene in all the pictur' is when evenin' comes, when all the lamps are lit in the parlour, when the neighbours come in, and when there is music and singing an' games. An' it's this part o' the pictur' that makes me homesick now and fills my heart with a longin' I never had before; an' yet it sort o' mellows and comforts me, too. Miss Serena Cadwell, whose beau was killed in the war, plays on the melodeon, and we all sing--all on us: men, womenfolks, an' children. Sam Merritt is there, and he sings a tenor song about love. The women sort of whisper round that he's goin' to be married to a Palmer lady nex' spring, an' I think to myself I never heard better singin' than Sam's. Then we play games--proverbs, buzz, clap-in-clap-out, copenhagen, fox-an'-geese, button-button-who's-got-the-button, spin-the-platter, go-to-Jerusalem, my-ship's-come-in; and all the rest. The ol' folks play with the young folks just as nat'ral as can be; and we all laugh when Deacon Hosea Cowles hez to measure six yards of love ribbon with Miss Hepsey Newton, and cut each yard with a kiss; for the deacon hez been sort o' purrin' round Miss Hepsey for goin' on two years. Then, aft'r a while, when Mary and Helen bring in the cookies, nutcakes, cider, an' apples, Mother says: 'I don't believe we're goin' to hev enough apples to go round; Ezry, I guess I'll have to get you to go down cellar for some more.' Then I says: 'All right, Mother, I'll go, providin' some one 'll go along an' hold the candle.' An' when I say this I look right at Laura, an' she blushes. Then Helen, jest for meanness, says: 'Ezry, I s'pose you ain't willin' to have your fav'rite sister go down cellar with you and catch her death o' cold?' But Mary, who hez been showin' Hiram Peabody the phot'graph album for more'n an hour, comes to the rescue an' makes Laura take the candle, and she shows Laura how to hold it so it won't go out.

"The cellar is warm an' dark. There are cobwebs all between the rafters an' everywhere else except on the shelves where Mother keeps the butter an' eggs an' other things that would freeze in the butt'ry upstairs. The apples are in bar'ls up against the wall, near the potater bin. How fresh an' sweet they smell! Laura thinks she sees a mouse, an' she trembles an' wants to jump up on the pork bar'l, but I tell her that there shan't no mouse hurt her while I'm around; and I mean it, too, for the sight of Laura a-tremblin' makes me as strong as one of Father's steers. 'What kind of apples do you like best, Ezry?' asks Laura, 'russets or greenin's or crow-eggs or bellflowers or Baldwins or pippins?' 'I like the Baldwins best,' says I, "coz they got red cheeks just like yours.' 'Why, Ezry Thompson! how you talk!' says Laura. 'You oughter be ashamed of yourself!' But when I get the dish filled up with apples there ain't a Baldwin in all the lot that can compare with the bright red of Laura's cheeks. An' Laura knows it, too, an' she sees the mouse again, an' screams, and then the candle goes out, and we are in a dreadful stew. But I, bein' almost a man, contrive to bear up under it, and knowin' she is an orph'n, I comfort an' encourage Laura the best I know how, and we are almost upstairs when Mother comes to the door and wants to know what has kep' us so long. Jest as if Mother doesn't know! Of course she does; an' when Mother kisses Laura good-bye that night there is in the act a tenderness that speaks more sweetly than even Mother's words.

"It is so like Mother," mused Ezra; "so like her with her gentleness an' clingin' love. Hers is the sweetest picture of all, and hers the best love."

Dream on, Ezra; dream of the old home with its dear ones, its holy influences, and its precious inspiration!--Mother. Dream on in the faraway firelight; and as the angel hand of memory unfolds these sacred visions, with thee and them shall abide, like a Divine Comforter, the spirit of Thanksgiving.

CHIP'S THANKSGIVING[22]
BY ANNIE HAMILTON DONNELL.

Chip had plenty of nuts on Thanksgiving Day. The little lady
called Heart's Delight saw to that. Can you guess who Chip was?

They had got "way through," as Terry said, to the nuts. It had been a beautiful Thanksgiving dinner "so far." Grandmother's sweet face beamed down the length of the great table, over all the little crinkly grandheads, at grandfather's face. Everybody felt very thankful.

[Note 22: From the *Youth's Companion*, November 26, 1903.]

"I wish all the children this side o' the north pole had had some turkey, too, and squash and cram'bry--and things," said Silence quietly. Silence was always wishing beautiful things like that.

"An' some nuts," added Terry, setting his small white teeth into the meat of a big fat walnut. "It wouldn't seem Thanksgivingy 'thout nuts."

"I know somebody who would be thankful with just nuts," smiled grandfather. "Indeed, I think he'd rather have them for all the courses of his Thanksgiving dinner!"

"Just nuts! No turkey, nor puddin', nor anything?"

The crinkly grandheads all bobbed up from their plates and nut-pickers in amazement. Just nuts!

"Yes. Guess who he is?" Grandfather's laughing eyes twinkled up the long table at grandmother.

"I'll give you three guesses apiece, beginning with Heart's Delight. Guess number one, Heart's Delight."

"Chip," gravely. Heart's Delight had guessed it the very first guess.

"Chip!" laughed all the little grand girls and boys. Why, of course! Chip! He would rather have just nuts for Thanksgiving dinner!

"I wish he had some o' mine!" cried Silence.

"An' mine!" cried Terry; and all the others wished he had some of theirs. What a Thanksgiving dinner little Chip would have had!

"He's got plenty, thank you." It was the shy little voice of Heart's Delight. A soft pink colour had come into her round cheeks. Everybody looked at her inquiringly, for how did Heart's Delight know Chip had plenty of nuts? Then Terry remembered something.

"Oh, that's where her nuts went to!" he cried. "Heart's Delight gave 'em to Chip! We couldn't think what she'd done with 'em all."

The pink colour was growing pinker--very pink indeed.

"Yes, that's where," said Silence, leaning over to squeeze one of Heart's Delight's little hands. And sure enough, it was. In the beautiful nut month of October, when the children went after their winter's supply of nuts, little Heart's Delight had left all her little rounded heap just where bright-eyed, nut-loving squirrel Chip would be sure to find them and hurry them away to his winter hole. And Chip had found them, she was sure, for not one was left when she went back to see, the next day.

"Why, maybe this very minute--right now--Chip's cracking his Thanksgiving dinner!" Terry laughed.

"Same as we are! Maybe he's got to the nut cour--oh, they're all nut courses! But maybe he's sittin' up to his table with the rest of the folks, thanksgiving to Heart's Delight," Silence said.

Heart's Delight's little shy face nearly hid itself over her plate. This was dreadful! It was necessary to change the subject at once, and a dear little thought came to her aid.

"But I'm afraid he hasn't got any gran'father and gran'mother to his Thanksgiving," she said softly. "I shouldn't think anybody could thanksgive 'thout a gran'mother and gran'father."

THE MASTER OF THE HARVEST[23]
BY MRS. ALFRED GATTY.

A good old-fashioned story for the older boys and girls to read on the Sunday before Thanksgiving Day.

The Master of the Harvest walked by the side of his cornfields in the early year, and a cloud was over his face, for there had been no rain for several weeks, and the earth was hard from the parching of the cold east winds, and the young wheat had not been able to spring up.

[Note 23: From "Parables from Nature."]

So, as he looked over the long ridges that lay stretched in rows before him, he was vexed, and began to grumble, and say, "The harvest would be backward, and all things would go wrong." At the mere thought of which he frowned more and more, and uttered words of complaint against the heavens, because there was no rain; against the earth, because it was so dry and unyielding; against the corn, because it had not sprung up.

And the man's discontent was whispered all over the field, and all along the long ridges where the corn seeds lay; and when it reached them they murmured out, "How cruel to complain! Are we not doing our best? Have we let one drop of moisture pass by unused, one moment of warmth come to us in vain? Have we not seized on every chance, and striven every day to be ready for the hour of breaking forth? Are we idle? Are we obstinate? Are we indifferent? Shall we not be found waiting and watching? How cruel to complain!"

Of all this, however, the Master of the Harvest heard nothing, so the gloom did not pass away from his face. On the contrary, he took it with him into his comfortable home, and repeated to his wife the dark words that all things were going wrong; that the drought would ruin the harvest, for the corn was not yet sprung.

And still thinking thus, he laid his head on his pillow, and presently fell asleep.

But his wife sat up for a while by the bedside, and opened her Bible, and read, "The harvest is the end of the world, and the reapers are the angels."

Then she wrote this text in pencil on the flyleaf at the end of the book, and after it the date of the day, and after the date the words, "Lord, the husbandman, Thou waitest for the precious fruit Thou hast sown, and hast long patience for it! Amen, O Lord, Amen!"

After which the good woman knelt down to pray, and as she prayed she wept, for she knew that she was very ill.

But what she prayed that night was heard only in heaven.

And so a few days passed on as before, and the house was gloomy with the discontent of its master; but at last one evening the wind changed, the sky became heavy with clouds, and before midnight there was rain all over the land; and when the Master of the Harvest came in next morning, wet from his early walk by the cornfields, he said it was well it had come at last, and that, at last, the corn had sprung up.

On which his wife looked at him with a smile, and said, "How often things came right, about which one had been anxious and disturbed." To which her husband made no answer, but turned away and spoke of something else.

Meantime, the corn seeds had been found ready and waiting when the hour came, and the young sprouts burst out at once; and very soon all along the long ridges were to be seen rows of tender blades, tinting the whole field with a delicate green. And day by day the Master of the Harvest saw them and was satisfied; but because he was satisfied, and his anxiety was gone, he spoke of other things, and forgot to rejoice.

And a murmur arose among them: "Should not the Master have welcomed us to life? He was angry but lately, because the seed he had sown had not yet brought forth; now that it has brought forth, why is he not glad? What more does he want? Have we not done our best? Are we not doing it minute by minute, hour by hour, day by day? From the morning and evening dews, from the glow of the midday sun, from the juices of the earth, from the breezes which freshen the air, even from clouds and rain, are we not taking in food and strength, warmth and life, refreshment and joy; so that one day the valleys may laugh and sing, because the good seed hath brought forth abundantly? Why does he not rejoice?"

As before, however, of all they said the Master of the Harvest heard nothing; and it never struck him to think of the young corn blades' struggling life. Nay, once, when his wife asked him if the wheat was doing well, he answered, "Very fairly," and nothing more. But she then, because the evening was fine and the fairer weather had revived her failing powers, said she would walk out by the cornfields herself.

And so it came to pass that they went out together. And together they looked all along the long green ridges of wheat, and watched the blades as they quivered and glistened in the breeze which sprang up with the setting sun. Together they walked, together they looked; looking at the same things and with the same human eyes; even as they had walked, and looked, and lived together for years, but with a world dividing their hearts; and what was ever to unite them?

Even then, as they moved along, she murmured half aloud, half to herself, thinking of the anxiety that had passed away: "Thou visitest the earth, and blessest it; thou makest it very plenteous."

To which he answered, if answer it may be called, "Why are you always so gloomy? Why should Scripture be quoted about such common things?"

And she looked in his face and smiled, but did not speak; and he could not read the smile, for the life of her heart was as hidden to him as the life of the corn blades in the field.

And so they went home together, no more being said by either; for, as she turned round, the sight of the setting sun and of the young freshly growing wheat blades brought tears into her eyes.

She might never see the harvest upon earth again; for her that other was at hand, whereof the reapers were to be angels.

And when she opened her Bible that night she wrote on the flyleaf the text she had quoted to her husband, and after the text the date of the day, and after the date the words, "Bless me, even me also, oh, my Father, that I may bring forth fruit with patience!"

Very peaceful were the next few weeks that followed, for all nature seemed to rejoice in the weather, and the corn blades shot up till they were nearly two feet high, and about them the Master of the Harvest had no complaints to make.

But at the end of that time, behold, the earth began to be hard and dry again, for once more rain was wanted; and by degrees the growing plants failed for want of moisture and nourishment, and lost power and colour, and became weak and yellow in hue. And once more the husbandmen began to fear and tremble, and once more the brow of the Master of the Harvest was over-clouded with angry apprehension.

And as the man got more and more anxious about the fate of his crops, he grew more and more irritable and distrustful, and railed as before, only louder now, against the heavens because there was no rain; against the earth because it lacked moisture; against the corn plants because they had waxed feeble.

Nay, once, when his sick wife reproved him gently, praying him to remember how his fears had been turned to joy before, he reproached her in his turn for sitting in the house and pretending to judge of what she could know nothing about, and bade her come out and see for herself how all things were working together for ill.

And although he spoke it in bitter jest, and she was very ill, she said she would go, and went.

So once more they walked out together, and once more looked over the corn-fields; but when he stretched out his arm and pointed to the long ridges of blades, and she saw them shrunken and faded in hue, her heart was grieved within her, and she turned aside and wept over them.

Nevertheless, she said she durst not cease from hope, since an hour might renew the face of the earth, if God so willed; neither should she dare to complain, ***even the harvest were to fail***. At which words the Master of the Harvest stopped short, amazed, to look at his wife, for her soul was growing stronger as her body grew weaker, and she dared to say things now which she would have had no courage to utter before.

But of all this he knew nothing, and what he thought, as he listened, was that she was as weak in mind as in body; and what he said was that a man must be an idiot who would not complain when he saw the bread taken from under his very eyes!

And his murmurings and her tears sent a shudder all along the long ridges of sickly corn blades, and they asked one of another, "Why does he murmur? and, Why does she weep? Are we not doing all we can? Do we slumber or sleep, and let opportunities pass by unused? Are we not watching and waiting against the times of refreshing? Shall we not be found ready at last? Why does he murmur? and, Why does she weep? Is she, too, fading and waiting? Has she, too, a master who has lost patience?"

Meantime, when she opened her Bible that night, she wrote on the flyleaf the text, "Wherefore should a man complain, a man for the punishment of his sins?" and after the text the date of the day, and after the date the words, "Thou dost turn Thy face from us, and we are troubled; but, Lord, how long, how long?"

And by and by came on the long-delayed times of refreshing, but so slowly and imperfectly that the change in the corn could scarcely be detected for a while. Nevertheless, it told at last, and stems struggled up among the blades, and burst forth into flowers, which gradually ripened into ears of grain. But a struggle it had been, and continued to be, for the measure of moisture was scant, and the due amount of warmth in the air was wanting. Nevertheless, by struggling and effort the young wheat advanced, little by little, in growth; preparing itself, minute by minute, hour by hour, day by day, as best it could, for the great day of the harvest. As best it could! Would the Master of the Harvest ask more? Alas! he had still something to find fault with, for when he looked at the ears and saw that they were small and poor, he grumbled, and said the yield would be less than it ought to be, and the harvest would be bad.

And as more weeks went on, and the same weather continued, and the progress was very, very slow, he spoke out of his vexation to his wife at home, to his friends at the market, and to the husbandmen who passed by and talked with him about the crops.

And the voice of his discontent was breathed over the cornfield, all along the long ridges where the plants were labouring, and waiting, and watching. And they shuddered and murmured: "How cruel to complain! Had we been idle, had we been negligent, had we been indifferent, we might have passed away without bearing fruit at all. How cruel to complain!"

But of all this the Master of the Harvest heard nothing, so he did not cease to complain.

Meantime, another week or two went on, and people as they glanced over the land wished that a few good rainy days would come and do their work decidedly, so that the corn ears might fill. And behold, while the wish was yet on their lips, the sky became charged with clouds, darkness spread over the country, a wild wind rose, and the growling of thunder announced a storm. And such a storm! People hid from it in cellars and closets and dark corners, as if now, for the first time, they believed in a God, and were trembling at the new-found fact; as if they could never discover Him in His sunshine and blessings, but only thus in His tempests and wrath.

And all along the long ridges of wheat plants drove the rain-laden blast, and they bent down before it and rose up again, like the waves of a labouring sea. Ears over ears they bowed down; ears above ears they rose up. They bowed down as if they knew that to resist was destruction; they rose up as if they had a hope beyond the storm. Only here and there, where the whirlwinds were the strongest, they fell down and could not lift themselves again. So the damage done was but little, and the general good was great. But when the Master of the Harvest saw here and there patches of overweighted corn yet dripping from the thunder showers, he grew angry for them, and forgot to think of the long ridges that stretched over his fields, where the corn ears were swelling and rejoicing.

And he came in gloomy to his home, when his wife was hoping that now, at last, all would be well; and when she looked at him the tumult of her soul grew beyond control, and she knelt down before him as he sat moody in his chair, and threw her arms round him, and cried out: "It is of the Lord's mercies that we are not utterly consumed. Oh, husband! pray for the corn and for me, that it may go well with us at the last! Carry me upstairs!" And his anger was checked by fear, and he carried her upstairs and laid her on the bed, and said it must be the storm which had shaken her nerves. But whether he prayed for either the corn or her that night she never knew.

And presently came a new distress: for when the days of rain had accomplished their gracious work, and every one was satisfied, behold, they did not cease. And as hitherto the cry had gone up for water on the furrows, so now men's hearts failed them for fear lest it should continue to overflowing, and lest mildew should set in upon the full, rich ears, and the glorious crops should be lost.

And the Master of the Harvest walked out by his cornfields, his face darker than ever. And he railed against the rain because it would not cease; against the sun because it would not shine; against the wheat because it might perish before the harvest.

"But why does he always and only complain?" moaned the corn plants, as the new terror was breathed over the field. "Have we not done our best from the first? And has not mercy been with us, sooner or later, all along? When moisture was scant, and we throve but little, why did he not rejoice over that little, and wait, as we did, for more? Now that abundance has come, and we swell triumphant in strength and in hope, why does he not share our joy in the present, and wait in trust, as we do, for the future ripening change? Why does he always complain? Has he himself some hard master, who would fain reap where he has not sown, and gather where he has not strewed, and who has no pity for his servants who strive?"

But of all this the Master of the Harvest heard nothing. And when the days of rain had rolled into weeks and the weeks into months, and the autumn set in, and the corn still stood up green in the ridges, as if it never meant to ripen at all, the boldest and most hopeful became uneasy, and the Master of the Harvest despaired.

But his wife had risen no more from her bed, where she lay in sickness and suffering, yet in patient trust, watching the sky through the window that faced her pillow, looking for the relief that came at last. For even at the eleventh hour, when hope seemed almost over, and men had half learned to submit to their expected trial, the dark days began to be varied by a few hours of sunshine; and though these passed away, and the gloom and rain returned again, yet they also passed away in their turn, and the sun shone out once more.

And the poor sick wife, as she watched, said to those around her that the weather was gradually changing, and that all would come right at last; and sighing a prayer that it might be so with herself also, she had her Bible brought to the bed, and wrote in the flyleaf the text, "Some thirty, some sixty, some an hundredfold"; and after the text the date of the day, for on that day the sun had been shining steadily for many hours. And after the date the words, "Unto whom much is given, of him shall much be required; yet if Thou, Lord, be extreme to mark iniquity, O Lord, who may stand?"

And day by day, the hours of sunshine were more in number, and the hours of rain and darkness fewer, and by degrees the green corn ears ripened into yellow, and the yellow turned into gold, and the harvest was ready, and the labourers not wanting. And the bursting corn broke out into songs of rejoicing, and cried, "At least we have not waited and watched in vain! Surely goodness and mercy have followed us all the days of our life, and we are crowned with glory and honour. Where is the Master of the Harvest, that he may claim his own with joy?"

But the Master of the Harvest was bending over the bed of his dying wife.

And she whispered that her Bible should be brought, and he brought it, and she said, "Open it at the flyleaf at the end, and write, 'It is sown in corruption, it is raised in incorruption; it is sown in dishonour, it is raised in glory; it is sown in weakness, it is raised in power; it is sown a natural body, it is raised a spiritual body!'" And she bade him add the date of the day, and after the date of the day, the words, "O

Lord, in Thy mercy say of me--She hath done what she could!" And then she laid her hand in his, and so fell asleep in hope.

And the harvest of the earth was gathered into barns, and the gathering-day of rejoicing was over, and the Master of it all sat alone by his fireside, with his wife's Bible on his knee. And he read the texts and the dates and the prayers, from the first day when the corn seeds were held back by drought; and as he read a new heart seemed to burst out within him from the old one--a heart which the Lord of the other Harvest was making soft, and the springing whereof He would bless.

And henceforth, in his going out and coming in from watching the fruits of the earth, the texts and the dates and the prayers were ever present in his mind, often rising to his lips; and he murmured and complained no more, let the seasons be what they would and his fears however great; for the thought of the late-sprung seed in his own dry cold heart, and of the long suffering of Him who was Lord and Master of all, was with him night and day. And more and more as he prayed for help, that the weary struggle might be blessed, and the new-born watching and waiting not be in vain, so more and more there came over his spirit a yearning for that other harvest, where he and she who had gone before might be gathered in together.

And thus--in one hope of their calling--the long-divided hearts were united at last.

A THANKSGIVING DINNER[24]
BY EDNA PAYSON BRETT.

Ministers' sons, somehow, have a bad reputation. Little Johnnie was one and he thought it pretty hard to have to go to church on Thanksgiving Day. But the pink-frosted cakes--

"Oh, dear!" puffed a certain little boy one bright Thanksgiving morning, as he jerked his chubby neck into the stiffest of white collars. "Great fun, isn't it, having to sit up in meeting for a couple of hours straight as a telegraph pole when I might be playing football and beating the Haddam team all to hollow! This is what comes of your pa's being the minister, I s'pose."

[Note 24: From the *Youth's Companion*, November 29, 1900.]

But Johnnie, for that was his name, continued his dressing, the ten years of his young life having taught him how useless it is to make a fuss over what has to be done.

In a few minutes he had finished, and was quite satisfied with his appearance, but for his shoes. These he eyed for a moment, and concluding that they would not pass inspection, started for the woodshed to give them a shine.

On his way he passed the open dining-room door, and suddenly halted. "Oh! Why can't I have a nice little lunch during sermon time?"

He took a step back and peeped slyly into the room; then stole across to the old-fashioned cupboard, stealthily opening the doors, and such an array of good things you never beheld! Sally was the best cook in Brockton any day, but on Thanksgiving she could work wonders.

He looked with longing eyes from one dish to another. Now the big pies were out of the question, and the cranberry tarts--he felt of them lovingly--but no, they were altogether too sticky. He stood on tiptoe to see what was on the second shelf. To his delight he found a platter filled with just the daintiest little pink-frosted cakes you ever saw.

"O-oo, thimble cakes!" he exclaimed. "You are just the fellows I want! I'll take you along to church with me." He cast one quick glance around, then grabbed a handful of the tiny cakes and crammed them into his trousers' pocket.

"Lucky for me ma isn't going to meeting to-day," chuckled the naughty boy, "and I don't believe grandma'd ever tell on me if I carried along the turkey!"

The early bell had now begun to ring, and Johnnie started for the village church.

"Come, my son," said Doctor Goodwin, as they entered the meeting-house, "you are to sit in the front seat with grandma this morning: she is particularly anxious to hear every word of the sermon to-day. And where's your contribution, boy? You haven't forgotten that?"

"No, sir," meekly answered Johnnie, "it's tied up in my handkerchief." But his heart sank--the front seat! How ever was his lunch to come in now?

The opening hymn had been sung, the prayer of thanksgiving offered, and now, as the collection was about to be taken, the pastor begged his people to be especially generous to the poor on this day.

Up in the front pew sat Johnnie, but never a word of the notice did he hear, so busy was he planning out his own little affair. It wasn't such easy planning either, just supposing he got caught!

But what was that? Johnnie jumped as if he had been struck. However, it was nothing but the money plate under his nose, and the good Deacon Simms standing calmly by.

To the guilty boy it seemed as if the deacon must have been waiting for ten minutes at the least, and in a great flurry he began to fumble for his handkerchief. What *had* he done with it? Oh, there it was at last, way down in the depths of his right trousers' pocket.

He caught hold of the knotted corner, and out came the handkerchief with a whisk and a flourish, and scatter, rattle, helter-skelter, out flew a half-dozen pink thimble cakes, down upon the floor, back into Mrs. Smiley's pew, and to Johnnie's horror one pat into the deacon's plate!

The good man's eyes tried not to twinkle as he removed the unusual offering, and passed on more quickly than was his wont.

Miserable Johnnie, with his face as red as a rooster's comb and eyes cast down in shame, saw nothing but the green squares on the carpet and the dreadful pink-frosted cakes. He was sure that every one in the church was glaring at him; probably even grandma had forsaken him, and each moment he dreaded--he knew not what.

To his surprise, the service seemed to go right on as usual. Another hymn was sung, and then there was a general settling down for the sermon. Very soon he began to grow tired of just gazing at the floor, yet he dared not look up, and by and by the heavy eyes drooped and Johnny was fast asleep.

All was now quiet in the meeting-house save the calm, steady voice of the preacher. Pretty soon a wee creature dressed all in soft brown stole across the floor of a certain pew. She was a courageous little body indeed, but what mother would not venture a good deal for her hungry babies? Such a repast as this was certainly the opportunity of a lifetime. Looking cautiously around, then concluding that all was safe, she disappeared down a hole in a corner way under the seat. In a twinkling she was back again; this time, however, she was not alone. Four little ones pattered after Mamma Mouse, and eight bright eyes spied a dinner worth running for.

Never mind what they did; but when Johnnie awoke at the strains of the closing hymn and tried to remember what had gone wrong, he saw nothing of the pink-frosted cakes save some scattered crumbs.

What could have become of them, he thought, in bewilderment.

He hardly knew how he got out of the church that day, but he found himself rushing down the road a sadder and a wiser boy. Grandma and papa had remained to chat. Johnnie did not feel like chatting to-day.

When he reached the house he did not go in, but out to the hayloft, his favourite resort in time of trouble. When the dinner bell sounded, notwithstanding the delicious Thanksgiving odours which had been wafted even to the barn, it was an unwelcome summons; yet go he must, and walking sheepishly into the dining-room, he slunk into his chair.

"Well, John," said his father, as he helped him to turkey, "I understand that you did not forget the poor to-day. Eh, my son?"

"The poor?" What could he mean? Johnnie was too puzzled to speak.

Then his father went on to tell how little Mrs. Mouse and her babies had nibbled a wondrous dinner of pink thimble cakes on the floor of pew number one while Johnnie slept. Grandma and Mrs. Smiley had told him all about it on the way home; besides, he had seen enough himself from the pulpit.

Johnny bravely bore the laugh at his expense, and as the merriment died away heaved a deep sigh of relief, and exclaimed, "Well, I'm glad somebody had a feast, even if it wasn't the fellow 'twas meant for! Humph, *'twas* quite a setup for poor church mice, wasn't it? But they needn't be looking for another next year. You don't catch me trying that again--no-sir-ee!"

TWO OLD BOYS[25]
BY PAULINE SHACKLEFORD COLYAR.

Walter's two grandfathers were a pair of jolly chums, as boys. There is plenty of humour in this tale of a turkey hunt.

"Day after to-morrow will be Thanksgiving," said Walter, taking his seat beside

Grandpa Davis on the top step of the front gallery.

[Note 25: *From Lippincott's Monthly Magazine*, December, 1896.]

"And no turkey for dinner, neither," retorted Grandma Davis, while her bright steel needles clicked in and out of the sock she was knitting.

The old man was smoking his evening pipe, and sat for a moment with his eyes fixed meditatively upon the blue hills massed in the distance.

"Have we got so pore as all that, Mother?" he asked, after a while, glancing over his shoulder at his wife, who was rocking to and fro just back of him.

"I'm obleeged to own to the truth," answered the old lady dejectedly. "What with the wild varmints in the woods and one thing an' another, I'm about cleaned out of all the poultry I ever had. It's downright disheartenin'."

"Well, then," asserted Grandpa Davis, with an unmirthful chuckle, "it don't appear to me as we've got so powerful much to be thankful about this year."

"Why, Grandpa!" cried Walter, in shocked surprise, "I never did hear you talk like that before."

"Never had so much call to do it, mebbe," interposed the old man cynically.

The last rays of the setting sun touched the two silvered heads, and rested there like a benediction, before disappearing below the horizon.

Silence had fallen upon the little group, and a bullfrog down in the fishpond was croaking dismally.

"Why don't you go hunting, and try to kill you a turkey for Thanksgiving?" ventured Walter, slipping his arm insinuatingly through his grandfather's. "I saw a great big flock of wild ones down on the branch last week, and I got right close up to them before they flew."

"I reckon there ought to be a smart sight of game round and about them cane brakes along that branch," said the old man slowly, as though thinking aloud. "It used to be ahead of any strip of woods in all these parts, when me and Dick was boys. But nobody ain't hunted there, to my knowledge, not sence me and him fell out."

"I wish you and Grandpa Dun were friends," sighed Walter. "It does seem too bad to have two grandpas living right side by side, and not speaking."

"I ain't got no ill-will in my heart for Dick," replied Grandpa Davis, "but he is too everlastin' hard-headed to knock under, and I'll be blamed if I go more'n halfway toward makin' up."

"That's just exactly what Grandpa Dun says about you," Walter assured him very earnestly.

"Wouldn't wonder if he did," said the old man pointedly. "Dick is always ben a mighty hand to talk, and he'd drap dead in his tracks if he couldn't get in the last word."

Be this as it might, the breach had begun when the Davis cattle broke down the worn fence and demolished the Dun crop of corn, and it widened when the Dun hogs found their way through an old water gap and rooted up a field of the Davis sweet potatoes. Several times similar depredations were repeated, and then shotguns were used on both sides with telling effect. The climax was reached when John Dun eloped with Rebecca, the only child of the Davises.

The young couple were forbidden their respective homes, though the farm they rented was scarce half a mile away, and the weeks rolled into months without sign of their parents relenting.

When Walter was born, however, the two grandmothers stole over, without their husbands' knowledge, and mingled their tears in happy communion over the tiny blue-eyed mite.

It was a memorable day at each of the houses when the sturdy little fellow made his way, unbidden and unattended, to pay his first call, and ever afterward (though they would not admit it, even to themselves) the grandfathers watched for his coming, and vied with each other in trying to win the highest place in his young affections.

He had inherited characteristics of each of his grandsires, and possessed the bold, masterful manner which was common to them both. "Say, Grandpa," he urged, "go hunting to-morrow and try to kill a turkey for Thanksgiving, won't you? I know grandma would feel better to have one, and if you make a cane caller, like papa does, I'll bet you can get a shot at one sure."

The old man did not commit himself about going, but when Walter saw him surreptitiously take down his gun from the pegs on the wall across which it had lain for so many years, and began to rub the barrels and oil the hammers, he went home satisfied that he had scored another victory.

Perhaps nothing less than his grandson's pleading could have induced Grandpa

Davis to visit again the old hunting-ground which had been so dear to him in by-gone days, which was so rich in hallowed memories. It seemed almost a desecration of the happy past to hunt there now alone.

The first cold streaks of dawn were just stealing into the sky the next morning when, accoutred with shot-pouch, powder-flask, and his old double-barrelled gun, Grandpa Davis made his way toward the branch. A medley of bird notes filled the air, long streamers of gray moss floated out from the swaying trees, and showers of autumn leaves fluttered down to earth. Some of the cows were grazing outside the pen, up to their hocks in lush, fresh grass, while others lay on the ground content-edly chewing their cuds. All of them raised their heads and looked at him as he passed them by.

How like old times it was to be up at daybreak for a hunt! The long years seemed suddenly to have rolled away, leaving him once more a boy. He almost wondered why Dick had not whistled to him as he used to do. Dick was an early riser, and somehow always got ready before he did.

There was an alertness in the old man's face and a spring in his step as he lived over in thought the joyous days of his childhood. The clouds were flushed with pink when he came in sight of the big water oak on the margin of the stream, and recollected how he and Dick had loved to go swimming in the deep, clear water beneath its shade.

"We used to run every step of the way," he soliloquized, laughing, "unbuttonin' as we went, chuck our clothes on the bank, and 'most break our necks tryin' to git in the water fust. I've got half a notion to take a dip this mornin', if it wasn't quite so cool," he went on, but a timely twinge of rheumatism brought him to his senses, and he seated himself on the roots of a convenient tree.

Cocking his gun, he laid it across his knees, and waited there motionless, imi-tating the yelp of a turkey the while. Three or four small canes, graduated in size, and fitted firmly one into the other, enabled him to make the note, and so expert had he become by long practice that the deception was perfect.

After a pause he repeated the call; then came another pause, another call, and over in the distance there sounded an answer. How the blood coursed through the old man's veins as he listened! There it was again. It was coming nearer, but very slowly. He wondered how many were in the flock, and called once more. This time, to his surprise, an answer came from a different direction--a long, rasping sound, a sort of cross between a cock's crow and a turkey's yelp.

He started involuntarily, and very cautiously peeped around. Hardly twenty steps from him another gray head protruded itself from the hole of another tree, and Grandpa Davis and Grandpa Dun looked into each other's eyes.

"I'll be double-jumped-up if that ain't Dick!" cried Grandpa Davis, under his breath. "And there ain't a turkey as ever wore a feather that he could fool. A minute more, and he'll spile the fun. Dick," he commanded, "stop that racket, and sneak over here by me," beckoning mysteriously. "Sh-h-h! they are answerin' ag'in. Down on your marrow-bones whilst I call."

Flattening himself upon the ground as nearly as he could, and creeping behind the undergrowth, Grandpa Dun made his way laboriously to the desired spot. He had never excelled in calling turkeys, but he was a far better shot than Grandpa Davis.

Without demur the two old boys fell naturally into the *role* of former days. Breathless and excited, they crouched there, waiting for the fateful moment. Their nerves were tense, their eyes dilated, and their hearts beating like trip-hammers.

Grandpa Davis had continued to call, and now the answer was very near.

"Gimme the first shot, Billy," whispered Grandpa Dun. "I let you do the callin'; and, besides, you know you never could hit nothin' that wasn't as big as the side of a meetin'-house."

Before Grandpa Davis had time to reply, there came the "put-put-put" which signals possible danger. A stately gobbler raised his head to reconnoitre; two guns were fired almost simultaneously, and, with a whir and a flutter, the flock disappeared in the cane brake.

The two old boys bounded over the intervening sticks and stumps with an agility that Walter himself might have envied, and bending over the prostrate gobbler exclaimed in concert: "Ain't he a dandy, though!"

They examined him critically, cutting out his beard as a trophy, and measured the spread of his wings.

"But he's yourn, after all, Dick," said Grandpa Davis ruefully. "These here ain't none of my shot, so I reckon I must have missed him."

"I knowed you would, Billy, afore your fired," Grandpa Dun replied, with mock gravity, "but that don't cut no figger. He's big enough for us to go halvers and both have plenty. More'n that, you done the callin' anyhow."

Then they laughed, and as they looked into one another's faces, each seemed to realize for the first time that his quondam chum was an old man.

A moment before they had been two rollicking boys off on a lark together--playing hooky, perhaps--and in the twinkling of an eye some wicked fairy had waved her wand and metamorphosed them into Walter's two grandfathers, who had not spoken to each other since years before the lad was born.

Yet the humour of the situation was irresistible after all, and, without knowing just how it happened, or which made the first advance, Dick and Billy found themselves still laughing until the tears coursed down their furrowed cheeks, and shaking hands with as much vigour as though each one had been working a pump handle.

"I'll tell you what it is, Billy," said Dick at last; "you all come over to my house, and we'll eat him together on Thanksgivin'."

"See here, Dick," suggested Billy, abstracting a nickel from his trousers' pocket; "heads at your house, and tails at mine."

"All right," came the hearty response.

Billy tossed the coin into the air: it struck a twig and hid itself among the fallen leaves, where they sought it in vain.

"'Tain't settled yet," announced Dick; "but lemme tell you what let's do. S'posin' we all go over to-morrow--it'll be Thanksgivin', you know--and eat him at John's house."

"Good!" cried Billy, with beaming face. "You always did have a head for thinkin' up things, Dick, and this here'll sorter split the difference, and ease matters so as--"

"Yes, and our two old women can draw straws, if they've got a mind to, and see which of them is obligated to make the fust call," interrupted Dick.

"Jist heft him, old feller," urged one of them.

"Ain't he a whopper, though!" exclaimed the other.

"Have a chaw, Dick?" asked Billy, offering his plug of tobacco.

"Don't keer if I do," acquiesced Dick, biting off a goodly mouthful.

Seating themselves upon a fallen hickory log, they chewed and expectorated, recalling old times, and enjoying their laugh with the careless freedom of their childhood days.

"Dick, do your ricolleck the fight you and a coon had out on the limb of that tree over yonder, one night?" queried Billy, nudging his companion in the ribs. "He come mighty nigh gittin' the best of you."

"He tore one sleeve out of my jacket, and mammy gimme a beatin' besides," giggled Dick. "And say, Billy, wasn't it fun the day we killed old man Lee's puddle ducks for wild ones? I don't believe I ever run as fast in my life."

"And, Dick, do you remember the night your pappy hung the saddle up on the head of the bed to keep you from ridin' the old gray mare to singin' school, and you rid her, bareback, anyway? You ricolleck you was stoopin' over, blowin' the fire, next mornin', when he seen the hairs on your britches, an' come down on you with the leather strop afore you knowed it."

Thus one adventure recalled another, and the two old boys laughed uproariously, clapping their hands and holding their sides, while the sun climbed up among the treetops.

"Ain't we ben two old fools to stay mad all this time?" asked one of them, and the other readily agreed that they had, as they once more grasped hands before parting.

Walter had arranged the Thanksgiving surprise for his parents, but when he brought home the big gobbler he was unable longer to keep the secret, and divulged his share in what had happened.

"I didn't really believe either one of them could hit a turkey," he confided to his father, "but I wanted to have them meet once more, for I knew if they did they would make friends."

The parlour was odorous with late fall roses next morning, the table set, and Walter and his parents in gala attire, when two couples, walking arm in arm, appeared upon the stretch of white road leading up to the front gate.

One couple was slightly in advance of the other, and Grandpa Davis, who was behind, whispered to his wife:

"Listen, Mary, Dick is actually tryin' to sing, and he never could turn a tune, but somehow it does warm up my heart to hear him: seems like old times ag'in."

After dinner was over--and such a grand dinner it was--Grandpa Davis voiced the sentiment of the rest of the happy family party when he announced, quite without warning:

"Well, this here has ben the thankfulles' Thanksgivin' I ever seen, and I hope the good Lord will spar' us all for yet a few more."

A THANKSGIVING DINNER THAT FLEW AWAY[26]
BY HEZEKIAH BUTTERWORTH.

A Cape Cod story about a wise old gander whose adventure on   the sea insured him against the perils of the Thanksgiving   hatchet. For boys or girls.

There is one sound that I shall always remember. It is "Honk!"

[Note 26: From "Zigzag Journeys in Acadia and New France," Lothrop, Lee & Shepard Company.]

I spun around like a top, one summer day when I heard it, looking nervously in every direction.

I had just come down from the city to the Cape with my sister Hester for my third summer vacation. I had left the cars with my arms full of bundles, and hurried toward Aunt Targood's.

The cottage stood in from the road. There was a long meadow in front of it. In the meadow were two great oaks and some clusters of lilacs. An old, mossy stone wall protected the grounds from the road, and a long walk ran from the old wooden gate to the door.

It was a sunny day, and my heart was light. The orioles were flaming in the old orchards; the bobolinks were tossing themselves about in the long meadows of timothy, daisies, and patches of clover. There was a scent of new-mown hay in the air.

In the distance lay the bay, calm and resplendent, with white sails and specks of boats. Beyond it rose Martha's Vineyard, green and cool and bowery, and at its wharf lay a steamer.

I was, as I said, light-hearted. I was thinking of rides over the sandy roads at the close of the long, bright days; of excursions on the bay; of clambakes and picnics.

I was hungry, and before me rose visions of Aunt Targood's fish dinners, roast chickens, and berry pies. I was thirsty, but ahead was the old well sweep, and behind the cool lattice of the dairy window were pans of milk in abundance.

I tripped on toward the door with light feet, lugging my bundles, and beaded with perspiration, but unmindful of all discomforts in the thought of the bright days and good things in store for me.

"Honk! honk!"

My heart gave a bound!

Where did that sound come from?

Out of a cool cluster of innocent-looking lilac bushes I saw a dark object cautiously moving. It seemed to have no head. I knew, however, that it had a head. I had seen it; it had seized me once in the previous summer, and I had been in terror of it during all the rest of the season.

I looked down into the irregular grass, and saw the head and a very long neck running along on the ground, propelled by the dark body, like a snake running away from a ball. It was coming toward me, and faster and faster as it approached.

I dropped my bundles.

In a few flying leaps I returned to the road again, and armed myself with a stick from a pile of cordwood.

"Honk! honk! honk!"

It was a call of triumph. The head was high in the air now. My enemy moved grandly forward, as became the monarch of the great meadow farmyard.

I stood with beating heart, after my retreat.

It was Aunt Targood's gander.

How he enjoyed his triumph, and how small and cowardly he made me feel!

"Honk! honk! honk!"

The geese came out of the lilac bushes, bowing their heads to him in admiration. Then came the goslings--a long procession of awkward, half-feathered things; they appeared equally delighted.

The gander seemed to be telling his admiring audience all about it: how a strange lad with many bundles had attempted to cross the yard; how he had driven him back, and had captured his bundles, and now was monarch of the field. He clapped his wings when he had finished his heroic story, and sent forth such a "Honk!" as might have startled a major-general.

Then he, with an air of great dignity and coolness, began to examine my baggage.

Among my effects were several pounds of chocolate caramels done up in brown paper. Aunt Targood liked caramels, and I brought her a large supply.

He tore off the wrappers quickly. He bit one. It was good. He began to distribute the bonbons among the geese, and they, with much liberality and good-will, among the goslings.

This was too much. I ventured through the gate, swinging my cordwood stick.

"Shoo!"

He dropped his head on the ground, and drove it down the walk in a lively waddle toward me.

"Shoo!"

It was Aunt Targood's voice at the door.

He stopped immediately.

His head was in the air again.

"Shoo!"

Out came Aunt Targood with her broom.

She always corrected the gander with her broom. If I were to be whipped I should choose a broom--not the stick.

As soon as he beheld the broom he retired, although with much offended pride and dignity, to the lilac bushes; and the geese and goslings followed him.

"Hester, you dear child," she said to my sister, "come here. I was expecting you, and had been looking out for you, but missed sight of you. I had forgotten all about the gander."

We gathered up the bundles and the caramels. I was light-hearted again.

How cool was the sitting-room, with the woodbine falling about the open window!

Aunt brought me a pitcher of milk, and some strawberries, some bread and honey, and a fan.

While I was resting and taking my lunch, I could hear the gander discussing the affairs of the farmyard with the geese. I did not greatly enjoy the discussion. His tone of voice was very proud, and he did not seem to be speaking well of me.

I was suspicious that he did not think me a very brave lad. A young person likes to be spoken well of, even by the gander.

Aunt Targood's gander had been the terror of many well-meaning people, and of some evildoers, for many years. I have seen tramps and pack peddlers enter the gate, and start on toward the door, when there would sound that ringing warning like a war blast, "Honk, honk!" and in a few minutes these unwelcome people would be gone. Farmhouse boarders from the city would sometimes enter the yard, thinking to draw water by the old well sweep; in a few minutes it was customary to hear shrieks, and to see women and children flying over the walls, followed by air-rending "Honks!" and jubilant cackles from the victorious gander and his admiring family.

Aunt Targood sometimes took summer boarders. Among those that I remember was the Rev. Mr. Bonney, a fervent-souled Methodist preacher. He put the gander to flight with the cart whip, on the second day after his arrival, and seemingly to aunt's great grief; but he never was troubled by the feathered tyrant again.

Young couples sometimes came to Father Bonney to be married; and one summer afternoon there rode up to the gate a very young couple, whom we afterward learned had "run away," or rather, had attempted to get married without their parents' approval. The young bridegroom hitched the horse, and helped from the carriage the gayly dressed miss he expected to make his wife. They started up the walk upon the run, as though they expected to be followed and haste was necessary to prevent the failure of their plans.

"Honk!"

They stopped. It was a voice of authority.

"Just look at him!" said the bride. "Oh, oh!"

The bridegroom cried "Shoo!" but he might as well have said "Shoo" to a steam engine. On came the gander, with his head and neck upon the ground. He seized the lad by the calf of his leg, and made an immediate application of his wings. The latter seemed to think he had been attacked by dragons. As soon as he could shake him off he ran. So did the bride, but in another direction; and while the two were thus perplexed and discomfited, the bride's father appeared in a carriage, and gave her a most forcible invitation to ride home with him. She accepted it without discussion. What became of the bridegroom, or how the matter ended, we never knew.

"Aunt, what makes you keep that gander year after year?" said I one evening, as we were sitting on the lawn before the door. "Is it because he is a kind of watchdog, and keeps troublesome people away?"

"No, child, no; I do not wish to keep most people away--not well-behaved people--nor to distress nor annoy any one. The fact is, there is a story about that gander that I do not like to speak of to every one--something that makes me feel tender toward him; so that if he needs a whipping I would rather do it. He knows something that no one else knows. I could not have him killed or sent away. You have heard me speak of Nathaniel, my oldest boy?"

"Yes."

"That is his picture in my room, you know. He was a good boy to me. He loved his mother. I loved Nathaniel--you cannot think how much I loved Nathaniel. It was on my account that he went away.

"The farm did not produce enough for us all--Nathaniel, John, and me. We worked hard, and had a hard time. One year--that was ten years ago--we were sued for our taxes.

"'Nathaniel,' said I, 'I will go to taking boarders.'

"Then he looked up to me and said--oh, how noble and handsome he appeared to me:

"'Mother, I will go to sea.'

"'Where?' asked I, in surprise.

"'In a coaster.'

"I turned white. How I felt!

"'You and John can manage the place,' he continued. 'One of the vessels sails next week--Uncle Aaron's; he offers to take me.'

"It seemed best, and he made preparations to go.

"The spring before Skipper Ben--you have met Skipper Ben--had given me some goose eggs; he had brought them from Canada, and said that they were wild goose eggs.

"I set them under hens. In four weeks I had three goslings. I took them into the house at first, but afterward made a pen for them out in the yard. I brought them up myself, and one of those goslings is that gander.

"Skipper Ben came over to see me the day before Nathaniel was to sail. Aaron came with him.

"I said to Aaron:

"'What can I give Nathaniel to carry to sea with him to make him think of home? Cake, preserves, apples? I haven't got much; I have done all I can for him, poor boy.'

"Brother looked at me curiously, and said:

"'Give him one of those wild geese, and we will fatten it on shipboard and will have it for our Thanksgiving dinner.'

"What Brother Aaron said pleased me. The young gander was a noble bird, the handsomest of the lot; and I resolved to keep the geese to kill for my own use, and to give *him* to Nathaniel.

"The next morning--it was late in September--I took leave of Nathaniel. I tried to be calm and cheerful and hopeful. I watched him as he went down the walk with the gander struggling under his arms. A stranger would have laughed, but I did not feel like laughing; it was true that the boys who went coasting were usually gone but a few months, and came home hardy and happy. But when poverty compels a mother and son to part, after they have been true to each other, and shared their feelings in common, it seems hard, it seems hard--though I do not like to murmur or complain at anything allotted to me.

"I saw him go over the hill. On the top he stopped and held up the gander. He disappeared; yes, my own Nathaniel disappeared. I think of him now as one who disappeared.

"November came. It was a terrible month on the coast that year. Storm followed storm; the sea-faring people talked constantly of wrecks and losses. I could not sleep on the nights of those high winds. I used to lie awake thinking over all the happy hours that I had lived with Nathaniel.

"Thanksgiving week came.

"It was full of an Indian-summer brightness after the long storms. The nights were frosty, bright, and calm.

"I could sleep on those calm nights.

"One morning I thought I heard a strange sound in the woodland pasture. It was like a wild goose. I listened; it was repeated. I was lying in bed. I started up--I thought I had been dreaming.

"On the night before Thanksgiving I went to bed early, being very tired. The moon was full; the air was calm and still. I was thinking of Nathaniel, and I wondered if he would indeed have the gander for his Thanksgiving dinner, if it would be cooked as well as I would have cooked it, and if he would think of me that day.

"I was just going to sleep when suddenly I heard a sound that made me start up and hold my breath.

"'*Honk*!'

"I thought it was a dream followed by a nervous shock.

"'*Honk! honk!*'

"There it was again, in the yard, I was surely awake and in my senses.

"I heard the geese cackle.

"'*Honk! honk! honk!*'

"I got out of bed and lifted the curtain. It was almost as light as day.

"Instead of two geese there were three. Had one of the neighbours' geese stolen away?

"I should have thought so, and should not have felt disturbed, but for the reason that none of the neighbours' geese had that peculiar call--that hornlike tone that I had noticed in mine.

"I went out of the door.

"The ***third*** goose looked like the very gander I had given Nathaniel. Could it be?

"I did not sleep. I rose early and went to the crib for some corn.

"It ***was*** a gander--a 'wild gander'--that had come in the night. He seemed to know me.

"I trembled all over as though I had seen a ghost. I was so faint that I sat down on the meal chest.

"As I was in that place, a bill pecked against the door. The door opened. The strange gander came hobbling over the crib stone and went to the corn bin. He stopped there, looked at me, and gave a sort of glad 'Honk' as though he knew me and was glad to see me.

"I was certain that he was the gander I had raised and that Nathaniel had lifted into the air when he gave me his last recognition from the top of the hill.

"It overcame me. It was Thanksgiving. The church bell would soon be ringing as on Sunday. And here was Nathaniel's Thanksgiving dinner and Brother Aaron's--had it flown away? Where was the vessel?

"Years have passed--ten. You know I waited and waited for my boy to come back. December grew dark with its rainy seas; the snows fell; May lighted up the hills, but the vessel never came back. Nathaniel--my Nathaniel--never returned.

"That gander knows something he could tell me if he could talk. Birds have memories. *He* remembered the corncrib--he remembered something else. I wish he *could* talk, poor bird! I wish he could talk. I will never sell him, nor kill him, nor have him abused. He *knows*!"

MON-DAW-MIN, OR THE ORIGIN OF INDIAN CORN[27] BY H. R. SCHOOLCRAFT.

This is the real Indian fairy tale of the birth of Mon-daw-min. Readers of Longfellow will remember his treatment of the same subject in "Hiawatha."

In Times past, a poor Indian was living with his wife and children in a beautiful part of the country. He was not only poor, but inexpert in procuring food for his family, and his children were all too young to give him assistance. Although poor, he was a man of a kind and contented disposition. He was always thankful to the Great Spirit for everything he received. The same disposition was inherited by his eldest son, who had now arrived at the proper age to undertake the ceremony of the Ke-ig-uish-im-o-win, or fast, to see what kind of a spirit would be his guide and guardian through life. Wunzh, for this was his name, had been an obedient boy from his infancy, and was of a pensive, thoughtful, and mild disposition, so that he was beloved by the whole family. As soon as the first indications of spring appeared, they built him the customary little lodge at a retired spot, some distance from their own, where he would not be disturbed during this solemn rite. In the meantime he prepared himself, and immediately went into it, and commenced his fast. The first few days he amused himself, in the mornings, by walking in the woods and over the mountains, examining the early plants and flowers, and in this way prepared himself to enjoy his sleep, and at the same time stored his mind with pleasant ideas for his dreams. While he rambled through the woods, he felt a strong desire to know how the plants, herbs, and berries grew without any aid from man, and why it was that some species were good to eat and others possessed medicinal or poisonous juices. He recalled these thoughts to mind after he became too languid to walk about, and had confined himself strictly to the lodge; he wished he could dream of something that would prove a benefit to his father and family, and to all others. "True!" he thought, "the Great Spirit made all things, and it is to him that we owe our lives. But could he not make it easier for us to get our food than by hunting animals and taking fish? I must try to find out this in my visions."

[Note 27: From "The Myth of Hiawatha."]

On the third day he became weak and faint, and kept his bed. He fancied, while thus lying, that he saw a handsome young man coming down from the sky and advancing toward him. He was richly and gayly dressed, having on a great many garments of green and yellow colours, but differing in their deeper or lighter shades. He had a plume of waving feathers on his head, and all his motions were graceful.

"I am sent to you, my friend," said the celestial visitor, "by that Great Spirit who made all things in the sky and on the earth. He has seen and knows your motives in fasting. He sees that it is from a kind and benevolent wish to do good to your people, and to procure a benefit for them, and that you do not seek for strength in war or the praise of warriors. I am sent to instruct you, and show you how you can do your kindred good." He then told the young man to arise, and prepare to wrestle with him, as it was only by this means that he could hope to succeed in his wishes. Wunzh knew he was weak from fasting, but he felt his courage rising in his heart, and immediately got up, determined to die rather than fail. He commenced the trial, and after a protracted effort was almost exhausted when the beautiful stranger said, "My friend, it is enough for once; I will come again to try you"; and, smiling on him, he ascended in the air in the same direction from which he came. The next day the celestial visitor reappeared at the same hour and renewed the trial. Wunzh felt that his strength was even less than the day before, but the courage of his mind seemed to increase in proportion as his body became weaker. Seeing this, the stranger again spoke to him in the same words he used before, adding, "To-morrow will be your last trial. Be strong, my friend, for this is the only way you can overcome me, and obtain the boon you seek." On the third day he again appeared at the same time and renewed the struggle. The poor youth was very faint in body, but grew stronger in mind at every contest, and was determined to prevail or perish in the attempt. He exerted his utmost powers, and after the contest had been continued the usual time, the stranger ceased his efforts and declared himself conquered. For the first time he entered the lodge, and sitting down beside the youth, he began to deliver his instructions to him, telling him in what manner he should proceed to take advantage of his victory.

"You have won your desires of the Great Spirit," said the stranger. "You have wrestled manfully. To-morrow will be the seventh day of your fasting, your father will give you food to strengthen you, and as it is the last day of trial, you will prevail. I know this, and now tell you what you must do to benefit your family and your tribe. To-morrow," he repeated, "I shall meet you and wrestle with you for the last time; and, as soon as you have prevailed against me, you will strip off my garments and throw me down, clean the earth of roots and weeds, make it soft, and bury me in the spot. When you have done this, leave my body in the earth, and do not disturb it, but come occasionally to visit the place, to see whether I have come to life, and be careful never to let the grass or weeds grow on my grave. Once a month cover me with fresh earth. If you follow my instructions, you will accomplish your object of doing good to your fellow-creatures by teaching them the knowledge I now teach you." He then shook him by the hand and disappeared.

In the morning the youth's father came with some slight refreshments, saying, "My son, you have fasted long enough. If the Great Spirit will favour you, he will do it now. It is seven days since you have tasted food, and you must not sacrifice your life. The Master of Life does not require that." "My father," replied the youth, "wait till the sun goes down. I have a particular reason for extending my fast to that hour." "Very well," said the old man. "I shall wait till the hour arrives, and you feel inclined to eat."

At the usual hour of the day the sky visitor returned, and the trial of strength was renewed. Although the youth had not availed himself of his father's offer of food, he felt that new strength had been given to him, and that exertion had renewed his strength and fortified his courage. He grasped his angelic antagonist with supernatural strength, threw him down, took from him his beautiful garments and plume, and finding him dead, immediately buried him on the spot, taking all the precautions he had been told of, and being very confident, at the same time, that his friend would again come to life. He then returned to his father's lodge, and partook sparingly of the meal that had been prepared for him. But he never for a moment forgot the grave of his friend. He carefully visited it throughout the spring, and weeded out the grass, and kept the ground in a soft and pliant state. Very soon he saw the tops of the green plumes coming through the ground; and the more careful he was to obey his instructions in keeping the ground in order, the faster they grew. He was, however, careful to conceal the exploit from his father. Days and weeks had passed in this way. The summer was now drawing toward a close, when one day, after a long absence in hunting, Wunzh invited his father to follow him to the quiet and lonesome spot of his former fast. The lodge had been removed, and the weeds kept from growing on the circle where it stood, but in its place stood a tall and graceful plant, with bright coloured silken hair, surmounted with nodding plumes and stately leaves, and golden clusters on each side. "It is my friend," shouted the lad; "it is the friend of all mankind. It is **Mondawmin**. We need no longer rely on hunting alone; for, as long as this gift is cherished and taken care of, the ground itself will give us a living." He then pulled an ear. "See, my father," said he, "this is what I fasted for. The Great Spirit has listened to my voice, and sent us something new, and henceforth our people will not alone depend upon the chase or upon the waters."

He then communicated to his father the instructions given him by the stranger. He told him that the broad husks must be torn away, as he had pulled off the garments in his wrestling; and having done this, directed him how the ear must be held before the fire till the outer skin became brown, while all the milk was retained in the grain. The whole family then united in feast on the newly grown ears, expressing gratitude to the Merciful Spirit who gave it. So corn came into the world.

A MYSTERY IN THE KITCHEN[28]
BY OLIVE THORNE MILLER.

The boy who has a sister and the girl who has a brother are the ones who will best like this story of the spirited twins, Jessie and Jack. Jessie wanted to take music lessons and Jack tried mining in Colorado.

Something very mysterious was going on in the Jarvis kitchen. The table was covered with all sorts of good things--eggs and butter and raisins and citron and spices; and Jessie, with her sleeves rolled up and a white apron on, was bustling about, measuring and weighing and chopping and beating and mixing those various ingredients in a most bewildering way.

[Note 28: From "Kristy's Surprise Party," Houghton, Mifflin Co.]

Moreover, though she was evidently working for dear life, her face was full of smiles; in fact, she seemed to have trouble to keep from laughing outright, while Betty, the cook, who was washing potatoes at the sink, fairly giggled with glee every few minutes, as if the sight of Miss Jessie working in the kitchen was the drollest thing in the world.

It was one of the pleasantest sights that big, sunny kitchen had seen for many a day, and the only thing that appeared mysterious about it was that the two workers acted strangely like conspirators. If they laughed--as they did on the slightest provocation--it was very soft and at once smothered. Jessie went often to the door leading into the hall, and listened; and if there came a knock on the floor, she snatched off her apron, hastily wiped her hands, rolled down her sleeves, asked Betty if there was any flour on her, and then hurried away into another part of the house, trying to look cool and quiet, as if she had not been doing anything.

On returning from one of these excursions, as she rolled up her sleeves again, she said:

"Betty, we must open the other window if it is cold. Mamma thought she smelled roast turkey!"

Betty burst into a laugh which she smothered in her apron. Jessie covered her mouth and laughed, too, but the window was opened to make a draught and carry out the delicious odours, which, it must be confessed, did fill that kitchen so full that no wonder they crept through the cracks, and the keyholes, and hung about Jessie's dress as she went through the hall, in a way to make one's mouth water.

"What did ye tell her?" asked Betty, as soon as she could speak.

"Oh, I told her I thought potpie smelled a good deal like turkey," said Jessie, and again both laughed. "Wasn't it lucky we had potpie to-day? I don't know what I should have said if we hadn't."

Well, it was not long after that when Jessie lined a baking-dish with nice-looking crust, filled it with tempting looking chicken legs and wings and breasts and backs and a bowlful of broth, laid a white blanket of crust over all, tucked it in snugly around the edge, cut some holes in the top, and shoved it into the oven just after Betty drew out a dripping pan in which reposed, in all the glory of rich brown skin, a beautiful turkey. Mrs. Jarvis couldn't have had any nose at all if she didn't smell that. It filled the kitchen full of nice smells, and Betty hurried it into the pantry, where the window was open to cool.

Then Jessie returned to the spices and fruits she had been working over so long, and a few minutes later she poured a rich, dark mass into a tin pudding-dish, tied the cover on tight, and slipped it into a large kettle of boiling water on the stove.

"There!" she said, "I hope that'll be good."

"I know it will," said Betty confidently. "That's y'r ma's best receipt."

"Yes, but I never made it before," said Jessie doubtfully.

"Oh, I know it'll be all right, 'n' I'll watch it close," said Betty; "'n' now you go'n sit with y'r ma. I want that table to git dinner."

"But I'm going to wash all these things," said Jessie.

"You go long! I'd ruther do that myself. 'Twon't take me no time," said Betty.

Jessie hesitated. "But you have enough to do, Betty."

"I tell you I want to do it," the girl insisted.

"Oh, I know!" said Jessie; "you like to help about it. Well, you may; and I'm much obliged to you, besides." And after a last look at the fine turkey cooling his heels (if he had any) in the pantry, Jessie went into the other part of the house.

When dinner time arrived and papa came from town, there duly appeared on the table the potpie before mentioned, and various other things pleasant to eat, but nothing was seen of the turkey so carefully roasted nor of the chicken pie, nor of the pudding that caused the young cook so much anxiety. Nothing was said about them, either, and it was not Thanksgiving nor Christmas, though it was only a few days before the former.

It was certainly odd, and stranger things happened that night. In the first place, Jessie sat up in her room and wrote a letter; and then, after her mother was in bed and everything still, she stole down the back stairs with a candle, quietly, as though she was doing some mischief. Betty, who came down to help her, brought a box in from the woodshed; and the two plotters, very silently, with many listenings at the door to see if any one was stirring, packed that box full of good things.

In it the turkey, wrapped in a snowy napkin, found a bed, the chicken pie and the plum pudding--beautiful looking as Betty said it would be--bore him company; and numerous small things, jam jars, fruits, etc., etc., filled the box to its very top. Then the cover, provided with screws so that no hammering need be done, was fastened on.

"Now you go to bed, Miss Jessie," whispered Betty. "I'll wait."

"No, you must be tired," said Jessie. "I'd just as lief."

"But I'd rather," said Betty shortly--"'n' I'm going to; it won't be long now."

So Jessie crept quietly upstairs, and before long there was a low rap on the kitchen door. Betty opened it, and there stood a man.

"Ready?" said he.

"Yes," answered Betty; "but don't speak loud; Miss Jarvis has sharp ears, 'n' we don't want her disturbed. Here's the card to mark it by," and she produced a card from the table.

The man put it in his pocket, shouldered the box, and Betty shut the door.

Not one of those good things ever went into the Jarvis dining-room!

The next morning things went on just as usual in the house. The kitchen door was left open and Mrs. Jarvis was welcome to smell any of the appetizing odours that wafted out into her room. Jessie resumed her study, and especially her practice, for she hoped some day to be a great musician. She waited on her mother and took charge of the housekeeping, so much as was necessary with the well-tried servant at the head of the kitchen. And though she had but sixteen years over her bright brown head, she proved herself to be what in that little New England town was called "capable."

But that box of goodies! Let us see where it went.

It was Thanksgiving morning in a rough-looking little mining settlement in Colorado. In a shanty rougher and more comfortless than the rest were two persons: one, a man of thirty, was deeply engaged in cleaning and oiling a gun which lay in pieces about him on the rough bench where he sat; the other, a youth of sixteen, was trying to make a fire burn in the primitive-looking affair that did duty as a stove. Both wore coarse miner's suits, and picks and other things about the room told that their business was to dig for the yellow dust we are all so greedy to have.

Evidently luck had not been good, for the whole place appeared run down, and the two looked absolutely hungry.

It was Thanksgiving morning, as I said, but no thankfulness shone in the two pale, thin faces. Both were sad, and the younger one almost hopeless.

"Jack," said the elder, pausing in his operations, "mind you give that old hen a good boil, or we won't be able to eat it."

"It'll be better'n nothing, anyway, I suppose," said Jack gloomily.

"Not much. 'Specially if you don't get the taste of sage brush out of it. Lucky I happened to get that shot at her, anyway," he went on, "I've seen worse dinners-- even Thanksgiving dinners--than a sage hen."

"I haven't," said Jack shortly; for the mention of Thanksgiving had brought up before him with startling vividness the picture of a bright dining-room in a certain town far away, a table loaded with good things, and surrounded by smiling faces, and the contrast was almost more than he could bear.

"Well, don't be down on your luck, boy, so long as you can get a good fat hen to eat, if she does happen to be too fond of seasoning before she's dead!" replied the other cheerfully; "we haven't struck it yet, but it's always darkest just before dawn, you know. We may be millionaires before this time to-morrow."

"We may," answered Jack; but he didn't look as if he had much hope of it.

A few hours later the occupants of the cabin sat down to their Thanksgiving dinner. It consisted of the hen aforesaid, cut in pieces and boiled--looking very queer, too--served in the kettle in which the operation had been performed. The table was at one end of the bench, the table service two jackknives and two iron spoons--absolutely nothing else.

The elder sat on the bench, the younger drew up a keg that had held powder, and the dinner was about to begin.

But that hen was destined never to be eaten, for just at that moment the door was pushed open in the rude way of the country, a box set down on the floor, and a rough voice announced:

"A box for Mr. Jack Jones."

Jack started up.

"For me, there must be a mistake! Nobody knows--" He stopped, for he had not mentioned that his name was assumed.

"Likely not!" said the man, with a knowing look, "but folks has a mighty queer way of findin' out," and he shut the door and left.

Jack stood staring at the box as if he had lost his wits. It could not be from home, for no one knew where he went when he stole out of the house one night six months ago, and ran away to seek his fortune. Not a line had he ever written--not even when very ill, as he had been; not even when without a roof to cover his head, as he had been more than once; not even when he had not eaten for two days, as also, alas, had been his experience.

He had deliberately run away, because--how trivial it looked to him now, and how childish seemed his conduct--because he thought his father too hard on him; would not allow him enough liberty; wanted to dictate to this man of sixteen; he intended to show him that he could get on alone.

Poor Jack, the only comfort he had been able to extract from his hard lot these many months of wandering, of work, of suffering such as he had never dreamed of--his only comfort was that his tender mother didn't know, his only sister would no more be worried by his grumbling and complaints, and his father would be convinced now that he wasn't a baby. Small comfort, too, to balance the hardships that had fallen to his lot since the money he had drawn from the savings bank--his little all--was used up.

"Why don't you open it?" The gruff but not unkind voice of his roommate, whom he called Tom, aroused him. "Maybe there's something in it better'n sage hen," trying to raise a smile.

But no smile followed. Mechanically Jack sought the tools to open it, and in a few moments the cover was off.

It *was* from home! On the very top was a letter addressed to Jack Jarvis in a hand that he well knew.

He hastily stuffed it into his pocket unopened. The layers of paper were removed, and as each one was thrown off, something new appeared. Not a word was spoken, but the kettle of sage hen was silently put on the floor by Tom as the bench began to fill up. A jar of cranberry sauce, another of orange marmalade, oranges and apples, a plum pudding, a chicken pie, and lastly, in its white linen wrapper, the turkey we saw browning in that far-off New England kitchen.

As one by one these things were lifted out and placed on the bench a deep silence reigned in the cabin. Jack had choked at sight of the letter, and memories of days far different from these checked even Tom's usually lively tongue. A strange unpacking it was; how different from the joyful packing at dead of night with those two laughing girl faces bending over it!

When all was done, and the silence grew painful, Jack blurted out: "Help yourself," and bustled about, busily gathering up the papers and folding them, and stuffing them back in the box, as though he were the most particular housekeeper in the world. But if Jack couldn't eat, something, too, ailed Tom. He said simply:

"Don't feel hungry. Believe I'll go out and see what I can find," and shouldering his gun, now cleaned and put together, he quickly went out and shut the door.

Jack sat down on the keg and looked at the things which so vividly brought home, and his happy life there, before him. He did not feel hungry, either. He sat and stared for some time. Then he remembered his letter. He drew it from his pocket and opened it. It was very thick; and when he pulled it out of the envelope the first thing he saw was the smiling face of his sister Jessie, his twin sister, his playmate and comrade, his confidante from the cradle. The loss of her ever-willing sympathy had been almost more to him than all the rest of his troubles.

This was another shock that brought something to his eyes that made him see the others through a mist. There were the pictures of his mother, whose gentle voice he could almost hear, and of his father, whose gray hairs and sad face he suddenly remembered were partly his work.

At last he read the letter. It began:

DEAR JACK:--I've just found out where you are, and I'm so

glad. I send you this Thanksgiving dinner. It was too bad
for you to go off so. You don't know how dreadful it was for
mamma; she was sick a long time, and we were scared to death
about her, but she's better now; she can sit up most all
day.

Oh, Jack! Father *cried*! I'm sure he did, and he almost ran
out of the room, and didn't say anything to anybody all day.
But I was determined I'd find you. I shan't tell you how I
did it, but Uncle John helped me, and now, Jack, he says he
wants just such a fellow as you to learn his business, and
he'll make you a very good offer. And, Jack, that's my
turkey--my Winnie--and nobody but Betty knows anything about
this box and this letter. I send you all my money out of the
savings bank (I didn't tell *anybody* that), and I *want*
you to come home. You'll find the money under the
cranberries. I thought it would be safe there, and I knew
you'd eat them all, you're so fond of cranberries. I didn't
tell anybody because I want to surprise them, and besides,
let them think you came home because you got ready. It's
nobody's business where you got the money anyway.

Now do come right home, Jack. You can get here in a week's
time, I know.
Your affectionate sister,
JESSIE.

Jack laid the letter down with a rush of new feelings and thoughts that overwhelmed him. He sat there for hours; he knew nothing of time. He had mechanically turned the cranberry jar upside down and taken from the bottom, carefully
wrapped in white paper, fifty dollars.

A pang went through him. Well did he know what that money represented to
his sister; by how many sacrifices she had been saving it for a year or two, with the

single purpose of taking the lessons from a great master that were to fit her to teach, to take an independent position in the world, to relieve her father, who had lost a large slice of his comfortable income, and who was growing old and sad under his burden. She had often talked it over with Jack.

Now she had generously given up the whole to him, all her hopes and dreams of independence; and he--he who should have been the support of his sister, the right arm of his father--he had basely deserted.

These thoughts and many more surged through his mind that long afternoon, and when Tom returned as the shadows were growing long, he sat exactly as he had been left.

On Tom's entrance he roused himself. There was a new light in his eye.

"Come, Tom," he said, "dinner's waiting. You must be hungry by this time."

"I am that," said Tom, who had been through his own mental struggles meanwhile.

The two sat down once more to their Thanksgiving dinner, and this time they managed to eat, though Jack choked whenever he thought of tasting a bit of Jessie's pet turkey, Winnie; and much as he liked turkey, and a home turkey at that, he could not touch it.

After the meal, when the provisions were stored away in the cupboard (a soap box) much too small for such a supply, it had grown quite dark, and the two, still disinclined to talk, went to their beds--if the rough bunks they occupied may be dignified by that name.

But not to sleep--at least not Jack, who tumbled and tossed all night and got up in the morning with an energy and life he had not shown for weeks.

After breakfast Tom shouldered his pick and said:

"I'll go on, Jack, while you clear up." Yet he felt in his heart he should never see Jack again; for there was a homestruck look in his face that the man of experience in the ways of runaway boys knew well.

He was not surprised that Jack did not join him, nor that when he returned at night to the cabin he found him gone and a note pinned up on the door:

I can't stand it--I'm off for home. You may have my share of everything.

JACK.

It was a cold evening in early December, and there seemed to be an undercurrent of excitement in the Jarvis household. The table was spread in the dining-room with the best silver and linen. Mrs. Jarvis was better, and had even been able to go into the kitchen to superintend the preparations for dinner.

Jessie went around with a shining face that no one understood and she could not explain.

Betty was strangely nervous, and had made several blunders that morning which mortified the faithful servant very much. An air of expectancy pervaded the whole house, though the two heads of it had not a hint of the cause.

Jessie heard the train she had decided to be the important one. She could hardly contain herself for expectation. She tried hard to sober herself now and then by the thought, "Perhaps he won't come," but she couldn't stay sobered, for she felt as certain that he would as that she lived.

You all know how it happened. The door opened and Jack walked in. One instant of blank silence, and then a grand convulsion.

Jack fell on his knees with his face in his mother's lap, though he had not thought a moment before of doing any such thing. Jessie hung over him, frantically hugging him. Mr. Jarvis, vainly trying to join this group, could only lay his hands on Jack's head and say in a broken voice: "My son! My son!" while Betty performed a war dance around the party, wildly brandishing a basting spoon in one hand and wiping her streaming eyes on the dishcloth which she held in the other.

It was long before a word could be spoken, and the dinner was totally ruined, as Betty declared with tears (though they were not for sorrow), before any one could calm down enough to eat.

Then the reaction set in, and justice was done to the dinner, while talk went on in a stream. Jack did not tell his adventures; he only said that he had come from the city, where he had made arrangements for a situation with Uncle John--at which

Jessie's eyes sparkled. His looks, even after a week of comfort and hope, spoke for his sufferings.

There is little more to tell. Jack Jarvis at seventeen was a different boy from the Jack who at sixteen started out to seek his fortune. You may be sure that Jessie had her music lessons after all, and that a new Winnie with a fine young brood at her heels stalked about the Jarvis grounds the next spring.

WHO ATE THE DOLLY'S DINNER?[29]
BY ISABEL GORDON CURTIS.

A good story for the Big Sister to read to the little boys
and girls. "Why can't dollies have a Thanksgiving dinner as well as real folks?" asked Polly Pine.

[Note 29: From "For the Children's Hour," Milton Bradley Company.]

"I don't know why," said mamma, laughing; "go and dress them in their best clothes, get the dolls' house swept and dusted and the table ready. Then I'll fix their dinner before we go downstairs."

"Oh, how nice!" said Polly Pine.

The doll house stood in the nursery. It was very big and very beautiful. It was painted red; it had tall chimneys, and a fine front door with R. Bliss on a brass plate. There were lace curtains at the windows, and two steps led up to the cunning little piazza. Polly Pine swept the rooms with her tiny broom and dusted them. Then she set the table in the dining-room with the very best dishes and the finest silver. She set a teeny vase in the middle of the table, with two violets in it, and she put dolly table napkins at each place.

When the house was all nice and clean she dressed Lavinia in her pink muslin, and Dora Jane in her gray velvet, and Hannah Welch in her yellow silk; then she seated them around the table, each one in her own chair. Polly was just telling them about company manners, how they must not eat with their knives, or leave their teaspoons in their cups when they drank their tea, when the door opened and in came mamma with a real dolls' Thanksgiving dinner.

There was a chicken bone to put on the platter before Hannah Welch, for Hannah always did the carving. There were cunning little dishes of mashed potato and cranberry sauce, and some celery in a tiny tumbler, and the smallest squash pie baked in a patty pan. Polly Pine just hopped up and down with delight when she saw it. She set everything on the table; then she ran away to put on her nicest muslin frock with the pink ribbons, and she went downstairs to her own dinner.

There were gentlemen there for dinner--gentlemen Polly was very fond of-- and she had a nice time visiting with one of them. He could change his table napkin into a white rabbit, and she forgot all about the dolls' Thanksgiving dinner until it was dessert-time, and the nuts and raisins came in.

Then Polly remembered, and she jumped down from her chair and asked mamma if she might go upstairs and see if the dolls had eaten their dinner. When mamma told about the doll house Thanksgiving, all the family wanted to go, too, to find out if the dolls had enjoyed their dinner.

The front door of the doll house was open, and there sat the dolls just as their little mistress had left them--only they had eaten nearly all the dinner! Everything was gone except the potato and the cranberry sauce. The chicken leg was picked bare, the bread was nibbled, and the little pie was eaten all around.

"Well, this is funny," said papa.

Just then they heard a funny, scratching noise in the doll house, and a little gray mouse jumped out from under the table. He ran out the front door of the doll house, and over the piazza, and down the steps before you could say "Jack Robinson." In a minute he was gone--nobody knew where. There was another tiny mouse in the doll house under the parlour sofa, and a third one under Lavinia's bed, with a poor, frightened gray tail sticking out. They all got away safe. Papa would not allow mamma to go for the cat. He said:

"Why can't a poor little mouse have a Thanksgiving dinner as well as we?"

AN OLD-FASHIONED THANKSGIVING[30]
BY ROSE TERRY COOKE.

A long story about a family of hardy New England pioneers in Revolutionary days. It will be most enjoyed by the older children.

"Pile in, Hannah. Get right down 'long o' the clock, so's to kinder shore it up. I'll fix in them pillers t'other side on't, and you can set back ag'inst the bed. Good-bye, folks! Gee up! Bright. Gee! I tell ye, Buck."

[Note 30: Adapted from "Huckleberries," Houghton, Mifflin Co.]

"Good-bye!" nodded Hannah, from the depths of the old calash which granny had given her for a riding-hood, and her rosy face sparkled under the green shadow like a blossom under a burdock leaf.

This was their wedding journey. Thirty long miles to be travelled, at the slow pace of an oxcart, where to-day a railroad spins by, and a log hut in the dim distance.

But Hannah did not cry about it. There was a momentary choking, perhaps, in her throat, as she caught a last view of granny's mob cap and her father's rough face, with the red head of her small stepbrother between them, grouped in the doorway. Her mother had died long ago, and there was another in her place now, and a swarm of children. Hannah was going to her own home, to a much easier life, and going with John. Why should she cry?

Besides, Hannah was the merriest little woman in the country. She had a laugh always lying ready in a convenient dimple.

She never knew what "blues" meant, except to dye stocking yarn. She was sunny as a dandelion and gay as a bobolink. Her sweet good nature never failed through the long day's journey, and when night came she made a pot of tea at the campfire, roasted a row of apples, and broiled a partridge John shot by the wayside, with as much enjoyment as if this was the merriest picnic excursion, and not a solitary camp in the forest, long miles away from any human dwelling, and by no means sure of safety from some lingering savage, some beast of harmful nature, or at least a visit from a shambling black bear, for bears were plentiful enough in that region.

But none of these things worried Hannah. She ate her supper with hearty appetite, said her prayers with John, and curled down on the featherbed in the cart, while John heaped on more wood, and, shouldering his musket, went to lengthen the ropes that tethered his oxen, and then mounted guard over the camp. Hannah watched his fine, grave face, as the flickering light illuminated it, for a few minutes, and then slept tranquilly till dawn. And by sunset next day the little party drew up at the door of the log hut they called home.

It looked very pretty to Hannah. She had the fairy gift, that is so rare among mortals, of seeing beauty in its faintest expression; and the young grass about the rough stone doorstep, the crimson cones on the great larch tree behind it, the sunlit panes of the west window, the laugh and sparkle of the brook that ran through the clearing, the blue eyes of the squirrel caps that blossomed shyly and daintily beside the stumps of new-felled trees--all these she saw and delighted in. And when the door was open, the old clock set up, the bed laid on the standing bedplace, and the three chairs and table ranged against the wall, she began her house-wifery directly, singing as she went. Before John had put his oxen in the small barn, sheltered the cart and the tools in it, and shaken down hay into the manger, Hannah had made a fire, hung on the kettle, spread up her bed with homespun sheets and blankets and a wonderful cover of white-and-red chintz, set the table with a loaf of bread, a square of yellow butter, a bowl of maple sugar, and a plate of cheese; and even released the cock and the hen from their uneasy prison in a splint basket, and was feeding them in the little woodshed when John came in.

His face lit up, as he entered, with that joyful sense of home so instinctive in every true man and woman. He rubbed his hard hands together, and catching Hannah as she came in at the shed door, bestowed upon her a resounding kiss.

"You're the most of a little woman I ever see, Hannah, I swan to man."

Hannah laughed like a swarm of spring blackbirds.

"I declare, John, you do beat all! Ain't it real pleasant here? Seems to me I never saw things so handy."

Oh, Hannah, what if your prophetic soul could have foreseen the conveniences of this hundred years after! Yet the shelves, the pegs, the cupboard in the corner, the broad shelf above the fire, the great pine chest under the window, and the clumsy settle, all wrought out of pine board by John's patient and skilful fingers, filled all her needs; and what can modern conveniences do more?

So they ate their supper at home for the first time, happy as new-nested birds, and far more grateful.

John had built a sawmill on the brook a little way from the house, and already owned a flourishing trade, for the settlement about the lake from which Nepasset Brook sprung was quite large, and till John Perkins went there the lumber had been all drawn fifteen miles off, to Litchfield, and his mill was only three miles from Nepash village. Hard work and hard fare lay before them both, but they were not daunted by the prospect....

By and by a cradle entered the door, and a baby was laid in it....

One baby is well enough in a log cabin, with one room for all the purposes of life; but when next year brought two more, a pair of stout boys, then John began to saw lumber for his own use. A bedroom was built on the east side of the house, and a rough stairway into the loft--more room perhaps than was needed; but John was called in Nepash "a dre'dful forecastin' man," and he took warning from the twins. And timely warning it proved, for as the years slipped by, one after another, they left their arrows in his quiver till ten children bloomed about the hearth. The old cabin had disappeared entirely. A good-sized frame house of one story, with a high-pitched roof, stood in its stead, and a slab fence kept roving animals out of the yard and saved the apple trees from the teeth of stray cows and horses.

Poor enough they were still. The loom in the garret always had its web ready, the great wheel by the other window sung its busy song year in and year out. Dolly was her mother's right hand now; and the twins, Ralph and Reuben, could fire the musket and chop wood. Sylvy, the fourth child, was the odd one. All the rest were sturdy, rosy, laughing girls and boys; but Sylvy had been a pining baby, and grew up into a slender, elegant creature, with clear gray eyes, limpid as water, but bright as stars, and fringed with long golden lashes the colour of her beautiful hair--locks that were coiled in fold on fold at the back of her fine head, like wreaths of undyed silk, so pale was their yellow lustre. She bloomed among the crowd of red-cheeked, dark-haired lads and lasses, stately and incongruous as a June lily in a bed of tulips. But Sylvy did not stay at home. The parson's lady at Litchfield came to Nepash one Sunday, with her husband, and seeing Sylvy in the square corner pew with the rest, was mightily struck by her lovely face, and offered to take her home with her the next week, for the better advantages of schooling. Hannah could not have spared Dolly; but Sylvia was a dreamy, unpractical child, and though all the dearer for being the solitary lamb of the flock by virtue of her essential difference from the rest, still, for that very reason, it became easier to let her go. Parson Everett was childless, and in two years' time both he and his wife adored the gentle, graceful girl; and she loved them dearly. They could not part with her, and at last adopted her formally as their daughter, with the unwilling consent of John and Hannah. Yet they knew it was greatly "for Sylvy's betterment," as they phrased it; so at last they let her go.

But when Dolly was a sturdy young woman of twenty-five the war-trumpet blew, and John and the twins heard it effectually. There was a sudden leaving of the plow in the furrow. The planting was set aside for the children to finish, the old musket rubbed up, and with set lips and resolute eyes the three men walked away one May morning to join the Nepash company. Hannah kept up her smiling courage through it all. If her heart gave way, nobody knew it but God and John. The boys she encouraged and inspired, and the children were shamed out of their childish tears by mother's bright face and cheery talk.

Then she set them all to work. There was corn to plant, wheat to sow, potatoes to set; flax and wool to spin and weave, for clothes would be needed for all, both absent and stay-at-homes. There was no father to superintend the outdoor work; so Hannah took the field, and marshalled her forces on Nepasset Brook much as the commander-in-chief was doing on a larger scale elsewhere. Eben, the biggest boy, and Joey, who came next him, were to do all the planting; Diana and Sam took on themselves the care of the potato patch, the fowls, and the cow; Dolly must spin and weave when mother left either the wheel or loom to attend to the general ordering of the forces; while Obed and Betty, the younglings of the flock, were detailed to weed, pick vegetables (such few as were raised in the small garden), gather berries, herbs, nuts, hunt the straying turkeys' nests, and make themselves generally useful. At evening all the girls sewed; the boys mended their shoes, having learned so much from a travelling cobbler; and the mother taught them all her small stock of schooling would allow. At least, they each knew how to read, and most of them to write, after a very uncertain fashion. As to spelling, nobody knew how to spell in those days.... But they did know the four simple rules of arithmetic, and could say the epigrammatic rhymes of the old New England Primer and the sibyllic formulas of the Assembly's Catechism as glibly as the child of to-day repeats "The House That Jack Built."

So the summer went on. The corn tasselled, the wheat ears filled well, the potatoes hung out rich clusters of their delicate and graceful blossoms, beans straggled half over the garden, the hens did their duty bravely, and the cow produced a heifer calf.

Father and the boys were fighting now, and mother's merry words were more rare, though her bright face still wore its smiling courage. They heard rarely from the army. Now and then a post rider stopped at the Nepash tavern and brought a few letters or a little news; but this was at long intervals, and women who watched and waited at home without constant mail service and telegraphic flashes, aware that news of disaster, of wounds, of illness, could only reach them too late to serve or save, and that to reach the ill or the dying involved a larger and more disastrous journey than the survey of half the world demands now--these women endured pangs beyond our comprehension, and endured them with a courage and patience that might have furnished forth an army of heroes, that did go far to make heroes of that improvised, ill-conditioned, eager multitude who conquered the trained bands of their oppressors and set their sons "free and equal," to use their own dubious phraseology, before the face of humanity at large.

By and by winter came on with all its terrors. By night wolves howled about the lonely house, and sprung back over the palings when Eben went to the door with his musket. Joe hauled wood from the forest on a hand-sled, and Dolly and Diana took it in through the kitchen window when the drifts were so high that the woodshed door could not be opened. Besides, all the hens were gathered in there, as well for greater warmth as for convenience in feeding, and the barn was only to be reached with snowshoes and entered by the window above the manger.

Hard times these were. The loom in the garret could not be used, for even fingers would freeze in that atmosphere; so the thread was wound off, twisted on the great wheel, and knit into stockings, the boys learning to fashion their own, while Hannah knit her anxiety and her hidden heartaches into socks for her soldier boys and their father.

By another spring the aching and anxiousness were a little dulled, for habit blunts even the keen edge of mortal pain. They had news that summer that Ralph had been severely wounded, but had recovered; that John had gone through a sharp attack of camp-fever; that Reuben was taken prisoner, but escaped by his own wit. Hannah was thankful and grateful beyond expression. Perhaps another woman would have wept and wailed, to think all this had come to pass without her knowledge or her aid; but it was Hannah's way to look at the bright side of things. Sylvia would always remember how once, when she was looking at Mount Tahconic, darkened by a brooding tempest, its crags frowning blackly above the dark forest at its foot and the lurid cloud above its head torn by fierce lances of light, she hid her head in her mother's checked apron, in the helpless terror of an imaginative child; but, instead of being soothed and pitied, mother had only laughed a little gay laugh, and said gently, but merrily:

"Why, Sylvy, the sun's right on the other side, only you don't see it."

After that she always thought her mother saw the sun when nobody else could. And in a spiritual sense it was true.

Parson Everett rode over once or twice from Litchfield that next summer to fetch Sylvia and to administer comfort to Hannah. He was a quaint, prim little gentleman, neat as any wren, but mild-mannered as wrens never are, and in a moderate way kindly and sympathetic. When the children had haled their lovely sister away to see their rustic possessions, Parson Everett would sit down in a high chair, lay aside his cocked hat, spread his silk pocket handkerchief over his knees, and prepare to console Hannah.

"Mistress Perkins, these are trying times, trying times. There is a sound of a going in the tops of the mulberry-trees--h-m! Sea and waves roaring of a truth--h-m! h-m! I trust, Mistress Perkins, you submit to the Divine Will with meekness."

"Well, I don't know," replied Hannah, with a queer little twinkle in her eye. "I don't believe I be as meek as Moses, parson. I should like things fixed different, to speak truth."

"Dear me! Dear me--h-m! h-m! My good woman, the Lord reigneth. You must submit; you must submit. You know it is the duty of a vessel of wrath to be broken to pieces if it glorifieth the Maker."

"Well, mebbe 'tis. I don't know much about that kind o' vessel. I've got to submit because there ain't anything else to do, as I see. I can't say it goes easy--not'n' be honest; but I try to look on the bright side, and to believe the Lord'll take care of my folks better'n I could, even if they was here."

"H-m! h-m! Well," stammered the embarrassed parson, completely at his wit's end with this cheerful theology, "well, I hope it is grace that sustains you, Mistress Perkins, and not the vain elation of the natural man. The Lord is in His holy temple; the earth is His footstool--h-m!" The parson struggled helplessly with a tangle of texts here; but the right one seemed to fail him, till Hannah audaciously put it in:

"Well, you know what it says about takin' care of sparrers, in the Bible, and how we was more valerable than they be, a lot. That kind o' text comes home these times, I tell ye. You fetch a person down to the bedrock, as Grandsir Penlyn used to say, and then they know where they be. And ef the Lord is really the Lord of all, I expect He'll take care of all; 'nd I don't doubt but what He is and does. So I can fetch up on that."

Parson Everett heaved a deep sigh, put on his cocked hat, and blew his nose ceremonially with the silk handkerchief. Not that he needed to: but as a sort of shaking off of the dust of responsibility and ending the conversation, which, if it was not heterodox on Hannah's part, certainly did not seem orthodox to him.... He did not try to console her any more, but contented himself with the stiller spirits in his own parish, who had grown up in and after his own fashion.

Another dreadful winter settled down on Nepasset township. There was food enough in the house and firewood in the shed; but neither food nor fire seemed to assuage the terrible cold, and with decreased vitality decreased courage came to all. Hygienics were an unforeseen mystery to people of that day. They did not know that nourishing food is as good for the brain as for the muscles. They lived on potatoes, beets, beans, with now and then a bit of salt pork or beef boiled in the pot with the rest; and their hearts failed, as their flesh did, with this sodden and monotonous diet. One ghastly night Hannah almost despaired. She held secret council with Dolly and Eben, while they inspected the potato bin and the pork barrel, as to whether it would not be best for them to break up and find homes elsewhere for the winter. Her father was old and feeble. He would be glad to have her with him and Betty. The rest were old enough to "do chores" for their board, and there were many families where help was needed, both in Nepash and Litchfield, since every available man had gone to the war by this time. But while they talked a great scuffling and squawking in the woodhouse attracted the boys upstairs. Joe seized the tongs and Diana the broomstick. An intruding weasel was pursued and slaughtered; but not till two fowls, fat and fine, had been sacrificed by the invader and the tongs together. The children were all hungry, with the exhaustion of the cold weather, and clamoured to have these victims cooked for supper. Nor was Hannah unmoved by the appeal. Her own appetite seconded. The savoury stew came just in time. It aroused them to new life and spirits. Hannah regained courage, wondering how she could have lost heart so far, and said to Dolly, as they washed up the supper dishes:

"I guess we'll keep together, Dolly. It'll be spring after a while, and we'll stick it out together."

"I guess I would," answered Dolly. "And don't you believe we should all feel better to kill off them fowls--all but two or three? They're master hands to eat corn, and it does seem as though that biled hen done us all a sight o' good to-night. Just hear them children."

And it certainly was, as Hannah said, "musical to hear 'em." Joe had a cornstalk fiddle, and Eben an old singing book, which Diana read over his shoulder while she kept on knitting her blue sock; and the three youngsters--Sam, Obed, and Betty--with wide mouths and intent eyes, followed Diana's "lining out" of that quaint hymn "The Old Israelites," dwelling with special gusto and power on two of the verses:

"We are little, 'tis true,
And our numbers are few,
And the sons of old Anak are tall;
But while I see a track
I will never go back,
But go on at the risk of my all.

"The way is all new,
As it opens to view,
And behind is the foaming Red Sea;
So none need to speak
Of the onions and leeks
Or to talk about garlics to me!"

Hannah's face grew brighter still. "We'll stay right here!" she said, adding her voice to the singular old ditty with all her power:

"What though some in the rear
Preach up terror and fear,
And complain of the trials they meet,
Tho' the giants before
With great fury do roar,
I'm resolved I can never retreat."

And in this spirit, sustained, no doubt, by the occasional chickens, they lived the winter out, till blessed, beneficent spring came again, and brought news, great news, with it. Not from the army, though. There had been a post rider in Nepash during the January thaw, and he brought short letters only. There was about to be a battle, and there was no time to write more than assurances of health and good hopes for the future. Only once since had news reached them from that quarter. A disabled man from the Nepash company was brought home dying with consumption. Hannah felt almost ashamed to rejoice in the tidings he brought of John's welfare, when she heard his husky voice, saw his worn and ghastly countenance, and watched the suppressed agony in his wife's eyes. The words of thankfulness she wanted to speak would have been so many stabs in that woman's breast. It was only when her eight children rejoiced in the hearing that she dared to be happy. But the other news was from Sylvia. She was promised to the schoolmaster in Litchfield. Only to think of it! Our Sylvy!

Master Loomis had been eager to go to the war; but his mother was a poor bedrid woman, dependent on him for support, and all the dignitaries of the town combined in advising and urging him to stay at home for the sake of their children, as well as his mother. So at home he stayed, and fell into peril of heart, instead of life and limb, under the soft fire of Sylvia's eyes, instead of the enemy's artillery. Parson Everett could not refuse his consent, though he and madam were both loth to give up their sweet daughter. But since she and the youth seemed to be both of one mind about the matter, and he being a godly young man, of decent parentage, and in a good way of earning his living, there was no more to be said. They would wait a year before thinking of marriage, both for better acquaintance and on account of the troubled times.

"Mayhap the times will mend, sir," anxiously suggested the schoolmaster to Parson Everett.

"I think not, I think not, Master Loomis. There is a great blackness of darkness in hand, the Philistines be upon us, and there is moving to and fro. Yea, Behemoth lifteth himself and shaketh his mane--h-m! ah! h-m! It is not a time for marrying and giving in marriage, for playing on sackbuts and dulcimers--h-m!"

A quiet smile flickered around Master Loomis's mouth as he turned away, solaced by a shy, sweet look from Sylvia's limpid eyes, as he peeped into the keeping-room, where she sat with madam, on his way out. He could afford to wait a year for such a spring blossom as that, surely. And wait he did, with commendable patience, comforting his godly soul with the fact that Sylvia was spared meantime the daily tendance and care of a fretful old woman like his mother; for, though Master Loomis was the best of sons, that did not blind him to the fact that the irritability of age and illness were fully developed in his mother, and he alone seemed to have the power of calming her. She liked Sylvia at first, but became frantically jealous of her as soon as she suspected her son's attachment. So the summer rolled away. Hannah and her little flock tilled their small farm and gathered plenteous harvest. Mindful of last year's experience, they raised brood after brood of chickens, and planted extra acres of corn for their feeding, so that when autumn came, with its vivid, splendid days, its keen winds and turbulent skies, the new chicken yard, which the boys had worked at through the summer, with its wattled fence, its own tiny spring, and lofty covered roofs, swarmed with chickens, ducks, and turkeys. Many a dollar was brought home about Thanksgiving time for the fat fowls sold in Litchfield and Nepash; but dollars soon vanished in buying winter clothes for so many children, or rather, in buying wool to spin and weave for them. Mahala Green, the village tailoress, came to fashion the garments, and the girls sewed them. Uncouth enough was their aspect; but fashion did not yet reign in Nepash, and if they were warm, who cared for elegance? Not Hannah's rosy, hearty, happy brood. They sang and whistled and laughed with a force and freedom that was kin to the birds and squirrels among whom they lived; and Hannah's kindly, cheery face lit up as she heard them, while a half sigh told that her husband and her soldier boys were still wanting to her perfect contentment.

At last they were all housed snugly for winter. The woodpile was larger than ever before, and all laid up in the shed, beyond which a rough shelter of chinked logs had been put up for the chickens, to which their roosts and nest boxes, of coarse wicker, boards nailed together, hollow bark from the hemlock logs, even worn-out tin pails, had all been transferred. The cellar had been well banked from the outside, and its darksome cavern held good store of apples, pork, and potatoes. There was dried beef in the stairway, squashes in the cupboard, flour in the pantry, and the great gentle black cow in the barn was a wonderful milker. In three weeks Thanksgiving would come, and even Hannah's brave heart sank as she thought of her absent husband and boys; and their weary faces rose up before her as she numbered over to herself her own causes for thankfulness, as if to say: "Can you keep Thanksgiving without us?" Poor Hannah! She did her best to set these thankless thoughts aside, but almost dreaded the coming festival. One night, as she sat knitting by the fire, a special messenger from Litchfield rode up to the door and brought stirring news. Master Loomis's mother was dead, and the master himself, seeing there was a new levy of troops, was now going to the war. But before he went there was to be a wedding, and, in the good old fashion, it should be on Thanksgiving Day, and Madam Everett had bidden as many of Sylvy's people to the feast as would come.

There was great excitement as Hannah read aloud the madam's note. The tribe of Perkins shouted for joy, but a sudden chill fell on them when mother spoke:

"Now, children, hush up! I want to speak myself, ef it's a possible thing to git in a word edgeways. We can't all go, fust and foremost. 'Tain't noways possible."

"Oh, Mother! Why? Oh, do! Not go to Sylvy's wedding?" burst in the "infinite deep chorus" of youngsters.

"No, you can't. There ain't no team in the county big enough to hold ye all, if ye squeeze ever so much. I've got to go, for Sylvy'd be beat out if mother didn't come. And Dolly's the oldest. She's got a right to go."

Loud protest was made against the right of primogeniture, but mother was firm.

"Says so in the Bible. Leastways, Bible folks always acted so. The first-born, ye know. Dolly's goin', sure. Eben's got to drive, and I must take Obed. He'd be the death of somebody, with his everlastin' mischief, if I left him to home. Mebbe I can squeeze in Betty, to keep him company. Joe and Sam and Dianner won't be more'n enough to take care o' the cows and chickens and fires, and all. Likewise of each other."

Sam set up a sudden howl at his sentence, and kicked the mongrel yellow puppy, who leaped on him to console him, till that long-suffering beast yelped in concert.

Diana sniffed and snuffled, scrubbed her eyes with her checked apron, and rocked back and forth.

"Now, stop it!" bawled Joe. "For the land's sake, quit all this noise. We can't all on us go; 'n' for my part, I don't want to. We'll hev a weddin' of our own some day!" and here he gave a sly look at Dolly, who seemed to understand it and blushed like an apple-blossom, while Joe went on: "Then we'll all stay to 't, I tell ye, and have a right down old country time."

Mother had to laugh.

"So you shall, Joe, and dance 'Money Musk' all night, if you want to--same as you did to the corn huskin'. Now, let's see. Betty, she's got that chintz gown that was your Sunday best, Dolly--the flowered one, you know, that Dianner outgrowed. We must fix them lawn ruffles into 't; and there's a blue ribbin laid away in my chest o' drawers that'll tie her hair. It's dreadful lucky we've got new shoes all round; and Obed's coat and breeches is as good as new, if they be made out of his pa's weddin' suit. That's the good o' good cloth. It'll last most forever. Joe hed 'em first, then Sam wore 'em quite a spell, and they cut over jest right for Obey. My black paduasoy can be fixed up, I guess. But, my stars! Dolly, what hev' you got?"

"Well, Mother, you know I ain't got a real good gown. There's the black lutestring petticoat Sylvy fetched me two years ago; but there ain't any gown to it. We calculated I could wear that linsey jacket to meeting, under my coat; but 'twouldn't do rightly for a weddin'."

"That's gospel truth. You can't wear that, anyhow. You've got to hev somethin'. 'Twon't do to go to Sylvy's weddin' in linsey woolsy; but I don't believe there's more'n two hard dollars in the house. There's a few Continentals; but I don't count on them. Joe, you go over to the mill fust thing in the morning and ask Sylvester to lend me his old mare a spell to-morrer, to ride over to Nepash, to the store."

"Why don't ye send Doll?" asked Joe, with a wicked glance at the girl that set her blushing again.

"Hold your tongue, Joseph, 'n' mind me. It's bedtime now, but I'll wake ye up airly," energetically remarked Hannah. And next day, equipped in cloak and hood, she climbed the old mare's fat sides and jogged off on her errand; and by noon-mark was safe and sound home again, looking a little perplexed, but by no means cast down.

"Well, Dolly," said she, as soon as cloak and hood were laid aside, "there's the beautifulest piece of chintz over to the store you ever see--jest enough for a gown. It's kind of buff-coloured ground, flowered all over with roses, deep-red roses, as nateral as life. Squire Dart wouldn't take no money for 't. He's awful sharp about them new bills. Sez they ain't no more'n corn husks. Well, we ain't got a great lot of 'em, so there's less to lose, and some folks will take 'em; but he'll let me have the chintz for 'leven yards o' soldier's cloth--blue, ye know, like what we sent pa and the boys. And I spent them two silver dollars on a white gauze neck-kercher and a piece of red satin ribbin for ye, for I'm set on that chintz. Now hurry up 'nd fix the loom right off. The web's ready, then we'll card the wool. I'll lay ye a penny we'll have them 'leven yards wove by Friday. To-day's Tuesday, Thanksgiving comes a Thursday week, an' ef we have the chintz by sundown a Saturday there'll be good store of time for Mahaly Green and you to make it afore Wednesday night. We'll hev a kind of a Thanksgiving, after all. But I wisht your pa----" The sentence ended in Hannah's apron at her eyes, and Dolly looked sober; but in a minute she dimpled and brightened, for the pretty chintz gown was more to her than half a dozen costly French dresses to a girl of to-day. But a little cloud suddenly put out the dimples.

"But, Mother, if somebody else should buy it?"

"Oh, they won't. I've fixed that. I promised to fetch the cloth inside of a week, and Squire Dart laid away the chintz for me till that time. Fetch the wool, Dolly, before you set up the web, so's I can start."

The wool was carded, spun, washed, and put into the dye tub, one "run" of yarn that night; and another spun and washed by next day's noon--for the stuff was to be checked, and black wool needed no dyeing. Swiftly hummed the wheel, merrily flew the shuttle, and the house steamed with inodorous dye; but nobody cared for that, if the cloth could only be finished. And finished it was--the full measure and a yard over; and on Saturday morning Sylvester's horse was borrowed again, and Hannah came back from the village beaming with pleasure, and bringing besides the chintz a yard of real cushion lace, to trim the ruffles for Dolly's sleeves, for which she had bartered the over yard of cloth and two dozen fresh eggs. Then even busier times set in. Mahala Green had already arrived, for she was dressmaker as well as tailoress, and was sponging and pressing over the black paduasoy that had once been dove-coloured and was Hannah's sole piece of wedding finery, handed down from her grandmother's wardrobe at that. A dark green grosgrain petticoat and white lawn ruffles made a sufficiently picturesque attire for Hannah, whose well-silvered hair set off her still sparkling eyes and clear healthy skin. She appeared in this unwonted finery on Thanksgiving morning to her admiring family, having added a last touch of adornment by a quaint old jet necklace, that glittered on the pure lawn neckkerchief with as good effect as a chain of diamonds and much more fitness. Betty, in her striped blue-and-white chintz, a clean dimity petticoat, and a blue ribbon round her short brown curls, looked like a cabbage rosebud--so sturdy and wholesome and rosy that no more delicate symbol suits her.

Obed was dreadful in the old-fashioned costume of coat and breeches, ill-fitting and shiny with wear, and his freckled face and round shock head of tan-coloured hair thrown into full relief by a big, square collar of coarse tatten lace laid out on his shoulders like a barber's towel, and illustrating the great red ears that stood out at right angles above it. But Obed was only a boy. He was not expected to be more than clean and speechless; and, to tell the truth, Eben, being in the hobbledehoy stage of boyhood--gaunt, awkward, and self-sufficient--rather surpassed his small brother in unpleasant aspect and manner. But who would look at the boys when Dolly stood beside them, as she did now, tall and slender, with the free grace of an untrammelled figure, her small head erect, her eyes dark and soft as a deer's, neatly clothed feet (not too small for her height) peeping from under the black lutestring petticoat, and her glowing brunette complexion set off by the picturesque buff-and-garnet chintz gown, while her round throat and arms were shaded by delicate gauze and snowy lace, and about her neck lay her mother's gold beads, now and then tangling in the heavy black curls that, tied high on her head with a garnet ribbon, still dropped in rich luxuriance to her trim waist.

The family approved of Dolly, no doubt, though their phrases of flattery were as homely as heartfelt.

"Orful slick-lookin', ain't she?" confided Joe to Eben; while sinful Sam shrieked out: "Land o' Goshen! ain't our Dolly smart? Shan't I fetch Sylvester over?"

For which I regret to state Dolly smartly boxed his ears.

But the pung was ready, and Sam's howls had to die out uncomforted. With many parting charges from Hannah about the fires and fowls, the cow, the hasty pudding, already put on for its long boil, and the turkey that hung from a string in front of the fire and must be watched well, since it was the Thanksgiving dinner, the "weddingers," as Joe called them, were well packed in with blankets and hot stones and set off on their long drive.

The day was fair and bright, the fields of snow purely dazzling; but the cold was fearful, and in spite of all their wraps, the keen winds that whistled over those broad hilltops where the road lay seemed to pierce their very bones, and they were heartily glad to draw up, by twelve o'clock, at the door of the parsonage and be set before a blazing fire, and revived with sundry mugs of foaming and steaming flip, made potent with a touch of old peach brandy; for in those ancient days, even in parsonages, the hot poker knew its office and sideboards were not in vain.

There was food, also, for the exhausted guests, though the refection was slight and served informally in the kitchen corner, for the ceremonial Thanksgiving dinner was to be deferred till after the wedding. And as soon as all were warmed and refreshed they were ushered into the great parlour, where a Turkey carpet, amber satin curtains, spider-legged chairs and tables, and a vast carved sofa, cushioned also with amber, made a regal and luxurious show in the eyes of our rustic observers.

But when Sylvy came in with the parson, who could look at furniture? Madam Everett had lavished her taste and her money on the lovely creature as if she were her own daughter, for she was almost as dear to that tender, childless soul. The girl's lustrous gold-brown hair was dressed high upon her head in soft puffs and glittering curls, and a filmy thread-lace scarf pinned across it with pearl-headed pins. Her white satin petticoat showed its rich lustre under a lutestring gown of palest rose brocaded with silver sprigs and looped with silver ribbon and pink satin roses. Costly lace clung about her neck and arms, long kid gloves covered her little hands and wrists and met the delicate sleeve ruffles, and about her white throat a great pink topaz clasped a single string of pearls. Hannah could scarce believe her eyes. Was this her Sylvy?--she who even threw Madam Everett, with her velvet dress, powdered hair, and Mechlin laces, quite into the background!

"I did not like it, Mammy dear," whispered Sylvy, as she clung round her astonished mother's neck. "I wanted a muslin gown; but madam had laid this by long ago, and I could not thwart or grieve her, she is so very good to me."

"No more you could, Sylvy. The gown is amazing fine, to be sure; but as long as my Sylvy's inside of it I won't gainsay the gown. It ain't a speck too pretty for the wearer, dear." And Hannah gave her another hug. The rest scarce dared to touch that fair face, except Dolly, who threw her arms about her beautiful sister, with little thought of her garments, but a sudden passion of love and regret sending the quick blood to her dark brows and wavy hair in a scarlet glow.

Master Loomis looked on with tender eyes. He felt the usual masculine conviction that nobody loved Sylvy anywhere near as much as he did; but it pleased him to see that she was dear to her family. The parson, however, abruptly put an end to the scene.

"H-m! my dear friends, let us recollect ourselves. There is a time for all things. Yea, earth yieldeth her increase--h-m! The Lord ariseth to shake visibly the earth--ahem! Sylvia, will you stand before the sophy? Master Lummis on the right side. Let us pray."

But even as he spoke the words a great knocking pealed through the house: the brass lion's head on the front door beat a reveille loud and long. The parson paused, and Sylvia grew whiter than before; while Decius, the parson's factotum, a highly respectable old negro (who, with his wife and daughter, sole servants of the house, had stolen in to see the ceremony), ambled out to the vestibule in most undignified haste. There came sounds of dispute, much tramping of boots, rough voices, and quick words; then a chuckle from Decius, the parlour door burst open, and three bearded, ragged, eager men rushed in upon the little ceremony.

There was a moment's pause of wonder and doubt, then a low cry from Hannah, as she flew into her husband's arms; and in another second the whole family had closed around the father and brothers, and for once the hardy, stern, reticent New England nature, broken up from its foundations, disclosed its depths of tenderness and fidelity. There were tears, choking sobs, cries of joy. The madam held her lace handkerchief to her eyes with real need of it; Master Loomis choked for sympathy; and the parson blew his nose on the ceremonial bandanna like the trumpet of a cavalry charge.

"Let us pray!" said he, in a loud but broken voice; and holding fast to the back of the chair, he poured out his soul and theirs before the Lord with all the fervour and the fluency of real feeling. There was no stumbling over misapplied texts now, no awkward objections in his throat, but only glowing Bible words of thankfulness and praise and joy. And every heart was uplifted and calm as they joined in the "Amen."

John's story was quickly told. Their decimated regiment was disbanded, to be reformed of fresh recruits, and a long furlough given to the faithful but exhausted remnant. They had left at once for home, and their shortest route lay through Litchfield. Night was near when they reached the town, but they must needs stop to get one glimpse of Sylvy and tidings from home, for fear lay upon them lest there might be trouble there which they knew not of. So they burst in upon the wedding. But Master Loomis began to look uneasy. Old Dorcas had slipped out, to save the imperilled dinner, and Pokey, the maid (*nee* Pocahontas!) could be heard clinking glass and silver and pushing about chairs; but the happy family were still absorbed in each other.

"Mister Everett!" said the madam, with dignity, and the little minister trotted rapturously over to her chair to receive certain low orders.

"Yes, verily, yes--h-m! A--my friends, we are assembled in this place this evening--"

A sharp look from madam recalled him to the fact that this was not a prayer-meeting.

"A--that is--yes, of a truth our purpose this afternoon was to--"

"That's so!" energetically put in Captain John. "Right about face! Form!" and the three Continentals sprung to their feet and assumed their position, while Sylvy and Master Loomis resumed theirs, a flitting smile in Sylvia's tearful eyes making a very rainbow.

So the ceremony proceeded to the end, and was wound up with a short prayer, concerning which Captain Perkins irreverently remarked to his wife some days after:

"Parson smelt the turkey, sure as shootin', Hannah. He shortened up so 'mazin' quick on that prayer. I tell you I was glad on't. I knew how he felt. I could ha' ate a wolf myself."

Then they all moved in to the dinner table--a strange group, from Sylvia's satin and pearls to the ragged fatigue-dress of her father and brothers; but there was no help for that now, and really it troubled nobody. The shade of anxiety in madam's eye was caused only by a doubt as to the sufficiency of her supplies for three unexpected and ravenous guests; but a look at the mighty turkey, the crisp roast pig, the cold ham, the chicken pie, and the piles of smoking vegetables, with a long vista of various pastries, apples, nuts, and pitchers of cider on the buffet, and an inner consciousness of a big Indian pudding, for twenty-four hours simmering in the pot over the fire, reassured her, and perhaps heartened up the parson, for after a long grace he still kept his feet and added, with a kindly smile:

"Brethren and friends, you are heartily welcome. Eat and be glad, for seldom hath there been such cause and need to keep a Thanksgiving!"

And they all said Amen!

1800 AND FROZE TO DEATH[31]
BY C. A. STEPHENS.

An exciting story of a battle with a crazy moose. It has a Thanksgiving flavour, too.

"What shall we have for Thanksgiving dinner?" was a question which distressed more than one household that year. Indeed, it was often a question what to have for dinner, supper, or breakfast on any day. For that was the strangely unpropitious, unproductive season of 1816, quaintly known in local annals as "1800 and Froze to Death."

[Note 31: From the **Youth's Companion**, November 26, 1908.]

It was shortly after the close of the War of 1812 with England. Our country was then poor and but little cultivated. There was no golden West to send carloads of wheat and corn; no Florida or California to send fruit; there were no cars, no railroads. What the people of the Eastern States had they must raise for themselves, and that year there were no crops.

Nothing grew, nothing ripened properly. Winter lingered even in the lap of May. As late as the middle of June there was a heavy snowstorm in New England. Frosts occurred every fortnight of the season. The seed potatoes, corn, and beans, when planted, either rotted in the ground or came up to be killed by the frosts. The cold continued through July and August. A little barley, still less wheat and rye, a few oats, in favourable situations, were the only cereals harvested, and these were much pinched in the kernel.

Actual starvation threatened hundreds of farmers' families as this singular summer and autumn advanced. The corn crop, then the main staple in the East, was wholly cut off. Two and three dollars a bushel--equal to ten dollars to-day--were paid for corn that year--by those who had the money to purchase it. Many of the poorer families subsisted in part on the boiled sprouts of raspberry and other shrubs. Starving children stole forth into the fields of the less indigent farmers by night, and dug up the seed potatoes and sprouted corn to eat raw.

Moreover, there appeared to be little or no game in the forest; many roving bears were seen, and wolves were bold. All wild animals, indeed, behaved abnormally, as if they, too, felt that nature was out of joint. The eggs of the grouse or partridge failed to hatch; even woodchucks were lean and scarce. So of the brooding hens at the settler's barn: the eggs would not hatch, and the hens, too, it is said, gave up laying eggs, perhaps from lack of food. Even the song birds fell into the "dumps" and neglected to rear young.

The dreary, fruitless autumn drew on; and Thanksgiving Day bade fair to be such a hollow mockery that in several states the governors did not issue proclamations.

Maine at that time was a part of the state of Massachusetts. My impression is that the governor appointed November 28th as Thanksgiving Day, but I am not sure. It is likely that not much unction attended the announcement. The notices of it did not reach many localities in Maine. In the neighbourhood where my grand-parents lived, in Oxford County, nothing was heard of it; but at a schoolhouse meet-ing, on November 21st, our nearest neighbour, Jonas Edwards, made a motion "that the people of the place keep the 28th of the month as Thanksgiving Day--the best they could."

The motion prevailed; and then the poor housewives began to ask the question, "What shall we have for Thanksgiving dinner?" At our house it is still remembered that one of my young great-uncles cried in reply, "Oh, if we could only have a good big johnnycake!"

And it was either that very night, or the night after, that the exciting news came of the arrival of a shipload of corn at Bath and Brunswick.

At Brunswick, seat of the then infant Bowdoin College, Freeport, Topsham, and other towns near the coast of Maine, where the people were interested in mari-time ventures, it had become known that a surplus of corn was raised in Cuba, and could be purchased at a fair price. An old schooner, commanded by one Capt. John Simmons, was fitted out to sail for a cargo of the precious cereal. For three months not a word was heard from schooner or skipper.

Captain Simmons had purchased corn, however, and loaded his crazy old craft full to the deck with it. Heavy weather and head winds held him back on his voy-age home. Water got to the corn, and some of it swelled to such an extent that the old schooner was like to burst. But it got in at last, early in November, with three thousand bushels of this West India corn.

How the news of this argosy flew even to towns a day's journey up from the coast!

A great hunger for corncake swept through that part of the state; and in our own little neighbourhood a searching canvass of the resources of the five log farm-houses followed. As a result of it, young Jonathan Edwards and my then equally youthful Great-uncle Nathaniel set off the next day to drive to Brunswick with a span of old white horses hitched in a farm wagon without springs, carrying four rather poor sheep, four bushels of barley, and fifteen pounds of wool, which they hoped to exchange for five bushels of that precious corn. On top of it all there were three large bagfuls of hay for the horses. The boys also took an axe and an old flint-lock gun, for much of the way was then through forest.

It was a long day's drive for horses in poor condition, but they reached Brunswick that night. There, however, they found the cargo of corn so nearly sold out, or bartered away, that they were able to get but three bushels to bring home.

The corn was reckoned at nine dollars, the four sheep at only six dollars, and it had been difficult "dickering" the fifteen pounds of wool and the two bushels of barley as worth three dollars more. The extra two bushels of barley went for their keep overnight. Such was produce exchange in 1816.

The next morning they started for home, lightly loaded with their dearly bought corn. Their route lay along the Androscoggin River, and they had got as far on their way as the present factory town of Auburn, where the Little Androscoggin flows into the larger river of the same name, when they had an adventure which resulted in very materially increasing the weight of their load.

It was a raw, cloudy day, and had begun to "spit snow"; and as it drew toward noon, they stopped beside the road at a place where a large pine and several birches leaned out from the brink of the deep gorge through which the Little Androscoggin flows to join the larger stream. Here they fed their horses on the last of the three bagfuls of hay, but had nothing to cook or eat in the way of food themselves. The weather was chilly, and my young Great-uncle Nathaniel said to Jonathan:

"If you will get some dry birchbark, I will flash the pan. We will kindle a fire and warm up."

Jonathan brought the bark, and meanwhile Nathaniel drew the charge from the old "Queen's arm," then ignited some powder in the pan with the flintlock, and started a blaze going.

The blaze, however, had soon to be fed with dry fuel, and noticing a dead firtop lying on the ground a few steps away, Jonathan took the axe and ran to break it up; and the axe strokes among the dry stuff made a considerable crackling.

Throwing down the axe at last, Jonathan gathered up a large armful of the dry branches, and had turned to the fire, when they both heard a strange sound, like a deep grunt, not far away, followed by sharp crashes of the brush down in the basin.

"What's that?" Nathaniel exclaimed. "It's a bear I guess," and he snatched up the empty gun to reload it. Jonathan, too, threw down his armful of boughs and turned back to get the axe.

Before they could do either, however, the strange grunts and crashes came nearer, and a moment later a pair of broad antlers and a huge black head appeared, coming up from the gorge.

At sight of the snorting beast, Jonathan turned suddenly. "It's a moose, Nat!" he cried. "A big bull moose! Shoot him! Shoot him!"

Nat was making frantic efforts, but the gun was not reloaded. Recharging an old "Queen's arm" was a work of time.

Fortunately for the boys, the attention of the moose was full fixed on the horses. With another furious snort, it gained the top of the bank and bounded toward where they stood hitched, chewing their hay.

The tired white horses looked up suddenly from their hay, and perceiving this black apparition of the forest, snorted and tugged at their halters.

With a frightful bellow, half squeal, half roar, the moose rose twelve feet tall on his hind legs, and rushed at the one hitched nearest. The horse broke its halter, ran headlong against its mate, recoiled, bumped into a tree trunk, and then--the trees standing thick in front of it--backed over the bank and went out of sight down the bluff, the moose bounding after it, still bellowing hoarsely.

The other horse had also broken its halter and ran off, while the two boys stood amazed and alarmed at this tremendous exhibition of animal ferocity.

"Nat! Nat! He will kill that horse!" Jonathan exclaimed, and they both ran to look over the bank. Horse and moose were now down near the water, where the river ran deep and swift under the steep bank, the horse trying vainly to escape through the tangled alder brush, the moose savagely pursuing.

The sight roused the boys to save their horse. Axe in hand, Jonathan ran and slid down the bluff side, catching hold of trees and bushes as he did so, to keep from going quite into the river. Nat followed him, with the gun which he had hastily primed. Both horse and moose were now thrashing amidst the alder clumps.

"Shoot him, shoot him!" Jonathan shouted. "Why don't you fire? Oh, let me have that gun!"

It is not as easy as an onlooker often thinks to shoot an animal, even a large one, in rapid motion, particularly among trees and brush; something constantly gets in the way. Both animals were now tearing along the brink of the deep stream, stumbling headlong one second, up the next, plunging on. As often as Nat tried to steady himself on the steep side of the bluff for a shot, either the horse was in the way or both animals were wholly concealed by the bushes. Moreover, the boys had to run fast through the brush to keep them in sight. Nat could not shoot with certainty, and Jonathan grew wild over the delay.

"Shoot him yourself, then!" Nat retorted, panting.

Jonathan snatched the gun and dashed forward, Nat picking up the axe and following after. On they ran for several hundred yards, barely keeping pace with the animals. Jonathan experienced quite as much difficulty in getting a shot as Nat had done.

At last he aimed and snapped--and the gun did not go off.

"You never primed it!" he exclaimed indignantly. Nat thought that he had done so, but was not wholly certain; and feeling that he must do his part somehow, he now dashed past Jonathan, and running on, attempted to head the horse off at a little gully down the bank to which they had now come. It was a brushy place; he fell headlong into it himself, and rolled down, still grasping hard at the axe. He was close upon the horse now, within a few yards of the water, and looking up, he saw the moose's head among the alder brush. The creature appeared to be staring at him, and regaining his feet, much excited, Nat threw the axe with all his strength at the moose's head.

By chance rather than skill, the poll of the axe struck the animal just above the eyes at the root of the antlers. It staggered, holding its head to one side a moment, as if half-stunned or in pain. Then, recovering, it snorted, and with a bound through the brush, jumped into the stream, and either swam or waded across to the low sandy bank on the other side. There it stood, still shaking its head.

Jonathan had caught up with Nat by this time, and they both stood watching the moose for some moments, hoping that the mad animal had now had enough of the fracas and would go his way. The horse was in the brush of the little gully, sticking fast there, or tired out by its exertions; and they now began considering how they could best extricate it and get it back up the bluff.

Just then, however, their other horse neighed long and shrill from the top of the bank, calling to its mate. The frightened horse beside them neighed back in reply.

These equine salutations produced an unexpected result. Another hoarse snort and a splash of the water was the response from across the stream.

"He's coming again!" exclaimed Jonathan. "Have you got the powder-horn, Nat? Give it to me quick, if you've got it!" Nathaniel had had the powder-horn up on the bank, but had dropped it there, or lost it out of his pocket in his scramble down the bluff.

There was no time to search for it. The moose was plunging through the narrow stream, and a moment later sprang ashore and came bounding up the gully toward the horse.

The boys shouted to frighten him off. The crazy creature appeared neither to hear nor heed. Jonathan hastily took refuge behind a rock; Nat jumped to cover of a tree trunk.

In his rush at the horse, the moose passed close to them. Again Nat hurled the axe at the animal's side. Jonathan, snatching up a heavy stone, threw it with all his might. The horse, too, wheeling in the narrow bed of the gully, kicked spitefully, lashing out its iron-shod hoofs again and again, planting them hard on the moose's front.

For some moments this singular combat raged there. Recovering the axe and coming up behind the animal, Nat now attempted to deal a blow. The moose wheeled, however, as if struck by sudden panic, and went clear over Nat, who was thrown headlong and slid down into the water.

The moose bounded clear over him, and again went splashing through the Little Androscoggin to the other side, where it turned as before, shaking its antlers and rending the brush with them.

Nathaniel had caught hold of a bush, and thus saved himself from going fully into the swift current. Jonathan helped him get out, and the two young fellows stared at each other. The encounter had given them proof of the mad strength and energy of the moose.

"Oh, if we could only find that powder-horn somewhere!" Jonathan exclaimed.

The horse up on the bluff sent forth again its shrill neigh, to which the one beside them responded.

And just as before, the moose, with an awful bellow, came plunging through the little river and bounding up the gully.

"My soul! Here he comes again!" Jonathan fairly yelled. "Get out o' the way!"

And Nat got out of the way as quickly as possible, taking refuge behind the same rock in the side of the gully.

Again the place resounded to a frightful medley of squeals, bellowings, and crashes in the brush. This time Jonathan had caught up the axe, and approaching the furious melee of whirling hoofs and gnashing teeth from one side, attempted to get in a blow. In their wild movements the enraged animals nearly ran over him, but he struck and stumbled.

The blow missed the moose's head, but fell on the animal's foreleg, just below the knee, and broke the bone. The moose reared, and wheeling on its hind legs, plunged down the gully, falling partly into the river, much as Nat had done.

A dozen times it now struggled to get up, almost succeeding, but fell back each time. With the ardour of battle still glowing in him, Jonathan rushed forward with the axe, and finally managed to deal the moose a deathblow; with a knife they then bled it, and stood by, triumphant.

"We've muttoned him! We've muttoned him!" Nat shouted. "But I never had such a fight as that before."

The horse, as it proved, was not seriously injured, but they were obliged to cut away the alder brush in the gully to get the animal back up the bluff, and were occupied for fully an hour doing so.

The body of the moose was a huge one; it must have weighed fully fourteen hundred pounds. The boys could no more have moved it than they could move a mountain. Moreover, it was now beginning to snow fine and fast.

Jonathan had a fairly good knife, however, and by using the axe they succeeded in rudely butchering the carcass and dismembering it. Even then the quarters were so heavy that their full strength was required to drag them up the bluff and load them into the wagon. The head, with its broad, branching antlers, was all that they could lift to the top of their now bulky load.

The task had taken till past four o'clock of that stormy November afternoon. Twilight was upon them, the wintry twilight of a snowstorm, before they made start; and it was long past midnight when they finally plodded home.

There were corncake and moose venison for Thanksgiving dinner.

The Codes Of Hammurabi And Moses
W. W. Davies

QTY

The discovery of the Hammurabi Code is one of the greatest achievements of archaeology, and is of paramount interest, not only to the student of the Bible, but also to all those interested in ancient history...

Religion   **ISBN:** *1-59462-338-4*

Pages:132
MSRP $12.95

The Theory of Moral Sentiments
Adam Smith

QTY

This work from 1749. contains original theories of conscience amd moral judgment and it is the foundation for systemof morals.

Philosophy   **ISBN:** *1-59462-777-0*

Pages:536
MSRP $19.95

Jessica's First Prayer
Hesba Stretton

QTY

In a screened and secluded corner of one of the many railway-bridges which span the streets of London there could be seen a few years ago, from five o'clock every morning until half past eight, a tidily set-out coffee-stall, consisting of a trestle and board, upon which stood two large tin cans, with a small fire of charcoal burning under each so as to keep the coffee boiling during the early hours of the morning when the work-people were thronging into the city on their way to their daily toil...

Pages:84

Childrens   **ISBN:** *1-59462-373-2*

MSRP $9.95

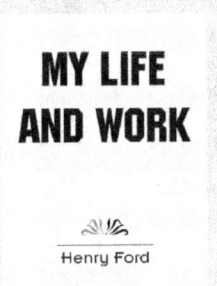

My Life and Work
Henry Ford

QTY

Henry Ford revolutionized the world with his implementation of mass production for the Model T automobile. Gain valuable business insight into his life and work with his own auto-biography... "We have only started on our development of our country we have not as yet, with all our talk of wonderful progress, done more than scratch the surface. The progress has been wonderful enough but..."

Pages:300

Biographies/   **ISBN:** *1-59462-198-5*

MSRP $21.95

The Art of Cross-Examination
Francis Wellman

QTY

I presume it is the experience of every author, after his first book is published upon an important subject, to be almost overwhelmed with a wealth of ideas and illustrations which could readily have been included in his book, and which to his own mind, at least, seem to make a second edition inevitable. Such certainly was the case with me; and when the first edition had reached its sixth impression in five months, I rejoiced to learn that it seemed to my publishers that the book had met with a sufficiently favorable reception to justify a second and considerably enlarged edition. ...

Reference   **ISBN: *1-59462-647-2***

Pages:412
MSRP $19.95

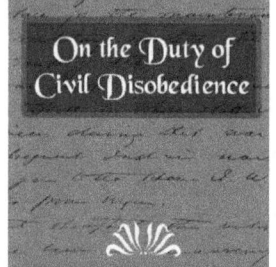

On the Duty of Civil Disobedience
Henry David Thoreau

QTY

Thoreau wrote his famous essay, On the Duty of Civil Disobedience, as a protest against an unjust but popular war and the immoral but popular institution of slave-owning. He did more than write—he declined to pay his taxes, and was hauled off to gaol in consequence. Who can say how much this refusal of his hastened the end of the war and of slavery ?

Law   **ISBN: *1-59462-747-9***

Pages:48
MSRP $7.45

Dream Psychology Psychoanalysis for Beginners
Sigmund Freud

QTY

Sigmund Freud, born Sigismund Schlomo Freud (May 6, 1856 - September 23, 1939), was a Jewish-Austrian neurologist and psychiatrist who co-founded the psychoanalytic school of psychology. Freud is best known for his theories of the unconscious mind, especially involving the mechanism of repression; his redefinition of sexual desire as mobile and directed towards a wide variety of objects; and his therapeutic techniques, especially his understanding of transference in the therapeutic relationship and the presumed value of dreams as sources of insight into unconscious desires.

Psychology   **ISBN: *1-59462-905-6***

Pages:196
MSRP $15.45

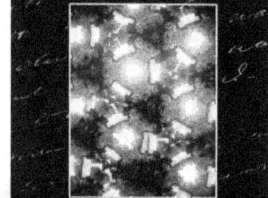

The Miracle of Right Thought
Orison Swett Marden

QTY

Believe with all of your heart that you will do what you were made to do. When the mind has once formed the habit of holding cheerful, happy, prosperous pictures, it will not be easy to form the opposite habit. It does not matter how improbable or how far away this realization may see, or how dark the prospects may be, if we visualize them as best we can, as vividly as possible, hold tenaciously to them and vigorously struggle to attain them, they will gradually become actualized, realized in the life. But a desire, a longing without endeavor, a yearning abandoned or held indifferently will vanish without realization.

Pages:360

Self Help   **ISBN: *1-59462-644-8***   *MSRP $25.45*

QTY

The Rosicrucian Cosmo-Conception Mystic Christianity by *Max Heindel* ISBN: *1-59462-188-8* **$38.95**
The Rosicrucian Cosmo-conception is not dogmatic, neither does it appeal to any other authority than the reason of the student. It is: not controversial, but is: sent forth in the, hope that it may help to clear... New Age/Religion Pages 646

Abandonment To Divine Providence by *Jean-Pierre de Caussade* ISBN: *1-59462-228-0* **$25.95**
"The Rev. Jean Pierre de Caussade was one of the most remarkable spiritual writers of the Society of Jesus in France in the 18th Century. His death took place at Toulouse in 1751. His works have gone through many editions and have been republished... Inspirational/Religion Pages 400

Mental Chemistry by *Charles Haanel* ISBN: *1-59462-192-6* **$23.95**
Mental Chemistry allows the change of material conditions by combining and appropriately utilizing the power of the mind. Much like applied chemistry creates something new and unique out of careful combinations of chemicals the mastery of mental chemistry... New Age Pages 354

The Letters of Robert Browning and Elizabeth Barret Barrett 1845-1846 vol II ISBN: *1-59462-193-4* **$35.95**
by *Robert Browning* and *Elizabeth Barrett* Biographies Pages 596

Gleanings In Genesis (volume I) by *Arthur W. Pink* ISBN: *1-59462-130-6* **$27.45**
Appropriately has Genesis been termed "the seed plot of the Bible" for in it we have, in germ form, almost all of the great doctrines which are afterwards fully developed in the books of Scripture which follow... Religion/Inspirational Pages 420

The Master Key by *L. W. de Laurence* ISBN: *1-59462-001-6* **$30.95**
In no branch of human knowledge has there been a more lively increase of the spirit of research during the past few years than in the study of Psychology, Concentration and Mental Discipline. The requests for authentic lessons in Thought Control, Mental Discipline and... New Age/Business Pages 422

The Lesser Key Of Solomon Goetia by *L. W. de Laurence* ISBN: *1-59462-092-X* **$9.95**
This translation of the first book of the "Lernegton" which is now for the first time made accessible to students of Talismanic Magic was done, after careful collation and edition, from numerous Ancient Manuscripts in Hebrew, Latin, and French... New Age/Occult Pages 92

Rubaiyat Of Omar Khayyam by *Edward Fitzgerald* ISBN: *1-59462-332-5* **$13.95**
Edward Fitzgerald, whom the world has already learned, in spite of his own efforts to remain within the shadow of anonymity, to look upon as one of the rarest poets of the century, was born at Bredfield, in Suffolk, on the 31st of March, 1809. He was the third son of John Purcell... Music Pages 172

Ancient Law by *Henry Maine* ISBN: *1-59462-128-4* **$29.95**
The chief object of the following pages is to indicate some of the earliest ideas of mankind, as they are reflected in Ancient Law, and to point out the relation of those ideas to modern thought. Religion/History Pages 452

Far-Away Stories by *William J. Locke* ISBN: *1-59462-129-2* **$19.45**
"Good wine needs no bush, but a collection of mixed vintages does. And this book is just such a collection. Some of the stories I do not want to remain buried for ever in the museum files of dead magazine-numbers an author's not unpardonable vanity..." Fiction Pages 272

Life of David Crockett by *David Crockett* ISBN: *1-59462-250-7* **$27.45**
"Colonel David Crockett was one of the most remarkable men of the times in which he lived. Born in humble life, but gifted with a strong will, indomitable courage, and unremitting perseverance... Biographies/New Age Pages 424

Lip-Reading by *Edward Nitchie* ISBN: *1-59462-206-X* **$25.95**
Edward B. Nitchie, founder of the New York School for the Hard of Hearing, now the Nitchie School of Lip-Reading, Inc, wrote "LIP-READING Principles and Practice". The development and perfecting of this meritorious work on lip-reading was an undertaking... How-to Pages 400

A Handbook of Suggestive Therapeutics, Applied Hypnotism, Psychic Science ISBN: *1-59462-214-0* **$24.95**
by *Henry Munro* Health/New Age/Health/Self-help Pages 376

A Doll's House: and Two Other Plays by *Henrik Ibsen* ISBN: *1-59462-112-8* **$19.95**
Henrik Ibsen created this classic when in revolutionary 1848 Rome. Introducing some striking concepts in playwriting for the realist genre, this play has been studied the world over. Fiction/Classics/Plays 308

The Light of Asia by *sir Edwin Arnold* ISBN: *1-59462-204-3* **$13.95**
In this poetic masterpiece, Edwin Arnold describes the life and teachings of Buddha. The man who was to become known as Buddha to the world was born as Prince Gautama of India but he rejected the worldly riches and abandoned the reigns of power when... Religion/History/Biographies Pages 170

The Complete Works of Guy de Maupassant by *Guy de Maupassant* ISBN: *1-59462-157-8* **$16.95**
"For days and days, nights and nights, I had dreamed of that first kiss which was to consecrate our engagement, and I knew not on what spot I should put my lips..." Fiction/Classics Pages 240

The Art of Cross-Examination by *Francis L. Wellman* ISBN: *1-59462-309-0* **$26.95**
Written by a renowned trial lawyer, Wellman imparts his experience and uses case studies to explain how to use psychology to extract desired information through questioning. How-to/Science/Reference Pages 408

Answered or Unanswered? by *Louisa Vaughan* ISBN: *1-59462-248-5* **$10.95**
Miracles of Faith in China Religion Pages 112

The Edinburgh Lectures on Mental Science (1909) by *Thomas* ISBN: *1-59462-008-3* **$11.95**
This book contains the substance of a course of lectures recently given by the writer in the Queen Street Hall, Edinburgh. Its purpose is to indicate the Natural Principles governing the relation between Mental Action and Material Conditions... New Age/Psychology Pages 148

Ayesha by *H. Rider Haggard* ISBN: *1-59462-301-5* **$24.95**
Verily and indeed it is the unexpected that happens! Probably if there was one person upon the earth from whom the Editor of this, and of a certain previous history, did not expect to hear again... Classics Pages 380

Ayala's Angel by *Anthony Trollope* ISBN: *1-59462-352-X* **$29.95**
The two girls were both pretty, but Lucy who was twenty-one who supposed to be simple and comparatively unattractive, whereas Ayala was credited, as her Bombwhat romantic name might show, with poetic charm and a taste for romance. Ayala when her father died was nineteen... Fiction Pages 484

The American Commonwealth by *James Bryce* ISBN: *1-59462-286-8* **$34.45**
An interpretation of American democratic political theory. It examines political mechanics and society from the perspective of Scotsman James Bryce Politics Pages 572

Stories of the Pilgrims by *Margaret P. Pumphrey* ISBN: *1-59462-116-0* **$17.95**
This book explores pilgrims religious oppression in England as well as their escape to Holland and eventual crossing to America on the Mayflower, and their early days in New England... History Pages 268

www.**bookjungle**.com *email: sales@bookjungle.com fax: 630-214-0564 mail: Book Jungle PO Box 2226 Champaign, IL 61825*

QTY

The Fasting Cure *by Sinclair Upton*   ISBN: *1-59462-222-1* **$13.95**
*In the Cosmopolitan Magazine for May, 1910, and in the Contemporary Review (London) for April, 1910, I published an article dealing with my experi-
ences in fasting. I have written a great many magazine articles, but never one which attracted so much attention...* New Age/Self Help/Health Pages 164

Hebrew Astrology *by Sepharial*   ISBN: *1-59462-308-2* **$13.45**
*In these days of advanced thinking it is a matter of common observation that we have left many of the old landmarks behind and that we are now pressing
forward to greater heights and to a wider horizon than that which represented the mind-content of our progenitors...* Astrology Pages 144

Thought Vibration or The Law of Attraction in the Thought World   ISBN: *1-59462-127-6* **$12.95**
by William Walker Atkinson   Psychology/Religion Pages 144

Optimism *by Helen Keller*   ISBN: *1-59462-108-X* **$15.95**
*Helen Keller was blind, deaf, and mute since 19 months old, yet famously learned how to overcome these handicaps, communicate with the world, and
spread her lectures promoting optimism. An inspiring read for everyone...* Biographies/Inspirational Pages 84

Sara Crewe *by Frances Burnett*   ISBN: *1-59462-360-0* **$9.45**
*In the first place, Miss Minchin lived in London. Her home was a large, dull, tall one, in a large, dull square, where all the houses were alike, and all the
sparrows were alike, and where all the door-knockers made the same heavy sound...* Childrens/Classic Pages 88

The Autobiography of Benjamin Franklin *by Benjamin Franklin*   ISBN: *1-59462-135-7* **$24.95**
*The Autobiography of Benjamin Franklin has probably been more extensively read than any other American historical work, and no other book of its kind
has had such ups and downs of fortune. Franklin lived for many years in England, where he was agent...* Biographies/History Pages 332

Name	
Email	
Telephone	
Address	
City, State ZIP	

☐ **Credit Card**   ☐ **Check / Money Order**

Credit Card Number	
Expiration Date	
Signature	

Please Mail to: Book Jungle
PO Box 2226
Champaign, IL 61825
or Fax to: *630-214-0564*

ORDERING INFORMATION

web: *www.bookjungle.com*
email: *sales@bookjungle.com*
fax: *630-214-0564*
mail: *Book Jungle PO Box 2226 Champaign, IL 61825*
or PayPal *to sales@bookjungle.com*

Please contact us for bulk discounts

DIRECT-ORDER TERMS

**20% Discount if You Order
Two or More Books**
Free Domestic Shipping!
Accepted: Master Card, Visa,
Discover, American Express

www.ingramcontent.com/pod-product-compliance
Lightning Source LLC
Chambersburg PA
CBHW080903020726

47502CB00008B/2331